Hellish
Book Three:
Unholy Religion

By Scott Dokey

ISBN: 978-0-9857036-7-7

Dedicated to my wonderful wife, Jennifer, for her constant support and belief in me and my dreams.

* * *

* * *

In shadows deep, a priest defiled,
Forsook the light, embraced the wild.
In forsaken halls where candles quake,
He whispers prayers the damned partake.

His faith now twisted, dark and grim,
Blessings turned to curses slim.
Hymns once holy, now are cries,
Echoing with lost souls' sighs.

Eyes gleam with forbidden lore,
Seeking ruin evermore.
To idols hungry, souls he gives,
In blood-soaked rites, his darkness lives.

Hope on altars, sacrificed,
Rituals of darkest vice.
Incense thick, obscures the truth,
Madness now his twisted youth.

Bound to void where shadows creep,
Hands reach for an endless sleep.
Salvation lost, in night he dwells,
A priest now chained to darkest spells.

CHAPTER 1

As the sun slipped below the horizon, casting a warm glow over the landscape, the cathedral stood tall against the evening sky. Its Gothic spires reached towards the heavens with a timeless elegance, while the surrounding foliage formed a lush backdrop, embracing the ancient structure in nature's gentle embrace.

A well-worn pathway led visitors to the cathedral's entrance, adorned with intricate carvings that spoke of stories untold. Inside, the air was filled with the sweet scent of incense, while an indistinct murmur from the congregants mingled with the soft rustle of their clothing as they settled into the pews.

Gideon, dressed in his white and gold vestments, stood nervously at the back of the nave, anticipation bubbling beneath the surface. As the congregation gathered, their whispered conversations and the distant notes of the organ created a symphony of reverence that filled the sacred space.

As the wooden doors creaked open, the crowd hushed. The soft rustling of hymnals and the occasional cough from a member of the audience echoed through the cavernous space, amplifying the tension that gripped the cathedral, while the last rays of sunlight filtered through the stained-glass windows, casting a kaleidoscope of colors across the stone floor.

Bishop Thomas, an older man with a stout frame, dressed in crimson and gold robes, began a slow trek down the aisle flanked by an array of altar boys until he took his place on the dais, an aura of authority and wisdom surrounding him.

Gideon stood nervously at the back, breathing deep to calm himself as he waited for the ceremony to start. Father Matthias, Gideon's friend and mentor, stood by his side with a reassuring hand on his shoulder. The elder priest's warm smile offered Gideon a silent affirmation of the long journey that had led them to this pivotal moment, yet beneath the surface, an unsettling tension lingered like a whisper of impending doom. He tried to shake the feeling, tossing it up to nerves as he wondered whether he was worthy of the mantle he was about to be bestowed, even though he had been assured by many that he was. But the impression persisted, like a premonition of things to come.

The organ's notes swelled, resonating through the hallowed space, bringing Gideon out of his thoughts and signaling the commencement of the ceremony. He began the solemn procession down the aisle flanked by his fellow clergy.

The congregation rose, their collective gaze fixed on the unfolding event. The scent of candle wax mingled with the lingering notes of incense, creating an aura of mystery that accompanied the procession as it moved steadily through the sanctuary.

The bishop's voice echoed through the cavernous space as he addressed those gathered to witness the spectacle, "Dear brethren, today we gather to witness the ordination of our brother, Gideon, into the sacred priesthood."

Bishop Thomas then began the solemn exchange of vows with Gideon. "Gideon, do you, in the presence of God and this congregation, solemnly promise to dedicate your life to the service of the Church and its people?"

Gideon, his voice, betraying the tiniest bit of fear, quivered slightly, "I do."

The echo of Gideon's response lingered in the sacred space as Bishop Thomas continued, "Will you strive to be a faithful minister of the mysteries of God, dispensing the Word and Sacraments with love and devotion?"

Gideon replied, "I will, with God's help."

"Will you endeavor to live a life of holiness, exemplifying the teachings of Christ in your thoughts, words, and actions?"

"I will, with the grace of God."

Bishop Thomas looked at Gideon, his eyes filled with pride, "Finally, will you promise to be obedient and submissive to your spiritual leaders, faithfully carrying out the duties entrusted to you by the Church?"

The exchange of vows between Gideon and the bishop reverberated overhead, the words carrying the weight of his solemn commitment. Gideon's voice held a subtle tremor as he fully measured the profound responsibility he was about to embrace.

"I will, in the name of the Father, the Son, and the Holy Spirit," Gideon replied confidently.

The church bells outside began to toll, marking the sacred transition taking place within the cathedral. The air seemed charged with an unimaginable energy, an acknowledgment from the divine of this momentous occasion.

Finally, Bishop Thomas placed his hands upon Gideon's head, imparting a solemn blessing. The congregation bowed their heads in unison, the atmosphere saturated with a sense of reverence.

With the last words of the benediction, Gideon turned toward the congregation as a newly ordained priest. The loud applause that erupted from the pews resonated fully through the sacred space.

***

As the cathedral basked in the dying embers of the sun's light, a sinister presence, unseen and unheard, slithered through the encroaching shadows outside. The unsuspecting congregation remained oblivious to the lurking darkness that had coiled itself just beyond their sanctuary, its icy touch seeping through the ancient stone walls.

With eyes like smoldering coals, the demon fixated on the vibrant stained-glass windows, its hunger stirred by the sacred rites unfolding within. Sinuous tendrils of shadow stretched out, ethereal fingers probing the sanctity that radiated from the hallowed halls.

Meanwhile, Gideon, his nerves frayed at the edges, lingered at the rear of the nave, blissfully unaware of the malignant presence lurking just beyond the glass.

The shadow demon writhed with unnatural glee, reveling in the purity it sought to corrupt. Its phantom appendages grazed the cold stone with a ghostly whisper, blending with the distant hymns to weave an unsettling melody through the air.

As the heavy wooden doors groaned open, a reverent hush fell over the congregation, while outside in the darkness, the demon's eyes gleamed with an insatiable hunger in anticipation of the chaos it would soon unleash.

CHAPTER 2

Mary watched the rain cascade down sadly, each drop a grim echo of the countless tears she had shed in the past, and that now flowed freely once more. She stood on the balcony of her small apartment looking out to a misty veil covering the city, the surrounding lights blurred into a dreary dance as her fingertips grazed the curve of her growing belly and the new life cradled within.

With a heavy heart, she clutched at the edge of her worn-out sweater, feeling the chill seeping into her bones as she walked back inside. She closed the sliding door behind her and shuffled to her bedroom, where a heavy silence hung in the air, disturbed only by the rhythmic cadence of the raindrops outside.

A long sigh escaped her lips as she lay on her bed and began tracing the outline of a photograph from the bedside table—a snapshot frozen in time, capturing a love that had transcended everything else. As she took in every small detail of the picture, recalling the moment the photograph was taken with precise clarity, another stream of tears drifted down her cheek and she whispered, "Michael, I miss you so much," yearning for the sound of his voice one more time.

For a moment, as Mary laid in the stillness, listening intently, she thought she heard him whisper her name. But she knew he was gone, and the only sound she had heard was the remembrance of his voice echoing through her mind. Another tear fell as she realized yet again that she was left all alone to face a future filled with uncertainty that the hellish nightmares they had endured were finally gone for good. The darkness surrounding her soul told her that they weren't.

As the night deepened around her, she found herself teetering on the edge of sleep, where she knew the shadows waited to embrace her in their dark songs, and she would be powerless to resist them.

***

Alone in a dark and desolate cemetery, Mary felt a cold sweat on her skin. The tombstones towered over her like twisted teeth, casting grotesque shadows in the pale moonlight. The air reeked of decay, and the ground seemed to squirm beneath her bare feet.

The moon's glow shined down on a sea of weathered graves surrounding her, some cracked open, revealing the rotting remains within. Mary could feel unseen eyes boring into her, like the graveyard itself hungered for her, eager to claim another soul for its unholy collection. A guttural moan, accompanied by distant muffled screams, filled the air as the tombstones seemed to close in.

She looked up to see a large gothic mausoleum looming ahead, like a gateway to the Underworld. Slowly, she made her way toward the foreboding structure, as if drawn there by some unnatural force. An icy wind rose up that carried the whispers of the dead through the air, surrounding her in a ghoulish choir.

As the entrance to the mausoleum drew closer, a ghostly figure slowly materialized from the shadows surrounding the death chamber. A dark aura surrounded the entity as it advanced toward Mary with a skeletal hand extended, its bony fingers reaching out to wrap around her throat in its icy grasp. The dead whispers surrounding her transformed into a maddening symphony of anguished screams that echoed through the necropolis.

She tried to run away, desperate to escape the nightmare, but the dirt floor suddenly collapsed beneath her feet, plummeting her into a chasm of darkness that swirled with the echoes of those same tormented spirits. A piercing scream flew from her mouth as she felt hundreds of icy, dead fingers grasping for her, their sharp claws ripping into her flesh while they dragged her further into Hell.

After what felt like an eternity of anguish, the descent into madness finally stopped and she found herself laying bloody and beaten on a cold stone floor in the middle of a large cave. Her breath came in ragged gasps as she looked around, her eyes wide with fear. The cave was dimly lit by an otherworldly, phosphorescent glow emanating from somewhere deep within the walls.

As Mary pushed herself up, she noticed that the stone beneath her felt strangely alive, pulsating with an eerie energy. The walls of the cave were covered with grotesque carvings depicting demonic figures and strange symbols etched into the rock, and a putrid scent hung in the air.

In the distance, she could make out the faint outlines of passages leading deeper into the subterranean abyss. As she stumbled forward, the cave seemed to stretch endlessly, twisting and turning in an inescapable labyrinth. Sinister whispers echoed through the passages murmuring words that clawed at her mind.

Mary hesitated at a fork in the cave, unsure which path to take. Suddenly, the air grew colder, and a distant rumble echoed through the tunnels. The walls trembled as if responding to an ancient force being woken from a long slumber. Unsure why, she chose the left passage and immediately the darkness swallowed her as she ventured deeper into the heart of this unholy realm.

With each step, the air grew thicker, almost suffocating. The distant cries of the tormented echoed louder, melding into a cacophony of despair that reverberated throughout.

Suddenly, the cave opened into a vast chamber adorned with twisted spires of rock jutting up from the floor and down from the ceiling. At the center, a pulsating, malignant blood-stained altar stood, surrounded by an ethereal mist. Shadows danced on the walls, and a figure emerged from the darkness—the same spectral being from the cemetery—with its hollow eyes that bore into Mary's soul.

"Welcome, Mary," the ghostly figure hissed, its voice an unsettling whisper. "I've been waiting for you."

***

With a gasp, Mary jolted awake. Beads of sweat glistened on her forehead as the haunting dreamscape slowly faded, leaving a lingering sense of dread surrounding her. She lay still for a moment, trying to anchor herself in the reality of her bedroom, hoping the darkness invading her soul would retreat. But the haunting echoes of the spectral being's hiss still reverberated in her mind, an unsettling whisper that refused to fade completely.

Slowly sitting up, Mary clutched the bed sheet tightly, her gaze darting around the room. The darkness seemed to hold a hint of the ethereal mist she had encountered in the dream, and she half-expected the ghostly figure to materialize from the shadows.

Welcome, Mary, I've been waiting for you. The ghostly whisper lingered in her ears, and she shook her head as if trying to dispel the haunting voice. The kicks from her unborn child intensified, as if the child sensed the residual fear that gripped his mother.

Mary hesitated after swinging her legs over the side of the bed, testing the solidity of the floor beneath her feet. The bitter touch of the hardwood against her skin reassured her.

As she made her way to the bedroom door, she couldn't shake off the feeling of being watched. Every creak of the floorboards echoed in her ears, and she half-expected the shadows to come alive. The fear that had seized her in the dream refused to loosen its grip, and a sense of foreboding accompanied her every step.

Opening the door, Mary stepped into the softly illuminated hallway. The nightmare may have ended, but its residue clung to her like a ghostly shroud. She longed for the warmth of her living room's lights, hoping it would banish the lingering specters of the dreamscape that had held her captive in the caverns of her own mind.

Bathed in the warm glow of the dimmed lights, Mary slowly lowered herself onto the plush couch. As she settled into the cushions, the fabric embraced her, a calm sorrow settling over her like a gentle mist.

With a sigh, Mary gazed across the room, her eyes fixated on an ethereal figure only she could see. In her mind's eye, Michael materialized, his laughter echoing in the recesses of her memory. Despite the heartbreaking reality that he was no longer there, she believed, if only for a fleeting moment, that he was sitting right beside her on the couch.

A bittersweet smile played on her lips as she initiated a

one-sided conversation with the ghost of her past. "Michael," she whispered, her voice carrying a blend of joy and longing. "We were pretty good together, weren't we?" The room held a sacred stillness, as if time itself were paying homage to their reunion.

In the silence, Mary could almost feel the warmth of his imaginary presence, as if he had never left her side. The illusion provided solace and a temporary escape from the harsh reality of his tragic death. It also served to shelter her from the encroaching darkness that sought to consume her. Tears welled up in her eyes, but this time, they were tears of happiness, a cathartic release of the emotions that had been pent up for so long.

She reached out, her fingers gently brushing against the air where she imagined his hand might be. "I miss you so much," she confessed, the ache in her heart momentarily alleviated by the illusion she had conjured.

As Mary continued to share her thoughts and dreams with the apparition of Michael, the echoes of their imaginary conversation lingered in the air, a tribute to a love that transcended the boundaries of life and death. And in that somber moment, bathed in the dim glow of their spectral reunion, Mary found herself teetering on the edge of sanity, her soul caught in a struggle between reality and make-believe.

CHAPTER 3

The roar of Priscilla's beat-up truck echoed through the quiet streets as she pulled into the parking space near the front of the apartment building on the outskirts of town. She crouched her head down to look through the windshield and studied the building for a moment before turning her head toward Jinx, her Yellow Lab sitting in the passenger seat. "Well, I guess there's no turning back now, is there, Jinxie?"

A soft bark issued from the dog's mouth before Priscilla reached up to pet her, scratching that magical spot right behind her ears.

A minute later, a moving truck rolled in behind her, its engine grumbling to a halt. With a soft sigh, Priscilla climbed out of her vehicle, leaving the door open, a leather jacket slung over her shoulder that blended in with her raven-black hair.

Three men wearing matching T-shirts that read 'Swift Movers' jumped out of their truck and walked toward her. "You must be Priscilla?" the driver said.

Priscilla nodded, "Thanks for coming on such short notice. I didn't know how long I was going to need to store my stuff before I found a place out here."

The crew leader offered a tired grin, his words uttered in a practiced script that felt forced, "No problem. Moving is our business, after all. We'll make it swift, just like our name says."

Priscilla chuckled, "I appreciate that. Let me show you where everything goes."

Priscilla called out to Jinx, who immediately jumped out of the vehicle and joined her as she led the movers inside the apartment. The men gathered around her as she pointed out the key pieces of furniture and explained where they should be placed. The crew leader scribbled notes on a clipboard, occasionally nodding in understanding.

"Got it," he said. "We'll get everything set up for you. Anything we should be extra careful with?"

"There's a box labeled 'fragile' in the back of my truck. Just that one. The rest should survive a little rough handling."

The movers exchanged glances, chuckling at Priscilla's easygoing attitude. With instructions in hand, they headed back to the truck, ready to tackle the unloading process.

As the first piece of furniture emerged from the moving truck, one of the movers, a young guy with a pleasant demeanor, approached Priscilla. "So, what brings you to this neck of the woods? Starting a new adventure?"

Priscilla nodded, her eyes misting over, "Something like that. Needed a change of scenery, you know?"

The mover grinned, "I get it. Sometimes you just gotta shake things up."

Priscilla agreed, watching as the crew worked. "Exactly. Hopefully, this town has a bit of magic waiting for me."

The mover chuckled, "Who knows? Small towns can surprise you."

As the crew continued their work, Priscilla stood outside, directing them. She couldn't help but notice the nosey neighbors peering out from behind their curtains and blinds, their curiosity piqued by the new arrival in town.

As her neighbors took in the excitement, a petite girl with a pixie haircut strolled by guided by a small terrier on a leash at her side. Spotting Priscilla, she offered a friendly smile. "Hey there! I'm Emily, and this is Trixie. Just moving in?"

Priscilla's gaze met Emily's, her stormy eyes betraying a hint of emotion. "I'm Priscilla, and this is Jinx. Yeah, I needed a change of scenery, and this town seemed like the right fit."

"Well, if you need anything, I'm in the next building, 33B," Emily offered kindly.

"Thank you. I'll keep that in mind," Priscilla replied gratefully.

As Jinx and Trixie engaged in the typical new-dog sniffing ritual, Priscilla's attention drifted to the figure standing behind Emily—a woman with a wide smile on her face. It was Priscilla's mother. Her smile couldn't mask the haunting memories Priscilla carried—the image of finding her mother's lifeless body lying on their living room floor not so long ago.

Emily sensed a shift in Priscilla's demeanor. "Is everything okay?" she asked.

Priscilla forced a smile. "Yeah, just adjusting to the new surroundings, you know?"

But Emily could see through the facade. "If you ever need to talk or anything, I'm here," she offered sincerely.

Priscilla nodded as Emily and Trixie scampered away.

"Come on, Jinx," she said. "Let's get settled into our new home."

Jinx let out a little bark as she followed Priscilla down the sidewalk toward the building. As she reached for the door handle, Priscilla turned toward the spot where her mother's spirit had appeared a moment ago, yearning for one last glimpse of her warm smile. But she was gone.

* * *

***

As Priscilla and Jinx neared the corner of the street, the streetlamp flickered erratically, filling the area with shadows that danced and twisted in eerie gaits along the pavement. A moment later, Emily approached from the opposite direction with Trixie in tow.

As the dogs circled each other once again, Priscilla's gaze flickered to the figure standing behind them. At first glance, it appeared to be her mother again, wearing a wide, welcoming smile. But as her eyes adjusted to the darkness, a chill crept down Priscilla's spine.

The smile was too wide, too manic, stretching unnaturally across her mother's face like a grotesque mask. Her eyes, cold, empty, devoid of any warmth or recognition, bore into Priscilla with a chilling intensity, sending shivers racing down her spine.

Suddenly, the scene shifted, the walls of reality warping and twisting like a nightmare come to life. Priscilla found herself standing in a familiar room, the air heavy with the scent of death and decay. It was her old house—the living room to be precise. And there, lying on the floor, was her mother.

Her lifeless body lay sprawled out before her, pale and motionless, a haunting echo of the tragedy that had shattered Priscilla's world. The memory flooded back with a visceral intensity; each detail etched into her mind like a scar.

But as Priscilla reached out to touch her mother's cold skin, the scene dissolved around her, melting away like wax in the heat. Darkness closed in, suffocating and oppressive, wrapping its tendrils around her like a suffocating embrace.

And then she heard it, a soft whisper echoing in the

darkness, a voice filled with malice and hatred. It was a voice she knew all too well, and as it whispered her name, each syllable dripped with venom, sending shivers racing down Priscilla's spine. "Hell won't stop me from violently ripping the life from your body just like you did mine, sister!"

Priscilla's heart hammered in her chest as she struggled to escape the suffocating grip of the nightmare. But no matter how hard she fought, the darkness only grew stronger, consuming her with its relentless hunger.

***

With a gasp, Priscilla shot up in bed, her body drenched in sweat, her heart pounding like a drum in her chest. It took her a moment to realize she was safe in her room, the nightmare fading into the recesses of her mind. But the terror lingered, clinging to her like a stubborn shadow, a reminder of the countless horrors that lurked just beneath the surface of past deeds unforgotten.

CHAPTER 4

The dim glow of candlelight flickered against the ancient wooden shelves in the church's library. Gideon, surrounded by towering bookcases filled with dusty tomes and weathered manuscripts, sat hunched over a worn wooden table. The scent of aging parchment and leather bindings filled the air as he immersed himself in the arcane writings. In the weeks that had passed since his ordination, he undertook his studies daily with an increased sense of purpose.

Eventually, weariness began to set in. He rubbed his tired eyes and let out a sigh, the weight of the knowledge he sought pressing down on him. The symbols on the pages seemed to blur, and the Latin words began to meld into an indistinct haze. He leaned back in his chair, stretching his cramped muscles, his eyes fixed on the flickering candle flames.

The door to the library creaked open, and Father Matthias entered, his silhouette outlined by the soft glow of the corridor beyond. He approached Gideon with a gentle smile, concern etched on his weathered face.

"Gideon, you've been at this for hours. Perhaps it's time to rest," Father Matthias said.

Gideon, looked up with a mixture of exhaustion and determination. "Father Matthias, these texts hold secrets that I need to understand if I'm to fulfill my responsibilities and provide the divine inspiration I was called to. I have to press on."

Father Matthias placed a comforting hand on Gideon's shoulder. "I admire your dedication, but even the strongest flame can be extinguished if it burns too long. Rest is just as essential as knowledge, my boy. You can't be expected to learn everything immediately. Even after a lifetime of studies, I still find myself an uneducated student at times."

Gideon nodded reluctantly. "You're right, Father. I'll take a break. I guess I just don't want to let anyone down."

Father Matthias gave a knowing smile. "Rest assured, Gideon, you have nothing to fear. Everything will come to you when the time is right. Now, get some fresh air. It'll help ease your mind."

As Father Matthias left the library, closing the door behind him, Gideon followed his advice and stepped outside into the cool night air. The moon hung high in the sky, casting a silvery glow over the church grounds.

Alone in the quiet courtyard, Gideon sat down on one of the concrete benches and closed his eyes, taking deep breaths to clear his mind. Then, an eerie stillness began to settle around him. The ambient sounds of the night suddenly went quiet, and an unsettling feeling gripped the air.

Gideon's eyes shot open when a soft whisper echoed through the darkness, sending a chill racing down his spine. The surrounding shadows seemed to come to life, twisting and undulating as if concealing some unseen force. His heart pounded in his chest as an ethereal figure materialized before him, its hollow eyes piercing into his very soul.

The figure spoke with a hiss in its voice, "Beware the path

you tread, Gideon. The answers you seek may consume more than you can fathom."

Gideon watched, frozen in fear, as the apparition then faded into the shadows. As soon as the spectral presence was gone, the courtyard returned to its normal calm, but Gideon was left with a lingering chill running through him.

On his way back to the library, guided by an unseen force, Gideon took a wrong turn that found him lost in a maze of corridors. Even though he had walked those halls hundreds of times in the past, the incident in the courtyard had left him disoriented. As he tried to calm himself, he suddenly stumbled upon a concealed doorway in the depths of the church. Hesitantly, he traced the outlines of the portal with his fingers, searching for a way to open it. His hand softly pressed on a small lever and a second later, he heard a slight 'click.'

Initially, Gideon hesitated to enter the space beyond, both out of fear and respect to the church's hidden secrets. But curiosity quickly overcame his hesitation and he silently slipped inside the darkness.

A switch on the wall brought a soft glow to the secret chamber, revealing countless shelves filled with ancient books, forgotten manuscripts, and dust-covered relics. The air within crackled with mystical energy, and Gideon realized he had uncovered a hidden archive of forbidden knowledge that perhaps even Father Matthias wasn't aware of. Little did he know that the secrets contained within would unravel the fabric of his reality, setting in motion a chain of events that would lead him down a perilous path.

***

The following night, as the sun dipped slowly below the

horizon, Gideon, with a flickering lantern in his hand, descended the narrow stairs leading to the church's hidden archives. His silhouette danced wildly against the walls as he approached the threshold. With a whispered prayer, he traced the outline of the entrance once more until he found the hidden latch and pushed open the creaking door. The dusty tomes, their spines adorned with cryptic symbols, beckoned him into a realm of knowledge concealed by the passage of time.

His nimble fingers traced the outlines of the arcane manuscripts, his eyes eager with curiosity. Although hesitant at first, Gideon quickly delved into these forbidden texts with an insatiable thirst. The soft, flickering light cast elongated shadows across his face as he absorbed the arcane wisdom, becoming a vessel through which the veil between the worldly and the mystical began to thin.

Compelled by an unseen force, he suddenly found himself drawn to a particularly aged tome hidden in the darkest corner of the chamber. He shuffled toward a large table in the back of the room and carefully sat the book down. With a delicate touch, he opened the cover. Immediately, the air crackled with an otherworldly energy. The flickering overhead light struggled against the gathering darkness, casting eerie shadows that danced across the symbols engraved on the pages. Gideon's eyes widened as ancient incantations revealed themselves, each word pulsating with a sinister resonance.

The forbidden wisdom, once dormant within the pages, now stirred as if recognizing a kindred spirit. Gideon held his breath as he traced the lines of ancient symbols with trembling fingers. The whispers of dark entities slithered into his mind, promising him power beyond mortal comprehension.

In the dim glow, Gideon hesitated, torn between the sacred teachings of the church and the seductive lure of the supernatural. A subtle voice echoed within, coaxing him to embrace the shadows that danced on the fringes of his faith. It spoke one word, "Vizibir."

The air suddenly went still, as if he were caught in the eye of a hurricane. The temperature of the room plummeted, sending a chill coursing through him that bit into his very soul. A vortex of swirling, black energy formed in the center of the room that posed as an inter-dimensional doorway to Hell. A second later, a dark figure stepped through the portal and advanced toward him.

As Gideon sought to back away from the menacing presence, the shadow bent down low and regarded him with a wide smile that erupted through its blackness. "Thank you," it hissed before it vanished as quickly as it had appeared.

Suddenly, the chamber seemed to exhale a sinister breath. Gideon's eyes, now reflecting the incandescent glow of demonic runes, revealed an internal transformation. The whispers now resonated within the recesses of his soul, etching the first lines of a dark pact.

Gideon closed the tome softly, his eyes now bearing witness to a dark metamorphosis taking place. The lantern's light flickered, as though protesting the unholy alliance forged in that sacred chamber. The shadows, now accomplices in Gideon's unholy communion, clung to him like tendrils in an insidious embrace.

CHAPTER 5

The following day, Priscilla found herself trying to settle into a new routine, albeit with a lingering sense of apprehension. Despite her best efforts to focus on unpacking and organizing her new apartment, memories of her mother continued to resurface, casting a shadow over her thoughts.

Finally, she decided to take a walk, hoping the fresh air and the allure of the secrets hidden in this new town would help ease her mind. "You wanna get out of here?" she said to Jinx.

Jinx's ears perked up before she trotted immediately to the door and snatched up the leash in her mouth.

Priscilla chuckled, "I guess that's a, yes?"

A minute later, they were embarking on an expedition to uncover all the riches this small town had to offer. Over the course of the next couple hours, they had traversed a wide section of town, stopping to admire a diverse selection of small shops and businesses along the way.

As Priscilla strolled past a small auto shop with a sign that read Robert's Garage hanging precariously over the shop's entrance, a foreboding chill settled over her, the air thick with an oppressive heaviness that seemed to press down on her from all sides. She wrapped her arms around herself, trying to shake off the sense of unease that clawed at the edges of her consciousness.

Robert, a pudgy middle-aged man with a greasy apron wrapped around his waist, glanced up from beneath the hood of a car, his eyes narrowing as they locked onto Priscilla's figure. Shadows danced across his face as his expression twisted into a grotesque parody of a smile.

"New in town, huh?" His voice was a low, guttural growl that sent a shiver down Priscilla's spine. "We're not used to folks like you around here."

Priscilla swallowed hard; her throat suddenly dry. She stepped closer, the gravel crunching beneath her feet. "Change can be a good thing, don't you think? I'm just here to live life a little differently."

Jinx gave a soft growl to echo Priscilla's statement.

Robert's laughter echoed through the garage, a harsh, grating sound that set Priscilla's teeth on edge. "You think you can just waltz in here and change things? You think you're special?" His voice took on a sinister edge, his eyes gleaming with an otherworldly light. "You have no idea what you're getting yourself into."

Priscilla's heart pounded in her chest, fear coursing through her veins like ice water. She took a step back, her breath coming in ragged gasps. "What do you mean? What's going on in this town?"

But Robert just grinned, his features twisting into a grotesque mask of madness. "You'll find out soon enough," he hissed, his voice echoing through the garage. "And when you do, you'll wish you'd never set foot in this cursed place."

With that, he turned away, his laughter fading into the darkness. Priscilla stood there, rooted to the spot, the weight of his words hanging heavy in the surrounding air.

A moment later, Robert turned his head toward her, oblivious to their previous interaction only a minute ago, eyeing her with a raised eyebrow. "New in town, huh? We're not used to folks like you around here."

When Priscilla didn't answer, Robert just grunted and resumed his work. As she stumbled away, the words echoed in her mind, *you'll wish you'd never set foot in this cursed place.*

Suddenly, the place that she had decided to call her new home seemed less like a sanctuary and more like a carnival of horrors.

As Priscilla and Jinx began the trek back toward their apartment, she spotted Emily chatting with a group of people outside a small coffee shop on a street corner near her apartment. Emily waved her over with a warm smile, and Priscilla hesitated for a moment before deciding to join them.

As she approached, Emily introduced Priscilla to the others and they exchanged pleasantries. Priscilla found herself drawn into the conversation, momentarily forgetting her troubles as she laughed and shared stories with her new acquaintances, while Jinx mingled among the group to their delight.

After a while, Emily pulled Priscilla aside. "How are you feeling today? I'm sure you're exhausted from moving, plus I got the feeling when we met yesterday that something was bothering you."

Priscilla hesitated, unsure how much to reveal to her new friend. But something about Emily's genuine concern put her at ease. "Honestly, it's been a rough few months," she admitted, her voice barely above a whisper.

Emily nodded. "I totally understand. I just want you to know that I'm here for you, Priscilla. Whatever you need."

"Thank you. I do have a question though. What's up with Robert and his garage? The place seems very dark."

Emily was quiet for a second before she answered, "Bob was a very strange man. Nobody really liked him much, but his was the only shop in town, so we had no other choice but to go to him if we needed help."

"You're talking about him like he's not around anymore."

"He died about a year ago. Some kind of freak accident in his shop."

Priscilla froze for a second. Not because she had seen his ghost—she had seen spirits since she was a little girl—but because she hadn't been able to tell that he had passed on. The veil between the living and the dead had been so thin that she had thought him alive, and that's what scared her the most.

CHAPTER 6

Night after night, Mary found herself ensnared in the same grotesque dreamscape, an otherworldly realm bleeding into the fragile tapestry of her mind. It always started out with her wandering through a forgotten cemetery, a thick fog clinging to the tombstones like tendrils of despair. The rain, heavy and cold, fell from a murky sky, mingling with the damp earth beneath her barren feet.

But this night was different. As Mary meandered through the ghoulish landscape, whispers hung in the air like ethereal apparitions. Again, the ghostly figure of a man emerged from the shadows, his form distorted and elongated. His eyes—vacant voids that seemed to absorb all light—were locked onto Mary with an intensity that sent shivers down her spine.

Suddenly, the graveyard came alive with the screams of those tortured souls who had departed the realm of the living and were now serving whatever hellish torment they had been awarded.

Mary sought to back away from the advancing figure, desperately turning to run, only to have dozens of bony claws reach up from the earth and grab at her. In seconds, she was overrun by skeletal figures, bound tightly and forced to watch in horror as the ghostly entity approached. The silhouette reached out its skeletal hand toward her, and as it did, large raven wings, as dark as the blackest sin, extended from its back, stretching out on each side to envelop her. It spoke her name with a sharp hiss in its voice, "Mary."

The figure bent its head down low, and Mary watched in horror as its face, which was nothing more than a veil of swirling black energy, shifted into focus and she was looking at a twisted version of Michael staring back at her. A wicked laugh erupted from his mouth as the darkness closed in on her.

In the blink of an eye, the dreamscape suddenly changed, and Mary found herself trapped inside a dark and dank crypt. The brick walls surrounding her were covered with moss and adorned with large cobwebs that stretched from corner to corner, while the stench of decay assaulted her nose and burned her eyes. The soft chittering of insects scurrying about echoed through the chamber as a thick fog seeped through the cracks in the stone like an insidious serpent.

As she backed away, her foot caught on the corner of a casket and she crashed to the floor. Daring a glance at the death box as she pushed herself up, she saw that the lid had been removed. When she saw herself lying inside, her face twisted in eternal agony, she tried to scream but no sound came out.

Then, Michael's ghostly figure was there once again. As he lunged for her, the mausoleum floor gave way beneath her, plunging her into a bottomless abyss. Mary's screams echoed into the void as she descended, the darkness swallowing her whole.

***

* * *

With a guttural gasp, Mary's eyes shot open. The remnants of the nightmare clung to her like a suffocating mist. A cold sweat drenched her trembling body, and the air in the room felt thick with an ominous dread.

As the moonlight filtered through the curtains, casting long, eerie shadows across the walls, Mary frantically looked around, as if she sensed a presence in the dark corners of the room.

With a shaky hand, she reached for her bedside lamp, bathing the room in a feeble, flickering light, but an unshakable terror still clung to her like a second skin. The distant echoes of the nightmare reverberated in her mind, the dark memory of Michael's ghostly figure lunging towards her leaving her breathless.

Clutching her belly, Mary tried to anchor herself in reality, but the chill of the dream persisted, seeping into her very bones. She could almost feel the mausoleum floor giving way beneath her once again, the sensation of plummeting into a bottomless abyss lingering as a haunting afterimage.

A heavy silence enveloped the room, broken only by the erratic cadence of Mary's breath. She couldn't shake the feeling that the nightmare had not released its hold on her entirely—that the tendrils of the supernatural ordeal still clung to the edges of her waking world—and that her dreams might be a harbinger of something far more sinister to come.

***

As the pale glow of the early morning light filtered through the curtains, Mary's hand groped once again for the bedside lamp. With a soft click, a warm light bathed the room that pushed back against the remnants of the darkness. In the gentle light, she stole a glance at the empty crib nestled in the corner, patiently awaiting her unborn child, and feared the world he may face.

Unable to shake the haunting images from her mind, Mary slipped out of bed and dressed, careful not to disturb the fragile peace that enveloped her swollen belly. She held her jacket tight against her body as she stepped into the crisp morning air, her breath hovering before her for a moment before dissolving.

The journey to St. Anthony's slowly transformed into an imperative pilgrimage, the dimly lit streets echoing with a hollow emptiness that mirrored her own as she approached the sacred grounds.

She paused for a moment, remembering the events that had happened outside this very structure not so long ago. The splintered door had been replaced with a new one, and the road in front of the building had been repaired, but to her discerning eye, a small trail of black stretched across the front of the highest tower. The construction crew had tried to paint over the evidence that an evil force had invaded their world, but a remnant lingered as a reminder that she needed to be ever vigilant against the darkness.

And that's what was really at the heart of everything. She knew it. She had experienced that darkness firsthand, and every ounce of her being feared that the same evil was waiting, biding its time until it could latch onto her son.

She pushed open the heavy door and made her way through the empty sanctuary. The soft flickering of candlelight danced upon the weathered pews, casting ethereal shadows along the walls. The scent of ancient wood and aged hymnals tried to offer a measure of solace as she walked towards the altar.

Father Donovan, an elderly priest with kind eyes that seemed to hold the wisdom of centuries, emerged from the shadows, his footsteps echoing softly on the worn stone floor. "Mary, my child. What brings you here at this early hour?" he said as he approached.

Mary's voice trembled as she spoke, "Father Donovan, I... I don't know what to do?" She stopped for a minute to pull herself together. "Every night I'm having these terrible nightmares. They're so dark and evil. And, even after I wake up, I feel like something's there, in the shadows waiting for me."

Father Donovan gestured for her to sit in the nearest pew. "Tell me about these dreams, Mary," he said as he sat down next to her. "Sometimes, our deepest fears take shape in the dark corners of our minds."

Tears welled in Mary's eyes as she recounted the nightmares that had wrapped around her like a relentless serpent. The chilling visions, the whispers that lingered in the corners of her consciousness—they all spilled out, painting a tapestry of fear and uncertainty. At first, she was hesitant to mention the dark version of Michael from these dreams, the one that had threatened to rip from her heart every good memory she had of him, but as she poured her soul out, she couldn't hold it in anymore.

Father Donovan placed a comforting hand on her shoulder. "Fear not, my child, for the Almighty watches over both the living and the unseen. These dreams, they stem from the depths of your love for your unborn child. The anticipation, the fear of the unknown, can manifest in haunting visions. But trust that God's protection extends to the tiniest miracles of life."

In the sacred hush of the church, Father Donovan offered a prayer, his voice invoking divine protection for Mary and her unborn child. The soft cadence of his words wrapped around her like a comforting cloak, momentarily dispelling the shadows that had taken refuge in her soul.

As Mary left the church, the air outside felt different—perhaps not lighter, but infused with a quiet resolve. She carried with her the priest's words, a fragile shield against the uncertainties that lurked in the shadows, hoping that they would be enough to fight the oncoming darkness. She feared they weren't.

CHAPTER 7

The moon hung low in the sky, casting eerie shadows across the empty street as Priscilla made her way home. As she approached her doorstep, she saw Emily sitting there with a cloud of despair hanging over her head.

"Emily?" Priscilla asked, her voice tinged with concern.

Emily looked up, her face drawn and pale, tears glistening in the dim light. "Priscilla," she whispered hoarsely, "I didn't know where else to go."

Priscilla's heart clenched at the sight of her friend in distress. Without hesitation, she ushered Emily inside.

Once settled on the couch, Emily's anguish spilled out like a torrential downpour. She spoke of her estranged father's passing, of the years lost to silence, and unresolved grievances. Tears streamed down her cheeks as she confessed her guilt and regret, the weight of her emotions threatening to consume her.

As Priscilla listened, her heart ached for her friend's pain. And then, in a moment of vulnerability, she revealed her own secret, a truth she had guarded closely for so long.

"Emily," Priscilla began, her voice barely above a whisper. "I need to tell you something. Something I've never shared with anyone other than my family before."

Emily looked up, her eyes wide with curiosity amidst the turmoil of her emotions.

"I can communicate with spirits," Priscilla confessed, her words hanging heavy in the air like thick smoke. "I have a gift, or perhaps it's better described as a curse, that allows me to bridge the gap between the living and the dead."

Emily's breath caught in her throat, disbelief mingling with hope in her eyes. "You're serious?" she asked, her voice trembling.

Priscilla nodded solemnly. "Yes. And I want to help. I want to offer you closure, a chance to speak to your father one last time."

A flicker of hope ignited within Emily's soul, illuminating the darkness that had threatened to consume her. With tearful gratitude, she accepted Priscilla's offer, clinging to the possibility of healing in the face of her grief.

***

The air in Priscilla's living room hung heavy with anticipation as she and Emily sat facing each other, hands clasped tightly together atop a weathered wooden table. A single candle flickered at the center, casting dancing shadows on the walls like restless spirits seeking solace.

Priscilla closed her eyes, allowing the darkness to envelop her senses as she delved into the depths of her gift. With each breath, she felt the barrier between the living and the dead grow thinner, a veil fluttering in the ethereal breeze.

"Focus on your father, Emily," Priscilla's voice echoed through the silence, soft yet commanded. "Let his presence guide you."

Emily nodded, her heart pounding like a drum in her chest

as she summoned memories of her father, his laughter echoing in the recesses of her mind like distant thunder.

Slowly, Priscilla began to chant, her words a haunting melody that wove through the room like tendrils of mist. She called out to the spirits, beckoning them forth from the shadows with a reverence born of years of practice.

As the candle flame flickered and danced, a shiver rippled through the air, sending goosebumps prickling along Emily's skin. And then, with a sudden gust of wind, the atmosphere shifted, crackling with an energy that seemed to hum with power.

A voice, soft and distant, whispered through the darkness, carrying with it a warmth that washed over Emily like a comforting embrace. "Emily," it murmured, the syllables tinged with a familiar cadence that sent tears streaming down her cheeks.

"Dad?" Emily's voice trembled with disbelief, her eyes wide with wonder as she reached out into the unknown.

"Yes, my sweet Em," the voice replied, its tone filled with love and regret. "I'm here."

The room seemed to hold its breath as Emily's voice quivered with emotion. "Dad," she whispered, her words barely audible over the gentle rustle of the wind outside. "I never got the chance to tell you I'm sorry... and that I love you."

A soft chuckle filled the air, warm and reassuring. "Oh, Emily," her father's voice enveloped her like a comforted blanket, "I've always known."

Tears welled in Emily's eyes as she reached out, as if trying to grasp hold of the fleeting memory of her father's touch. "I'm sorry," she choked out, her voice thick with regret. "I'm sorry for all the things I said, and everything left unsaid; for all the time wasted."

Her father's voice was filled with tenderness, "There's no need for apologies, Emily," he murmured. "Our time together may have been brief, but the love we shared endures."

A sense of peace slowly settled over Emily. "I miss you so much," she confessed, her voice trembling.

"I was never truly gone, my dear," her father's voice echoed through the room. "I'll always be with you, watching over you."

And in that sacred moment, Emily found solace in the knowledge that love transcends even the boundaries of death.

As the seance drew to a close, Priscilla gently guided Emily back to the present, her touch a grounding force in the midst of the swirling chaos of emotion. And as she sat in the quiet aftermath, Emily knew that she had touched something sacred, something that would linger in her heart long after the night had faded into memory.

CHAPTER 8

The quiet little town carried on with its daily affairs, blissfully unaware of the darkness that had infiltrated the heart of their once-virtuous priest. Gideon, standing at the pulpit in the dimly lit cathedral, found himself glancing nervously at the congregation. His normally confident voice now wavered as he delivered the morning sermon. The shadows seemed to dance eerily along the walls, mocking his internal turmoil.

With an unsteady smile he began to speak, his words coming out in stuttered syllables, "In this... humble town, let the Light guide your path."

The congregation exchanged nervous glances, a subtle unease settling among them, as Gideon's gaze flickered to the corners of the sanctuary, where the shadows hid the grotesque displays of the departed.

In the dimness, Gideon watched as the pews transformed into crypts, each seat harboring a silent specter. Lifeless eyes stared back at him, frozen in twisted expressions of pain and despair. Some clung to the rafters, their bodies contorted in ghastly poses, suspended in a macabre ballet. The air grew thick with the stench of decay, a morbid perfume that wafted through the unsuspecting assembly.

Gideon's hands trembled as he clutched the edges of the pulpit, desperately trying to maintain composure. The once-holy sanctum had become a nightmarish gallery, and the congregation remained blissfully ignorant, their attention fixed on the feeble attempts of their troubled priest.

The flickering candles cast elongated shadows, distorting the faces of the grotesque apparitions that only Gideon could see. Pale hands reached out from the darkness, as if pleading for release from their purgatorial prison. A chorus of phantom whispers echoed through the hallowed halls, creating a symphony of torment that went unheard by the unsuspecting faithful.

As Gideon continued his sermon, beads of cold sweat formed on his forehead and his voice wavered with an unsettling undertone. "Dear parishioners, in the embrace of the Father, we find solace and redemption. Yet, let us not be blind to the encroaching shadows that seek to engulf us."

A chorus of hushed whispers rose from the confused crowd as they looked around nervously.

"There is a darkness among us," Gideon said shakily, "lurking in the corners of our very souls. We must confront it, acknowledge its presence, for only then can the Father truly guide us through the treacherous paths that lay ahead."

The congregation shifted uncomfortably in their pews, exchanging puzzled glances, oblivious to the nightmarish reality that Gideon alone faced within the sanctuary.

Finally, Gideon, concluded his sermon, trying hard to look composed. "And so, my beloved congregation, let us bow our heads in reverence and unity, seeking the guidance of our ever-watchful Father. Let our collective prayers banish any lurking shadows, ensuring that our paths remain illuminated by the eternal grace that blesses us. As we stand together in this sanctuary, may the Light guide us towards the righteous way."

He looked out at the congregation, his eyes held low to avoid looking at the hellish nightmare that overtaken the sanctuary. "Let us join in prayer, thanking the Father for His unwavering presence among us."

The congregation obediently bowed their heads.

Gideon, his internal struggle hidden beneath a mask of tranquility, closed his eyes as a deceptive calm settled over the dimly lit sanctuary and began his prayer, "O, benevolent Spirit, as we partake in this moment of communal devotion, I implore you to extend your mercy upon this town. Grant us strength to overcome any unseen challenges that may threaten the harmony we cherish. Shield us from the shadows that I, as your humble servant, strive to confront. May your radiant glow envelop us all, guiding us towards a future bathed in the brilliance of your divine love."

A gurgled whisper rose up to Gideon's ear, causing him to open his eyes. He gasped as he watched a horde of demons emerge from the darkness. The air thickened with an otherworldly chill, and the once-hallowed space quickly twisted into a terrifying nightmare.

Gruesome creatures with twisted, skeletal-thin frames surrounded the unsuspecting parishioners, their skin a sickly shade of ashen gray. Their long, gnarled claws slashed through the air with bone-chilling sounds, sending sprays of blood in every direction, leaving gruesome trails in their wake. The insides of the holy place seemed to warp; its once-hallowed walls now painted with the splatter of death.

One demon, its form resembling a grotesque combination of twisted limbs and leathery wings, lunged toward Gideon with a guttural growl, landing inches away from his face. "Embrace us, Gideon," the demon hissed. "Swallow the darkness or become lost, just like those you pretend to lead."

Throughout the sanctuary, the demons reveled in a gruesome dance, tearing at human flesh with relentless ferocity. The congregation's anguished cries merged with the demonic howls, creating a cacophony of torment that dug into Gideon's very soul.

Suddenly, the scene shifted back to normal, the crowd completely unaware of the darkness that had just invaded their holy sanctuary. The demons vanished back into the shadows, leaving Gideon standing at the pulpit, drenched in cold sweat.

After a second, Gideon concluded the prayer with a visible shudder, "May our Heavenly Father protect us from the unseen forces that threaten to disrupt our sacred space. In its radiant glow, let us find solace and strength. Amen."

The congregation, unaware of the nightmarish bloodbath that had unfolded within their priest's tortured mind, opened their eyes, continuing the prayer with a sense of serene devotion.

"In your name, Heavenly Father, I offer this prayer for the well-being of our beloved community. Amen."

**

In the confessional later that morning, Gideon's hands trembled as he listened to the sins of his parishioners. The priest found himself struggling to offer words of comfort and forgiveness, his mind haunted by the sinister secrets hidden deep within the church.

One man, in his forties, with a long face and beady eyes, said in a low voice, "Father, I've been tormented by dark thoughts, and I fear I'm losing my way."

Gideon, his voice strained, replied, "Pray for guidance, my child. Pray for the Light to banish the shadows that threaten to consume your soul."

The man snickered in response, "You see, it's my neighbor's daughter. She just turned eighteen, and sometimes these thoughts enter my brain that I can't control."

"The temptations of the flesh are forever attacking man's soul. We must be vigilant against these attacks and quiet our mind so they fall away harmless."

"That's just it," the man said with a hint of malice in his voice. "It's too late. I'm afraid I've been a very bad boy. Yesterday, it got to where I couldn't help myself anymore."

Gideon's voice wavered, "There is no sin so great that it cannot be forgiven through prayer and penance."

The man's tongue slithered from his mouth and licked his lips like he was reliving his favorite meal. "The whispers in my head became so loud I couldn't shut them out, urging me to do terrible things. She was so young and juicy. Even when she was crying while I split her in two, I kept hearing the voices. They were relentless, repeating one word over and over." He paused for a second, as if afraid to voice the word, before he finally said, "Vizibir."

The confessional itself seemed to moan in response, as if the walls bore witness to the unholy communion between priest and penitent. Shadows danced within the cramped space, taking on ethereal forms that mirrored the sins confessed. Gideon fearfully peered through the lattice screen only to be met by a ghostly apparition, the face of a tormented soul etched into the dimly lit shadows.

Gideon's hands clenched the confessional's worn wood in an attempt to anchor himself against the rising tide of horror. His eyes widened as he glimpsed the tortured spirit manifesting in the confessional booth, a wraith-like figure clinging to the parishioner.

As he struggled to maintain the facade of a compassionate

priest, Gideon felt the tendrils of darkness weaving around his own soul. He swallowed hard as he continued, "I recommend twenty hail-Mary's and a week of fasting to cleanse your soul of this darkness."

"It won't do any good," the man said simply. "He gave me a message for you: He's coming. And you better make sure you're ready."

The man then got up and walked out of the confessional, leaving Gideon on his seat shaken and scared.

***

As evening descended, Gideon forced a smile while he mingled with the crowd in the church courtyard—a place that was once a haven of community and camaraderie, but now was shrouded in gloom. His smile strained even further as he felt the weight of the unspeakable horrors that lurked just beyond the perception of the unsuspecting group. The flickering lights cast grotesque shadows on his face, mirroring the contorted expressions of the tortured spirits that haunted the hallowed grounds.

A middle-aged woman slowly approached him, her eyes bright and cheerful. "Thank you, Father Gideon. Your guidance has brought light and joy into our lives. We are forever grateful."

Gideon, a flicker of conflict in his eyes, replied in a pre-occupied tone, "Yes, yes, the Light is our refuge."

As the people continued to express their gratitude, Gideon's eyes darted nervously, scanning the faces of those he had sworn to protect. Unknown to them, a spectral entourage surrounded them, as an icy wind whispered through the courtyard, carrying with it the mournful cries of tormented souls.

Gideon's internal conflict deepened with each word of praise, a contradiction between the priest they believed him to be and the harbinger of darkness he was becoming. The once-joyful laughter of his parishioners now sounded like distant echoes, distorted and haunting. He longed to warn them, to reveal the ghastly truth that lurked beneath their seemingly idyllic existence, but the forbidden knowledge clenched at his throat like a vise.

As the wind suddenly grew in intensity, Gideon's gaze flitted nervously toward the church, its silhouette looming ominously against the dimming sky. In that moment, he realized the twisted dance of shadows beneath the surface had grown more sinister, and he feared he was losing himself to the encroaching darkness.

With a final, forced nod and a half-hearted smile, Gideon retreated from the courtyard, leaving behind the mask of peace and serenity he had feebly worn.

***

As the moonlight streamed through the stained-glass windows, casting fractured patterns on the cold stone floor, Gideon kneeled before the altar. Beads of sweat formed on his forehead as he wrestled with conflicting prayers, torn between seeking divine intervention and succumbing to the seductive whispers of the forbidden knowledge.

With each strike of the church bell, Gideon grappled with the toll his actions were taking on his soul. The sound reverberated through the air, a haunting reminder of the irreversible path he was treading. The echoes seemed to amplify the internal struggle, the clash between the sacred and the profane.

Sleep became an elusive companion for Gideon.

Nightmares, vivid and unsettling, invaded his restless slumber. The scent of damp earth and decaying leaves pervaded his dreams, a manifestation of the darkness seeping into his subconscious.

Finally, Gideon shuffled from his dorm and walked back and forth nervously through the halls mumbling softly to himself as he tried to quiet the demons running rampant inside his mind. The foundation of faith that he had clung to his whole life was now crumbling beneath him, and he feared that he wouldn't be strong enough to pull himself from the abyss once it collapsed completely.

Bordering on the edge of panic and exhaustion, he reached for the door to his room only to realize that he was back in the forgotten hall where it had all began. The outline of the hidden door began to glow softly, beckoning to him. Like a siren song, the forbidden secrets contained within called out to him, drawing him closer, and before he could even comprehend his actions, he was inside the secret chamber, moving like an automaton toward the ancient volumes lining the shelves.

Alone in the room, the conflict raging inside Gideon reached a fever pitch. The flickering light reflected the turmoil etched across his face. The arcane tomes that once terrified him now beckoned, their secrets seducing him with promises of unrivaled power.

Gideon, his hands shaking, opened one of the forbidden books, tracing ancient symbols with trembling fingers. Whispers, soft and insidious, echoed in his mind, offering guidance on how to further tap into the dark forces he had unleashed.

The priest now stood at the precipice, the weight of his actions pulling him toward an irreversible darkness. For a brief second, he tried to force himself away from the madness, using the last ounce of faith he had left in an effort to regain control and break free. But the forces of evil that had taken hold of him were too strong.

A crackle of energy coursed through the room as the last wall protecting Gideon's soul crashed down and the darkness overtook him completely. With a fervent hunger, he devoured the secrets of the damned.

Gideon, who had promised to protect all that was holy, was no more.

CHAPTER 9

Days passed, but the nightmares continued to haunt Mary like a persistent specter, creeping into her mind even in moments of supposed peace. Each night, as she drifted into the realm of sleep, the darkness seemed to envelop her, suffocating and oppressive.

One evening, as Mary sat alone in the dimly lit living room, the soft glow of the lamp casting long shadows across the walls, she felt a presence—a whispering in the shadows that sent shivers down her spine.

She clutched her swollen belly protectively, her heart pounding with fear as the whispers grew louder, more insistent, as if the darkness itself had found a voice.

The air grew colder, thick with the weight of unseen cruelty. Shadows danced on the walls, twisting and contorting into grotesque shapes that seemed to leer at her with evil intent.

"Mary," the voice hissed, a chill wind brushing against her skin. "Mary, we're coming for him. We're coming for your son."

She tried to shake off the terror that gripped her, but the whispers only intensified, echoing through the empty rooms of the house like a sinister lullaby.

In desperation, Mary stumbled to her feet, her hands trembling as she fumbled for her phone. With shaking fingers, she dialed Father Donovan's number, praying that he would answer, that his voice would be a beacon of light in the suffocating darkness.

Each ring felt like an eternity, the silence broken only by the whispers that seemed to coil around her like serpents.

"Father Donovan," she gasped when he finally picked up, her voice trembling. "Please, you have to help me. The shadows... they're talking to me. They want my baby!"

There was a moment of silence on the other end of the line, and then Father Donovan's voice, calm and steady, filled the void. "Mary, listen to me carefully. Do not listen to the whispers of darkness. They seek only to sow fear and despair. Trust in the protection of the Almighty, for His light will always prevail over the shadows."

With those words echoing in her mind like a mantra, Mary closed her eyes and whispered a fervent prayer for divine intervention. And slowly, ever so slowly, the whispers began to fade, until all that remained was the gentle hum of the lamp and the steady beat of her own heart.

But even as the darkness receded, Mary knew that it would return—that the battle against the shadows was far from over. And as she cradled her unborn child in her arms, she vowed to do whatever it took to keep him safe from the encroaching darkness, no matter the cost.

With trembling hands, she reached for a blanket, wrapping it tightly around her shoulders as if to ward off the unseen chill that permeated the air. Every creak of the floorboards, every flicker of movement in the corner of her eye, sent her heart racing anew, a primal instinct urging her to flee, to escape the unseen threat that lurked in the shadows.

But she knew there was no escape—not from the darkness that had woven itself into the very fabric of her existence. It was a part of her now, a relentless force that would stop at nothing to claim what it believed was rightfully its own.

As the night wore on, Mary huddled in the flickering light of the lamp, her eyes fixed on the crib that stood silent and empty in the corner of the room. She prayed for morning to come, for the first light of dawn to banish the shadows once and for all.

But deep down, she knew that the darkness would never truly be vanquished—that it would always linger, a constant reminder of the fragile line between light and shadow, between hope and despair.

And as the whispers returned, faint and fleeting, Mary uttered a silent vow to her unborn child—a promise to protect him from the darkness that threatened to consume them both.

CHAPTER 10

Twilight descended on Priscilla's cozy living room like a shroud, casting long shadows that danced in the flickering candlelight. Emily sat opposite her, a glint of curiosity in her eyes that mirrored the restless energy crackling in the air.

"Priscilla," Emily began, her voice a soft whisper that seemed to echo in the silence, "I can't stop thinking about what happened the other night; what you did for me and my father. I want to learn all about your gifts. I want you to teach me what you know."

Priscilla regarded her friend with a smile, her eyes holding secrets that stretched far beyond the physical realm. "Are you sure, Emily?" she asked, her voice a low murmur. "What you're asking is not for the timid. Once the doors of the universe are opened, they're difficult to close."

Emily nodded, "I'm sure," she replied, her voice steady despite the tremor of excitement coursing through her veins. "I want to learn everything."

With a silent nod, Priscilla reached for a weathered deck of tarot cards resting on the table between them, their faded edges whispering of secrets long forgotten. "Then let's begin," she murmured, her fingers weaving a dance as she shuffled the cards with a practiced ease.

As the cards fell before them, Emily felt a thrill of anticipation coiling in the pit of her stomach, her heart pounding like a drum in the silence of the room. With a flick of her wrist, Priscilla spread the cards out like a map to the unknown, their images shimmering in the dim light.

"Now," Priscilla's voice was a mere whisper, "clear your mind, Emily. Focus on the question burning in your soul, and let the cards reveal their secrets."

Emily closed her eyes, allowing the darkness to envelop her as she reached out into the unknown, her question echoing in the depths of her mind like a prayer. With a slow exhale, she drew a single card from the spread, its surface cool against her fingertips.

As she turned over the card, a gasp escaped her lips, her eyes widening in awe at the image before her. "The High Priestess," she breathed. "What does it mean?"

Priscilla regarded the card with a knowing smile, her eyes gleaming. "The High Priestess represents intuition, mystery, and the subconscious," she explained. "She is a guide through the shadows, a guardian of secrets long forgotten."

Emily finally got it, like a lightbulb turning on in her head. "Thank you, Priscilla," she whispered, her voice carrying a hint of awe and appreciation.

"This is just a first step on a long winding road."

"Where did you get all this stuff?" Emily asked as she glanced around the room at all the charms and amulets mingled with scores of ominous looking books.

Priscilla was silent for a second before she replied, "My mother was a very special woman."

"She must've been to have a daughter like you."

Priscilla remained quiet as she pushed the tears away once more.

* * *

***

As the days melted into weeks, Priscilla and Emily's connection deepened, entwining like vines in a secret garden. Under Priscilla's tutelage, Emily embarked on a journey into the arcane, her thirst for knowledge igniting like a flame in the darkness. With each whispered incantation and flicker of candlelight, she delved deeper into the mysteries of divination, her senses attuned to the subtle vibrations that pulsed through the air like a siren's song.

Priscilla guided Emily through the intricate dance of spirit communication. Together, they peeled back the layers of reality, revealing the hidden truths that lurked beneath the surface of the mundane world.

As Emily absorbed each lesson eagerly, her excitement grew. With every new revelation, she felt herself drawing closer to the mystical elements that swirled unseen all around.

And with Emily by her side, shedding light on the shadows of her soul, Priscilla found the strength to face her own past ghosts. The two of them navigated through the maze of sorrow together, searching for comfort and redemption among the misty memories that haunted them both.

In her new life, Priscilla finally found peace from the storms inside her. The walls of her apartment wrapped around her like a friendly hug, shielding her from the chaos.

She wandered the streets regularly, often with Jinx at her side, her footsteps echoing in the empty spaces between shadows. With each adventure, she uncovered the town's hidden treasures, breathing life into forgotten spots with her presence.

As time passed, Priscilla became an integral part of the community, blending into their story like ink on a page. Once met with doubt, her quirks now intrigued them, drawing them in like a spellbinding melody.

One night under the twinkling lights of the local bar, Priscilla clinked glasses with her new friends, feeling the warmth of their companionship melting the cold in her heart. Amidst laughter and chatter, she found a sense of belonging, a glimmer of hope in the darkness.

Her eyes were suddenly drawn to a flyer on the corner of the bar. Emily followed her as she walked over and picked up the paper, absorbed in its bright colors and descriptive fonts that announced the upcoming Annual Arts Festival.

"We have the arts festival every year down at the park and the surrounding businesses. It's a lot of fun! You should totally set up a booth there," Emily said matter-of-factly as she took a swig of her beer. "That would be so cool!"

Priscilla raised an eyebrow. "I'm not so sure about that? I've never done anything in public like that before, plus people already think I'm weird enough as it is."

"Are you kidding me? People love you. They just had to get used to your uniqueness."

Priscilla chuckled. "My uniqueness?"

"You know what I mean," Emily said with a smile. "You're a free spirit, while most of the people in this town have a stick shoved up their ass."

Emily suddenly got excited, "I know... you can dress up like a gypsy, complete with large hoop earrings and a red scarf around your head. With your long, dark hair, you pretty much fit the part already. Picture a sign that reads, 'Zelda the All-Knowing.' People will think it's just a show without realizing the truth. You'll be helping them without them even knowing it."

"Let me think about it," Priscilla said. But inside, her mind was already made up, her mother sitting beside her nodding her on with a gentle smile.

51

CHAPTER 11

Gideon moved like a shadow through the labyrinthine halls, each step calculated to avoid even the slightest echo. The sacred tome he clutched seemed to pulse with a mysterious energy, amplifying the tension in the air. The walls whispered ancient secrets, and the flickering lights cast dancing shadows that seemed to conspire against him.

As he approached the entrance to the hidden chamber, Gideon's senses heightened. The sinister runes on the walls began to glow with an unsettling intensity that only he could see, and the air crackled with a foreboding energy. Then he felt the weight of Matthias' presence approaching like an impending storm.

Just as Gideon turned away from the concealed entrance, doubling back toward the main corridor, he heard the rhythmic footsteps of Father Matthias drawing near. The hooded figure emerged from the shadows, his piercing gaze fixing on Gideon like a hawk spotting its prey.

"Brother Gideon," Matthias spoke, his voice echoing through the corridor. "I was making my nightly security check and thought I heard something. Why are you wandering these halls at this hour? What troubles your spirit in the dead of night?"

Gideon turned to face Matthias with the sacred tome discreetly hidden beneath his robe. He bowed low, his eyes cast downward in feigned reverence. "Father Matthias, I seek solace in the sanctity of these hallowed halls. The weight of our sacred duties burdens my soul."

Matthias studied Gideon for a second, his eyes narrowing. "The path of devotion is not without its challenges, Brother. But beware, for darker forces may lurk in the shadows, tempting even the most steadfast."

Gideon nodded solemnly, his mind racing to maintain the illusion of innocence. "Your guidance is my anchor in these turbulent times, Father. I only hope to find enlightenment and strength to serve our sacred order."

Father Matthias held Gideon in a scrutinizing gaze, the silence stretching between them like a taut bowstring. Gideon could almost hear the elder priest's thoughts probing for any sign of deceit.

"May the spirits be your guide," Matthias finally said, breaking the silence before he continued his patrol, disappearing into the darkness.

Gideon released a pent-up breath, beads of sweat clinging to his forehead. He waited until Matthias's footsteps faded before moving stealthily back through the corridor, his footsteps barely audible. He tightly clutched the sacred tome in his trembling hands, feeling the coolness of its weathered pages against his skin. As he entered the hidden chamber, the air crackled with energy. Sinister runes adorned the walls, pulsating with an eerie light that cast haunting shadows. The sacred tome seemed to quiver in response, its ancient pages whispering promises of unimaginable power.

The ominous glow of the runes intensified as he sat the book down on the table and carefully opened its cover, stopping on a page with an image of a black-robed figure encircled by tendrils of dark magic. As he began to chant the incantation the air thickened with a palpable tension.

Gideon's voice quivered, each syllable of the incantation escaping his lips like a hesitant whisper yet carrying the weight of centuries-old secrets. "Ignis umbrae, malum veni," he chanted, the ancient words weaving a tapestry of arcane magic in the air. The acrid scent in the room thickened, an unsettling fragrance that spoke of both forbidden knowledge and the presence of forces long kept at bay.

As the ritual unfolded, the room's atmosphere shifted ominously. The runes on the walls pulsed with an eerie glow, their malevolence intensifying in response to Gideon's invocation. The temperature plummeted, and an icy wind began to swirl around him.

Undeterred, Gideon pressed on, his voice steady despite the fear and anticipation gripping him. "Tenebrae potentia, aperire portam inter mundos," he continued, the sacred words resonating with a dark energy that seemed to warp the fabric of reality itself. The sacred tome beneath his hands radiated an unholy light.

In the midst of the ritual's crescendo, a sudden surge of power rocketed through the room, causing the lights to crackle and hiss before going out, plunging everything into impenetrable darkness. Gideon's heart raced as he navigated the ritual by memory, the shadows now alive with a dark energy.

As the last words of the incantation left his lips, the sacred tome glowed with an intensity that bordered on blinding. The twisted silhouette of an otherworldly figure materialized.

Emerging from the shadows, the demonic entity took form, its eyes ablaze with an infernal light that pierced through the darkness. The very air seemed to quiver in the presence of this ancient force. The demon's voice echoed with a haunting melody, resonating deep within Gideon's soul.

"Gideon, servant of the light turned disciple of the dark," the demon hissed. "I offer you power beyond mortal comprehension."

Gideon's eyes widened, a mix of terror and perverse excitement coursing through him as he nodded fervently. "I am yours, master. Grant me the strength to fulfill my destiny."

The demon's grin widened, revealing teeth sharp as serrated blades, each one like a dagger poised to plunge into Gideon's very soul. The unholy light in the chamber intensified, casting elongated shadows that seemed to writhe with evil delight.

"So be it, Gideon," the demon hissed. "Embrace the shadows, and together, we will change the fate of the world."

As the demonic energy surged, it seized Gideon with a vise-like grip, sending waves of searing pain through every fiber of his being. He convulsed violently as his screams reached a crescendo, a symphony of torment that echoed through the accursed chamber. His body, bathed in an unholy light, contorted and twisted in ways that defied the natural order, resulting in bones snapping and then reforming. The pain, an unrelenting torrent, seemed to stretch into an eternity as his very essence was reshaped.

The air thickened with the scent of burning flesh, as if Gideon's very soul was being seared by the infernal power. His once-holy vestments clinging to his writhing form transformed into a cocoon of darkness that seemed to devour him from the inside out. The symbols of the abyss etched themselves into his flesh, each mark a searing brand that spoke of his unholy allegiance.

Finally, as the demonic ordeal reached its zenith, a

sickening silence descended upon the chamber. Gideon, now unrecognizable, stood hunched and panting. His eyes, now hollow and vacant, gleamed with an unsettling wickedness.

Gideon's form trembled, the echoes of his torment still reverberating through the room. As the unholy energy subsided, a shuddering gasp escaped his lips, and his eyes once again flickered with a trace of their former clarity.

As the energy in the room began to wane, a subtle transformation unfolded. Gideon's contorted form trembled, and the demonic symbols etched into his flesh began to fade, like tendrils of smoke dissipating into the air.

With a deep breath, Gideon steadied himself, the echoes of his screams fading into the shadows. He straightened his posture, the façade of his former self carefully reconstructed. Now standing in the aftermath of his infernal ordeal, he seemed to regain a semblance of composure. His eyes, though, still held a haunted look, a silent testimony to the horrors he had endured.

The chamber, bathed in an eerie stillness, bore witness to the unsettling transformation. His true self hidden behind this disguise, Gideon now stood as a paradox—a vessel that concealed the darkness within.

With newfound conviction, Gideon stepped out into the corridor, his eyes gleaming with an unholy light that seemed to pierce through the darkness. The demon slithered at his side, whispering dark secrets and planting seeds of evil in his mind.

CHAPTER 12

As the sun began its descent across the late afternoon sky, it cast a warm glow over the small town. The summer art festival was just beginning, and already lively music and laughter filled the air. Vibrant stalls adorned with colorful streamers and string lights lined the bustling streets, offering artisanal crafts and a variety of global cuisines. The air was filled with the scent of blooming flowers mixed with the alluring aroma of street food.

Priscilla, dressed in a long, white flowing blouse, wearing large hoop earrings and a red scarf wrapped around her forehead, looked like she belonged in another time and another place. She had set up a small booth at the edge of the lush park that was the main focal point of the festival, where she offered tarot readings to those curious enough to explore the mystic arts. Emily had painted an enormous banner that hung across the top that read 'Zelda, the All-Knowing' in big red letters, punctuated with magic symbols bordering the perimeter.

Amid the symphony of the festival noise, a hush fell over the crowd as Priscilla and Emily began to carefully unfold a vibrant tapestry onto the small wooden table that served as her booth. The fabric depicted intricate patterns of stars, moons, and swirling galaxies, mirroring the mysteries that surrounded her. Candles flickered in glass jars, casting dancing shadows on the tapestry, creating an otherworldly ambiance.

"Is it too late to back out?" Priscilla asked Emily nervously as the first group of patrons walked toward her booth.

Emily chuckled, "Just be yourself and you'll do fine. Remember, this is all for fun."

"I take my gifts very serious, Emily. You know that. I don't do it just for fun."

"That's not what I meant, and you know it. I meant, just relax and don't pressure yourself."

Priscilla took a deep breath and let it out slowly. "You're right. I'm sorry."

She was just about to take her seat at the table when Emily stopped her. "Just one more thing." She pulled the sleeves down on Priscilla's blouse to bare her shoulders, and then did the same with the front to show a little more cleavage. "There, now you look like a true gypsy."

"And a slutty one, at that," Priscilla snickered.

"Aren't those the best kind?" Emily replied with a sneer. "Now, time to put on a show," she said as she nudged Priscilla forward before exiting out the back of the tent.

As the crowd gathered nearby, watching Priscilla, in her chic, flowing outfit gently swaying with the afternoon breeze, her intense eyes scanned the intrigued faces around her.

As Priscilla arranged her tarot cards with a deliberate precision, curious onlookers began to gather. Some exchanged intrigued glances, while others whispered in hushed tones. Priscilla remained focused on her task, her hands moving with a grace that hinted at years of practiced skill.

A middle-aged woman approached the booth cautiously, eyeing the tarot cards with a mixture of skepticism and curiosity. "Are you the one they're all talking about?" she asked, her tone a blend of disbelief and fascination.

Priscilla looked up, her eyes penetrating and filled with a knowing glint. "I guess I am," she replied, her voice a soft melody that seemed to carry on the breeze. "Would you like a glimpse into the mysteries of the universe surrounding you?"

The woman hesitated for a moment, then nodded, intrigued. Priscilla motioned for her to sit across from the table, and as she began to shuffle the cards, the festival's lively ambiance seemed to fade into the background.

The woman took a seat across from Priscilla, looking at the tarot cards spread out before her with a hint of trepidation in her eyes. With a subtle gesture, Priscilla motioned for the woman to choose, "Pick three cards that speak to you."

As the woman picked her cards, Priscilla's fingers moved gracefully over the remaining deck. She studied the chosen cards carefully. "The Fool," she began, her voice carrying a mystical weight, "represents a leap into the unknown, a journey that may seem foolish to others but holds the key to profound wisdom for you."

She turned the next card. "The Tower," Priscilla continued, her gaze unyielding. "A disruption is on the horizon, a shaking of foundations. Embrace the chaos, for from destruction arises transformation."

The last card revealed itself, and Priscilla looked into the woman's eyes. "The Moon," she whispered, her voice a ghostly echo. "A path obscured by shadows, illusions dancing on the edges of your reality. Trust your intuition; the moonlit darkness conceals hidden truths."

The woman's skepticism lingered, but a flicker of curiosity

sparked in her eyes. Priscilla's words hung in the air, wrapped with mystery. The festival's sounds slowly returned, but the woman couldn't shake the cryptic feeling of the reading.

"It seems you have a big decision you've been thinking about for some time," Priscilla said. "Follow your heart, knowing that everything will work out for your benefit."

As the woman walked away from the booth, Priscilla looked up to see a flock of ravens lining the branches of a nearby tree, their collective eyes regarding her intently. One of them let out a soft 'caw' before they all flew away, leaving her with a sense of dread.

Amidst the bright lights of the festival, and the soft breeze of the summer air, she suddenly had a terrible feeling that a storm was coming.

CHAPTER 13

Andrew longed for relief from the unrelenting chaos of city life, craving a sanctuary where the frenetic pace could fade into the background. The constant noise and bustle had worn him down, leaving him weary and disillusioned. With a determined resolve, he set out on a journey to discover a sense of peace and tranquility that only a small town could offer.

As Andrew ventured deeper into the heart of this tranquil haven, he found that which had eluded him for far too long. The streets whispered stories of simplicity and serenity, while the warm embrace of the locals welcomed him with open arms. Against the backdrop of scenic landscapes, Andrew felt a weight lifted from his shoulders, replaced by a newfound sense of purpose and hope, as if the universe itself had conspired to guide him to this moment of peace amidst the chaos.

Almost immediately, Andrew found a job working at the local bookstore—a haven for book lovers and a hub of intellectual engagement. He found solace within the cozy confines of the small store. Growing up as a bookworm himself, he was instantly at home within its walls, and quickly formed personal bonds with many of its regular patrons.

Between tending to the bookstore, which had become his second home, and exploring the scenic surroundings, Andrew discovered a sense of peace that had eluded him for years, signaling the beginning of a new chapter in his life's journey.

***

Word of Priscilla's intriguing booth spread through the festival like wildfire, drawing a steady stream of curious onlookers. Some approached with skepticism, others with genuine interest, but all left with a spark of fascination kindled by her mysterious presence. And as the festival continued, Priscilla wove her own threads into the fabric of the community, leaving behind an indelible mark on the hearts and minds of those who dared to explore the mystic arts with her.

Intrigued by the commotion surrounding Priscilla's booth, Andrew found himself drawn to the spectacle. The vibrant colors of the tarot cards, the incense lingering in the air, and the curious gazes of fellow attendees created an atmosphere that intrigued and challenged Andrew's conservative nature.

Andrew hesitated at the edge of the bustling festival with his eyes fixated on Priscilla's booth. Yet a magnetic pull drew him closer, compelling him to explore the unknown.

As he approached, the lively chatter of the crowd and the strains of distant music enveloped him. Priscilla, sensing his arrival, looked up with a knowing smile that seemed to pierce through the layers of his reserved demeanor.

Their eyes met, and Priscilla silently invited Andrew to experience a reading. With a mix of curiosity and a touch of skepticism, he agreed, sitting across from Priscilla as she laid out the cards.

"Hello, Andrew," she greeted him, her voice a melodic whisper that carried an uncanny warmth.

"How do you know my name?" Andrew asked reservedly.

Priscilla smiled, "I know lots of things. Do you want the cards to show you?"

Andrew's expression revealed a mix of curiosity and apprehension. "I'm not sure about all this," he admitted, glancing at the tarot cards laid out on the table. "I've always been a bit more traditional in my beliefs."

"Tradition certainly has its place," Priscilla said, her gaze unwavering. "But sometimes, it's worth considering the uncharted waters to discover new horizons."

Despite his reservations, Andrew found himself drawn to the idea. He hesitated for a moment before finally nodding. The candles flickered as she began to shuffle the cards with a practiced elegance.

As the cards revealed their stories, Priscilla spoke in a gentle tone. She touched upon aspects of Andrew's life that seemed almost too personal to be mere chance, offering insights that stirred a complex mixture of emotions within him. In that moment, the boundaries between the conservative values he held dear and the mystic allure of Priscilla's insights began to blur.

As the reading concluded, Priscilla locked eyes with Andrew, their gaze holding steady in a brief display of romantic tension. "The tapestry of life is vast, and each thread adds its unique beauty," she finally said cryptically. "Sometimes, embracing the unknown can lead to unexpected surprises."

Andrew's mind was spinning as he left Priscilla's booth, the encounter lingering in his thoughts. The festival continued around him, but Priscilla's mystical presence had left an indelible mark on him, sparking a subtle shift in the tapestry of his own beliefs.

***

"What just happened here?" Emily said with a smile as she re-entered the rear of the tent while Priscilla took a break.

Feigning oblivion, Priscilla replied, "I have no idea what you're talking about?"

"The redness in your cheeks would suggest otherwise."

Priscilla tried to object further, but knew it was futile. "He was kinda cute, wasn't he?"

"I knew it! You felt something, didn't you?"

"Was it that obvious?"

Emily laughed. "Let's just say, any more sexual tension between you two and you would've needed a private room."

"Okay, break time's over. Get out of here, now."

A light squeal erupted from Emily's lips as Priscilla shooed her from the tent.

Priscilla took a deep breath as Andrew's image lingered in her mind, bringing a soft smile to her lips.

***

As Andrew left Priscilla's booth and made his way across the park toward another group of booths boasting an assortment of street-fair foods and handcrafts, he couldn't get Priscilla out of his mind. He had become enraptured by her from the first moment he entered her booth, not just from the arcane knowledge she carried within her, but from the carefree way she presented herself, letting herself be true in every moment. She was the opposite of him in every way, and she was perfect.

After a futile attempt to distract himself with a greasy Philly Cheesesteak, followed by the biggest Elephant Ear he'd ever seen, Andrew found himself drawn back toward the corner of the park. Standing at the back of the crowd, he watched spellbound as she dazzled the crowd with her mysticism. Then she looked directly at him and smiled.

As soon as Priscilla finished with her current reading and the recipient left with the familiar look of awe on their face, she closed up her booth—amidst a smattering of complaints from waiting customers—and walked directly toward Andrew, her steps filled with purpose.

Andrew tried to turn away, his face flushed with embarrassment, and nearly tripped over his own feet, causing him to stagger backward.

"If I didn't know any better, Andrew," Priscilla said, "I'd think you were stalking me."

Instantly tongue-tied, Andrew's words tripped over themselves as he struggled to talk, "It's not... I mean, I don't... It's just..."

Priscilla chuckled, "Relax. I'm just joking. But I am curious about why you came back to watch me?"

Andrew took a deep breath to calm the butterflies in his stomach. "To be honest," he finally said, "I'm not sure? The entire experience just kind of shook me somehow."

"You feel conflicted because of your faith."

"I've just never been exposed to anything like this before. It's certainly opened my eyes that there's more to this world than I had known."

"So, you came back because of my otherworldly insight?"

"No, that's not it. I mean, that's part of it, but..."

A playful smile sprung to her lips. "I'm just playing." Then she looked him directly in the eyes, and he was completely spellbound once more. "I felt the same thing," she said softly.

To his surprise, she reached out and took his hand, leading him further into the festival, where they continued their discourse into the mysteries of the universe amidst the lights and music of the surrounding celebration.

CHAPTER 14

The sun, a timid presence in the dawn sky, cast its first rays upon the town. Gideon, dressed in his pristine white and gold vestments, emerged from the rectory adjacent to the church. The morning air carried the scent of dew-kissed grass and blooming flowers as Gideon walked the narrow path to the church.

The aged wooden door groaned softly as he entered the sacred space. The morning Mass was a quiet affair, attended by the early risers and the devoted few. As he approached the pulpit, he could feel the tendrils of darkness that had taken hold of him writhing inside, just below the surface, waiting for its time to wreak havoc. He gently pushed the darkness down and took his place, standing beneath the soft hues of stained glass, and held his arms out wide to his unsuspecting congregation.

Gideon, with a benevolent smile that betrayed his true nature, said, "In this humble town, let the Spirit guide your path. Embrace one another with kindness, for in unity, we find strength."

The congregation, nestled in the familiar wooden pews, listened with reverence, unaware of the darkness that now lingered beneath their priest's charismatic veneer.

As the morning Mass concluded, Gideon transitioned towards the quiet confessional nestled in the corner of the church. The aged door, a silent keeper of innumerable secrets, groaned as it creaked open and closed, allowing parishioners to seek solace within its hallowed confines.

Within the confessional, the atmosphere shifted to one of intimate vulnerability. Gideon lowered himself into the confessional booth. His voice, a delicate blend of gentleness and calculated persuasion, flowed through the wooden partition as he offered absolution to those who dared to bare their souls.

Behind the privacy of the confessional curtain, the parishioners whispered their darkest confessions, trusting in Gideon's facade of compassion. Although the air was thick with the weight of remorse and the anticipation of redemption, instead, the confessional became the stage upon which Gideon orchestrated his subtle manipulations.

One parishioner, their voice hushed with guilt, confessed, "Father, I have coveted my neighbor's success."

Gideon, his voice a carefully crafted symphony of understanding, feigned compassion: "My child, forgiveness is the path to redemption. Your sins are absolved. Now, reflect on the love that binds your community together, realizing that with Him everything is possible. The success which another has should be yours to share just as well. If he will not offer it freely, then you must take that which belongs to you." His words, seemingly benevolent, carried a subtle undertone of influence as he skillfully redirected their focus, manipulating their emotions to serve his own hidden agenda.

He continued to exploit the sacred trust bestowed upon him by his parishioners. The confessional, once a symbol of repentance and absolution, now became a silent witness to the darker undercurrents coursing through the town. Unknown to the parishioners, their confessions fueled the shadows growing within Gideon.

*
* * *

As the sun descended beyond the horizon, its last rays casting a warm glow over the cathedral, Gideon emerged from the church out into the open courtyard, where a crowd of parishioners had gathered. He moved among them, flashing his charismatic smile while concealing the darkness that plotted beneath the surface.

After mingling with them for a time, he retreated to the dimly lit corridors beneath the church. The hidden chamber had become his sanctuary, a place where he could explore the darkest secrets of reality.

Alone with the shadows, he whispered sinister promises to the darker essence that lurked within him. "They trust me, believe in my righteousness. Little do they know that their faith in me will be their undoing."

In the secrecy of the night, Gideon delved into forbidden rituals, consulted ancient texts, and harnessed the dark energies surging around and through him. As the town slept, blissfully unaware of the dual existence of their priest, Gideon continued to weave a web of deception that, like a serpent in the shadows, slithered closer to shattering the delicate balance of their ordinary lives.

CHAPTER 15

Weeks had passed since Mary's horrific encounter with the shadows, yet the specter of fear still clung to her like a tattered shroud. Each night brought with it a new terror, a new nightmare that threatened to tear her sanity apart at the seams.

As she lay awake in the dead of night, the silence of her apartment pressing in on her, Mary couldn't shake the feeling that something was watching her, its unseen eyes lurking in the darkness, hungrily waiting for her.

She clutched the covers tightly to her chest, her heart pounding in her chest, screaming at her to run from the encroaching darkness that seeped through the cracks in her fragile reality.

And then, in the stillness of the night, she heard it—a soft rustling, like the whisper of moth wings against silk. It was a sound that sent a chill down her spine.

With trembling hands, Mary reached for the bedside lamp, her fingers fumbling with the switch as she prayed for the embrace of light to banish the shadows that danced on the edge of her vision.

When the light flooded the room, it revealed nothing. And

yet, the feeling persisted—a sense of unease that hung heavy in the air like a noose around her neck.

With a trembling hand, Mary reached for her phone, her fingers dancing over the screen as she hesitated before dialing the number—not the priest's, but a number she had stumbled upon by accident while surfing the internet in an attempt to find a way to fight the darkness tightening around her.

"Hello?" came a voice on the other end in a thick Haitian accent, crackling with static as if speaking from beyond the veil of reality.

Mary's breath caught in her throat as she heard the voice. "Please," Mary whispered, her voice barely more than a breath. "I need your help. Something is happening to me—something unnatural."

There was a pause on the other end of the line, a silence that seemed to stretch on for an eternity. And then, in a voice like the whisper of the wind through ancient trees, came the reply, "I will come to you. But be warned, child—there are forces at work here beyond your understanding. You tread a dangerous path."

With those ominous words ringing in her ears, Mary hung up the phone and waited, her heart pounding in her chest as she braced herself for whatever horrors awaited her in the darkness.

CHAPTER 16

As Emily stepped into Priscilla's apartment, the scent of lavender and sandalwood greeted her, instantly setting her at ease. Priscilla welcomed her with a warm smile, her long hair cascading in gentle waves down her back. Jinx trotted over and nearly pounced on Emily with excitement, slobbering all over her face as she bent down to pet her.

"Jinx, behave!" Priscilla scolded. "You're acting like you have no manners."

Emily just chuckled. "It's okay. She probably smells Trixie on me."

"I guess we should set up a play date for them in the near future, then?"

"That sounds great!"

Priscilla motioned for Emily to follow her. "I've set up the studio for our study session and meditation."

Emily followed Priscilla into the converted spare bedroom, where plush cushions adorned the floor around a low coffee table. A soft, ambient light filled the room, casting a tranquil glow. On the table lay numerology books, journals, and a deck of tarot cards.

Jinx tried to follow them inside the room but Priscilla

stopped her. "Not this time, Jinxie. You can stay out in the living room for now," she said as she closed the door.

"This looks amazing, Priscilla," Emily said, admired the setup. "I can't wait to dive into all this stuff with you!"

Priscilla grinned. "Me too! But let's not get ahead of ourselves. First, let's start with a brief meditation to clear our minds."

They settled onto the cushions, closing their eyes as Priscilla led them through a calming meditation, guiding their breaths and helping Emily find a sense of peace.

After the meditation, they opened their eyes, feeling refreshed and centered. Priscilla reached for the numerology books, eager to begin their study session. As they delved into the intricate meanings of numbers and their significance in personal and universal energies, the hours slipped by unnoticed.

Finally, they took a much-needed break, and as they sipped on drinks and nibbled on snacks, Emily couldn't contain her curiosity any longer. "So, how was your date with Andrew yesterday?" Emily asked with a playful grin.

Priscilla blushed, a smile spreading across her face. "It was amazing! He took me to this charming little romantic Italian restaurant downtown, with soft candlelight and live music in the background."

Emily leaned in, captivated by Priscilla's recounting of the evening. "What did you guys talk about?"

Priscilla's eyes lit up as she recalled their conversation. "We talked about everything under the sun, from our favorite books to our dreams and aspirations. He's such a great listener, Emily. There was an instant connection."

Emily nodded, a knowing smile on her lips. "Sounds like you two hit it off pretty well, then?"

Priscilla nodded enthusiastically. "We did! It felt like we've known each other for years. And the best part? We share a lot of the same values and beliefs, he's just a little more on the conservative side, if you get what I mean?"

Emily grinned. "I'm so happy for you, Priscilla. You deserve someone who appreciates you for who you are."

Priscilla reached out and squeezed Emily's hand. "Thank you, Em. Your support means the world to me."

As they resumed their study session, Priscilla sifted through her notes that she'd jotted down. "So, are you ready to learn how to do your own Tarot readings?"

Emily's eyes lit up. "That would be awesome!"

Priscilla removed her cards from their leather pouch and shuffled them before spreading them out on the coffee table. "Alright, let's start with the basics. First, you need to understand the symbolism of each card and its interpretations."

They spent the next hour going through the cards, Priscilla explained the meaning behind each one and how it could be interpreted in different contexts. Emily took diligent notes, absorbing the information eagerly.

"Now, let's practice with a simple spread," Priscilla suggested, laying out three cards on the table. "We'll start with a past, present, and future reading."

Emily nodded, feeling a mixture of nerves and excitement. She carefully shuffled the deck and then selected three cards, laying them out in front of her.

Priscilla guided her through the interpretation of each card, encouraging Emily to trust her intuition and explore the deeper meanings behind the symbols.

As they delved deeper into the reading, Emily began to feel a sense of connection with the cards, as if they were speaking to her on a subconscious level.

A sudden breeze swept through the room, causing the

candles to flicker and casting strange shadows on the walls. Emily glanced around, feeling a tingling sensation run down her spine.

"Do you feel that, Priscilla?" Emily asked, her voice trembling.

Priscilla furrowed her brow. "Yeah, it's like the energy in the room shifted drastically."

Suddenly, a loud crash echoed from the living room. Then they heard Jinx barking with a low growl rumbling in her throat. Both women froze.

"What was that?" Emily whispered nervously.

Priscilla jumped up quickly. "I'll go check it out. Just stay here."

Priscilla raced to the living room, and as she rounded the corner, she gasped in horror. The living room carpet was littered with shattered glass from the broken window, and a cold draft filled the room, but the actual terror was the enormous figure crouched on the floor in front of the window that Jinx was barking incessantly at.

Priscilla shouted, "Emily, call the police!"

Emily grabbed her phone and dialed 911 as quickly as she could. Panic surged through her as she relayed the situation to the dispatcher, her hands shaking.

Priscilla approached the figure cautiously, her heart pounding in her chest. The creature in the room was unlike anything she had ever seen before. It was humanoid in shape, but its skin seemed to shimmer with an otherworldly iridescence, and its eyes glowed with an eerie light.

"Stay back!" Priscilla shouted.

The creature crouched lower, emitting a low, guttural growl that sent shivers down her spine, while Jinx continued to bark ferociously, her hackles raised, as she circled the intruder.

Priscilla edged closer, glancing around the room, searching for anything she could use as a weapon.

Suddenly, the creature leaped forward with startling speed. Priscilla barely had time to react, diving out of the way just as its claws raked the air where she had been standing a second before.

She scrambled to her feet, and in one swift motion grabbed a heavy lamp from a nearby table, then swung it at the creature with all her strength.

The lamp connected with a sickening thud, sending the creature stumbling backwards with a pained hiss. But it recovered quickly, its eyes narrowing in fury as it prepared to strike again.

Emily rushed into the room and immediately screamed when she saw the demon, drawing the attention of the creature.

As the creature advanced toward Emily, Priscilla's eyes landed on a small, intricately carved wooden box tucked away on a shelf. A soft glow emanated from within, and she suddenly smelled the sweet scent of Lavender flowing through the room—the telltale sign that her grandma was present.

She reached for the box frantically, her fingers trembling as she opened it. Inside, nestled among ancient charms and talismans, she found a small, glowing crystal. Clutching the stone tightly in her hand, Priscilla hurled the crystal toward the shadow demon. A blinding flash erupted as it struck the creature, causing it to recoil in agony.

The demon let out a piercing shriek, its form wavering and flickering. With a final, desperate wail, it vanished into thin air, leaving behind nothing but a lingering smell of sulfur.

Emily stared in disbelief at the spot where the shadow demon had stood just moments before, her breath coming in ragged gasps. She turned to Priscilla with eyes wide from fear. Her lips trembled as she spoke, "What the hell was that thing?"

Priscilla's voice quivered as well as she answered, "I think it was a shadow demon."

"Where did it come from, and why did it attack us?" Emily cried.

Priscilla wrapped Emily tight in her arms. "I don't know?"

Emily pulled back and looked at her through frightened eyes, "Will it come back?"

Priscilla put on her most confident face, trying to convince herself just as much as Emily. "No, it's dead. It won't be coming back." But something inside her suggested otherwise.

CHAPTER 17

Mary waited quietly in her dimly lit living room, her nerves frayed like the edges of an old and worn tapestry. The air was charged with electricity, crackling with the announcement of something ancient approaching.

And then she heard it—a soft knock. Mary slowly rose from her seat, her heart pounding in her chest as she made her way to the door. She hesitated for a moment, her hand shaking as it hovered over the knob, before summoning the courage to pull it open.

Standing before her was the figure of a woman referred to on her website simply as Nyx, her presence as enigmatic as the moonlight filtering through the window. She was tall and slender, with dark skin and eyes that seemed to hold the secrets of the universe within their depths.

"Mary," Nyx said, her thick voice a whisper that sent shivers down her spine. "I have come as you requested. Tell me, child, what troubles you?"

Mary swallowed hard, the weight of her fear pressing down on her like a leaden cloak. "The darkness," she said, her voice barely more than a breath. "It haunts me—nightmares, whispers in the shadows. I fear for my unborn child, for whatever horrors are waiting for him. His father was plagued by the same demons and I'm afraid he's cursed to follow the same fate."

The witch nodded, her expression grave, then closed her eyes for a moment. When she opened them again, there was a hint of surprised contained within. "Your son has been touched by the angels, hasn't he?"

Mary's eyes misted over when she thought of Michael and nodded solemnly.

"I sense the darkness that surrounds you and your child. But fear not, for there is power in knowledge, and I have knowledge that may aid you in your struggle."

With a graceful gesture, the witch stepped further into the room, her presence seeming to fill the space with an otherworldly energy. She reached into her cloak and pulled out a small talisman, its surface shimmering with a warm glow.

"This," she said, holding out the talisman to Mary, "is a ward against the darkness—a talisman of protection crafted from the ancient magics of my ancestors. Carry it close to your heart and let its power be a shield against the shadows that seek to consume you."

Mary took the talisman with trembling hands. "Thank you," she whispered as she held it tightly in her grasp, afraid to let it go for fear that it might quickly vanish. "Thank you for giving me hope to face this darkness."

The witch offered her a small, reassuring smile. "Remember, child, that the light exists even in the darkest of nights. Trust in the strength of your own spirit, and know that you are not alone in your struggle."

"But what if I'm not strong enough?" Mary whimpered. "What if I can't save my baby?"

Nyx reached out and put her hands on Mary's temples and

closed her eyes. "Close your eyes and relax, child," she said.

Mary felt Nyx reaching into her brain, her psychic fingers pushing forward like wriggling worms squirming through the dirt in search of food, until they took hold and became conduits that uploaded a lifetime of memories into the witch's mind.

Time stood still as Nyx infiltrated the deep recesses of Mary's mind, drinking in every moment of her life, before she finally withdrew her hands. "You too have been touched by the Divine, and that is why the darkness seeks to destroy you. Know that there will be a time when both of your lives will hang in the balance. But as long as you have faith, the darkness will not succeed. Use that power within you to drive away that which threatens you."

Nyx turned to leave and then stopped, "When you reach that point where you have nothing but despair surrounding you, call me and I will be there."

Mary stood there in shock for a moment. "But how do I reach you? Your website isn't available anymore."

"Silly child," Nyx replied, "I don't use things such as the internet. You found me the first time because you needed my help, and now I'm here. Simple as that. Speak my name into the amulet and I'll come, but only do so when there is no other hope."

With those words ringing in her ears, Mary watched as the witch faded into the night, her form melting into the shadows like mist in the morning sun. And as she held the talisman of protection in her hands, she felt a glimmer of hope—a flicker of light in the suffocating darkness that threatened to consume her.

With renewed determination, she vowed to do whatever it took to protect her unborn child from the encroaching shadows, drawing strength from the guidance of the witch and the promise of a brighter tomorrow.

As Mary sat alone in the quiet of her living room, the talisman clutched tightly in her hand, she felt a sense of peace wash over her—a feeling of empowerment that she hadn't felt in for a long time. She knew that the road ahead would be fraught with danger and uncertainty, but with the guidance of the witch and the protection of her magic, she felt ready to face whatever darkness awaited her.

CHAPTER 18

As they huddled together, trembling in fear, the sound of approaching sirens cut through the tense silence of the room. Emily and Priscilla each exhaled a sigh of relief before Priscilla opened the door for the police.

Seconds later, a team of officers flooded into the room, each one on high alert as they surveyed the scene of shattered glass and overturned furniture.

"Is everyone okay?" one officer asked.

Priscilla nodded, forcing a reassuring smile. "Yeah, we're fine. Just a bit shaken up."

The officers began to assess the damage, noting the broken window and scattered debris. Emily watched nervously, her mind still racing from the attack.

"We heard a loud noise and called the police right away," Priscilla said. "It looks like someone tried to break in, but we scared them off before they could do any actual damage."

"Did you get a good look at the intruder?" the officer asked.

"No, they ran away when Jinx started barking."

The officer nodded, jotting down notes as they surveyed the scene. "We'll make sure to increase patrols in the area.

And if you notice anything suspicious, don't hesitate to give us a call."

As the police prepared to leave, Emily slowly felt a slight sense of relief. The shadow demon may have been defeated, but its presence lingered like a dark cloud in the back of her mind.

As soon as the police had left, Priscilla and Emily worked quickly to clean up the debris and patch up the broken window as best they could, relegated to trash bags and duct tape as a temporary fix. The resulting repair looked ridiculous, putting a little levity into the air.

"There, good as new," Priscilla quipped as she took a seat on the couch.

Emily immediately sat down next to her, cuddling in tight, her body still tense.

"It's okay, Emily. We're safe now," Priscilla said as she brushed Emily's hair from her forehead in an attempt to calm her down. "You were incredibly brave tonight."

Emily nodded, but her hands still trembled. "I don't know if I can do this, Priscilla," she admitted, her voice wavering. "I thought I wanted to learn about all this mystical stuff, but after tonight... I'm not so sure."

Priscilla's heart went out to her friend, understanding the weight of the ordeal they'd just faced. "It's natural to feel scared after something like this," she said, her tone gentle but firm. "But you can't let fear hold you back. Learning can be a powerful tool for understanding ourselves and the world around us."

Emily hesitated, her mind torn between her desire for knowledge and the lingering fear from their encounter with the shadow demon. But as she looked into Priscilla's eyes, she saw a flicker of determination and strength that inspired her.

Taking a deep breath, Emily snuggled against Priscilla a

little tighter. "I guess you're right. I can't let fear dictate my choices," she said, her voice a little steadier now.

***

As Emily trudged through the dimly lit street toward her nearby apartment, the shadows seemed to twist and coil around her, whispering secrets she dared not listen to. Every creak of a distant branch, every flicker of a streetlight threatened to unleash a terror beyond her imagination.

Her heart pounded like a drum in her chest, each step echoing in the hollow silence of the night. The darkness pressed in around her, suffocating and oppressive, as if it hungered for her very soul.

As she turned the corner, Emily's breath caught in her throat, her eyes darting nervously from one shadowy alcove to the next. She knew she was being watched, felt the weight of unseen eyes boring into her flesh.

Then, from the depths of the darkness, a figure emerged— a twisted silhouette that seemed to writhe and contort with unnatural grace. Emily froze, her blood turning to ice in her veins as the figure drew closer.

But just as terror threatened to consume her, the figure morphed into the familiar form of her neighbor, Mrs. Henderson, walking her dog. Relief flooded through Emily like a tidal wave, but the sense of unease lingered like a stain upon her soul.

"Emily, dear, you look like you've seen a ghost," Mrs. Henderson said, her voice tinged with concern as she approached.

Emily forced a shaky smile, trying to mask the fear that clawed at her insides. "Just... a rough night," she managed to whisper, her words barely audible over the pounding of her heart.

Mrs. Henderson studied her for a moment, her eyes narrowed with suspicion. "Well, if you ever need someone to talk to, you know where to find me."

With a grateful nod, Emily watched as Mrs. Henderson disappeared into the safety of her apartment building, leaving her alone once more with the shadows that stalked after her.

As she reached her doorstep and fumbled for her keys, she couldn't shake the feeling of eyes boring into her from the darkness. As Emily crossed the threshold into her apartment, the weight of the night's events draped over her like a cloak of despair. Each creak of the floorboards, each flicker of a shadow, whispered secrets of unspeakable dread, sending shivers down her spine. She knew all too well that even within the sanctuary of her own home, the darkness held sway.

Her hands trembled as she flicked on every light in the apartment, banishing the oppressive darkness that threatened to suffocate her. Yet, despite the artificial warmth flooding the room, a bone-chilling cold lingered in the shadows, clawing at the edges of her sanity.

As the relentless march of time wore on and exhaustion gnawed at her frayed nerves, Emily found herself ensnared in the vise-like grip of fear. The mere thought of sleep filled her with a primal dread, for she knew all too well that within the twisted corridors of her dreams, the shadows held dominion.

But despite her best efforts, fatigue proved to be her most formidable adversary, dragging her ever closer to the abyss of unconsciousness. With a whispered plea to whatever gods might listen, she reluctantly surrendered to the embrace of her bed.

As she drifted off to sleep, Emily clung desperately to the

fleeting hope that her dreams would offer respite from the horrors that haunted her waking hours, praying for a glimpse of light amidst the suffocating darkness.

Yet, as she drifted into the depths of unconsciousness, the nightmares seized her like ravenous beasts, pulling her into a realm of unimaginable torment.

In her dream, Emily found herself standing on a desolate plain, where the earth lay barren and lifeless before her. The air was heavy with a sense of impending doom, and the shadows danced to a hellish song, whispering sinister promises of anguish and despair.

Suddenly, from the depths of the abyss, a grotesque figure emerged—a twisted abomination with limbs contorted and eyes ablaze with hatred. It stalked toward her with a low growl issuing from somewhere inside its twisted body.

Emily attempted to flee, her movements sluggish and labored as if ensnared by invisible chains. With each faltering step, the darkness closed in around her, suffocating and oppressive, until she found herself ensnared in the creature's clutches.

Its putrid breath washed over her, a foul stench that choked the very air from her lungs. Its jagged claws tore through flesh and bone with a sickening crunch.

She screamed, a primal sound of terror and agony that echoed across the desolate landscape. But there was no escape from the relentless horror that enveloped her.

And then, with a jolt, Emily was torn from the clutches of her nightmare, her heart racing and her body drenched in a cold sweat. She lay there, trembling and disoriented, the echoes of her torment still reverberating through her consciousness.

Snuggling up to Emily, Trixie emitted a small whine and showered her with nervous kisses, as if trying to chase away the lingering effects of the nightmare.

But even with Trixie's protective presence beside her as the first fingers of dawn crept over the horizon, Emily knew that she could never fully escape the shadows that now haunted her dreams.

***

Priscilla paced the living room of her apartment, her nerves frayed and her heart heavy with the weight of the night's events. The memory of the encounter with the shadow demon sent a shiver down her spine, and she couldn't shake the feeling of lingering dread that clung to her like a suffocating fog.

With trembling hands, Priscilla reached for her phone and dialed Andrew's number. She didn't want to face the darkness alone, not after what she'd just gone through. She had put on a brave face for Emily, trying her best to look strong for her friend, when in truth she was scared shitless.

"Hello?" Andrew answered.

"Andrew, it's Priscilla," she said, her words rushed and desperate. "Can you come over? Something happened. I'm... scared."

Andrew replied immediately, his tone soft and reassured. "Of course. I'll be there right away."

When Andrew arrived minutes later, Priscilla practically threw herself at him, wrapping her arms around him and holding him tight, her body shaking as the tears fell. After a few minutes, she led him into the living room, where they settled onto the couch in silence, Priscilla snuggling next to him for strength.

"I'm here for you, Priscilla," Andrew said as he reached out to take her hand. "Whatever you need, just ask."

Priscilla nodded somberly. "Thank you, Andrew."

As they sat together in the dimly lit room, Priscilla slowly felt the weight of her fear begin to lift, replaced by a sense of comfort and security in Andrew's presence.

And then, with a heavy sigh, she began to recount the events of the night—the shattered glass, the barking dog, the looming figure in the darkness. She told him about the shadow demon, about the terror that had gripped her heart as she faced the unknown.

Andrew listened in stunned silence, his eyes widening at the horrors Priscilla described. But through it all, he remained steadfast and unwavering, his presence a beacon of light in the midst of the darkness.

As Priscilla finished her tale, she looked to Andrew with a mixture of fear and hope. "I know it sounds crazy, but... it was real. And I don't think it was the only one. There's something else here in this town that we don't know about. I'm just glad you're here with me now."

Andrew squeezed her hand reassuringly. "We'll get through this together, Priscilla. I promise."

Priscilla snuggled against him a little tighter, "Can you stay here with me tonight? I don't want to be alone."

"Of course, I'll stay," Andrew replied.

She lifted her head and looked at him through desperate eyes before she reached up and kissed him long and hard.

CHAPTER 19

For the next couple of days, Emily found herself paralyzed by fear, unable to shake the lingering feeling that had taken hold of her since their encounter with the shadow demon. The mere thought of returning to Priscilla's apartment filled her with a gnawing sense of unease, and she couldn't bear to face the possibility of confronting the darkness once again.

Each passing hour seemed to weigh heavier on her shoulders, the memories of their harrowing ordeal haunting her every waking moment. She tried to distract herself with mundane tasks, but the fear lurked just beneath the surface, threatening to consume her at any moment.

Amidst the oppressive weight of her fear, Emily found herself adrift in a sea of uncertainty. At night, she lay awake, tormented by the memories of their harrowing escape. But this time, as she drifted into a fitful sleep, a dream swept over her like a gentle tide, carrying her to a place of comfort and solace.

This time in her dream, Emily found herself standing in a sunlit meadow, with wildflowers swaying in the breeze and the sounds of birds filling the air. And there, standing before her, was her father, his warm smile lighting up the world around them.

"Dad?" Emily whispered, her voice trembling as she reached out to him.

Her father's eyes twinkled as he took her hand, his touch reassuring and familiar. "I'm here, Emily," he said, his voice a soothing melody in the stillness of the dream.

Tears welled in Emily's eyes as she gazed up at her father, the weight of her fear lifting like a heavy burden from her shoulders. In that moment, she knew that she was not alone, that her father's love would guide her through even the darkest of nights.

Emily took her father's hand and together they walked through the meadow, the sunlight casting a warm glow over their path. They shared memories of moments they cherished, laughter echoing through the meadow like a sweet melody.

As they walked, Emily's father put his arm around her shoulder, pulling her closer, "You're stronger than you know, Em," he said, his voice gentle but firm. "You have the power to overcome any obstacle, to face any fear that comes your way. Trust in yourself, and trust in the love that surrounds you."

With each step, Emily felt a sense of peace wash over her, the love and support of her father giving her the strength she needed to carry on. As they reached the edge of the meadow, Emily turned to her father, hoping for one more embrace, but he was already gone.

When Emily woke the next morning, the memory of her dream lingered like a gentle caress. She knew that her father's presence would always be with her, a beacon of light in the darkness, guiding her through even the most daunting of trials.

With a deep breath, Emily resolved to confront her

anxieties and take the first step towards reclaiming her sense of courage. She wrapped herself in her coat, the fabric offering little comfort against the chill of the morning air, and made her way to Priscilla's apartment.

Standing before the door, Emily hesitated for a moment, fear threatening to overwhelm her. But she clenched her jaw and forced herself to push through it.

With a determined resolve, Emily knocked on the door, the sound echoing through the air with a hollow thud. A minute later, the door swung open.

"Emily!" Priscilla exclaimed. "Is everything okay?"

Emily stepped inside, the warmth of Priscilla's apartment enveloping her like a comforting embrace, even though the black garbage bag still clung to the window as a grim reminder of the past nightmare. "I've been avoiding coming over, but I think I'm ready to start again," she confessed, her voice tinged with uncertainty. "I want to learn everything, and I know that facing my fear is the only way forward."

There was a moment of understanding that passed between them, and Priscilla smiled, a reassuring light in her eyes. "I'm proud of you, Emily," she said, embracing her in a tight hug. "Facing your fears takes a lot of courage, and I'm here to support you every step of the way."

With a sense of relief flooding her veins, Emily nodded, a newfound sense of determination coursing through her. "Thank you. I'm ready to continue anytime if you're not busy. Although I was hoping the window had been fixed by now."

"Yeah, me too," Priscilla stated. "They had to order a replacement window. It was supposed to be here yesterday, but it came in broken. Maintenance said another one would be here tomorrow."

Suddenly, the door to the bedroom creaked open, and

Andrew emerged, a smile spreading across his face as he joined them in the living room.

"Morning, ladies," Andrew greeted them warmly.

Priscilla turned to Emily with a grin. "Emily, this is Andrew," she introduced, gesturing towards him. "Andrew, meet Emily."

Emily offered Andrew a friendly wave. "Nice to see you again, Andrew," Emily said with a smile.

Andrew returned the greeting, his eyes twinkling with recognition. "Likewise, Emily. Priscilla's told me a lot about you."

As they exchanged pleasantries, Andrew's phone chimed, and he checked the screen with a furrowed brow.

"Sorry to interrupt, ladies, but duty calls," Andrew said with an apologetic smile. "Looks like I've got to head into work early today."

Priscilla nodded understandingly, albeit with a slight frown on her face, as he walked toward the door. "Too bad you have to go. You could've joined our meditation session."

"As awesome as that sounds, I'm afraid I'll have to take a rain-check."

Before Andrew left, Priscilla leaned in and pressed her lips gently to his. "I'll call you later," she said softly, her eyes meeting his with a passionate warmth.

Andrew's face lit up with a smile. "I'll be waiting."

With a wave goodbye, Andrew disappeared through the door, leaving Emily and Priscilla alone once more.

As the door closed behind him, Emily couldn't hide her excitement. "Looks like things are going well with you two," she teased, a mischievous twinkle in her eye.

Priscilla's cheeks flushed pink, and she couldn't conceal the smile that tugged at the corners of her lips. "Yeah, they are," she admitted.

"You have to give me all the juicy details!" Emily exclaimed.

Priscilla replied, "I most certainly do not. Now, let's start our session and maybe after I'll fill you in a little."

"Like, how is he in bed?"

Priscilla raised an eyebrow, but remained silent as a smile spread over her face, causing a little shriek to fly from Emily's lips.

"Okay, enough of that," Priscilla said as she grabbed Emily's hand.

As they settled into the living room, a peculiar energy filled the air, thick and charged with an unsettling anticipation. Priscilla guided Emily to the couch. "Close your eyes," she murmured, her voice a whisper that seemed to echo from far away. "Forget everything. Let go."

Emily obeyed, her eyelids sealing shut against the world, surrendering herself to Priscilla's enigmatic guidance. With each breath, she felt the room fade away, replaced by a hazy dreamscape of whispered promises and lurking shadows.

"Now, picture yourself at the edge of a sprawling forest." Priscilla's voice drifted through Emily's mind, weaving a tapestry of imagery that seemed to shimmer with an otherworldly glow. "Listen to the trees. Hear the stories they have to tell."

Emily's imagination took flight, conjuring visions of towering pines and winding paths that disappeared into the gloom. She hesitated at the forest's edge, feeling a primal fear clawing at the edges of her consciousness.

"Feel the ground beneath your feet," Priscilla's voice was a distant murmur, as if spoken from the depths of a forgotten cavern. "You are part of this place now. Embrace it."

As Emily surrendered to the vision, a sense of unease crept over her, a whisper of ancient secrets and hidden dangers lurking just beyond the trees. Yet, she pressed forward, drawn by an irresistible pull into the heart of the darkness.

And then, in the depths of her meditation, Emily felt a flicker of something stir within her, a spark of light amidst the encroaching shadows. It danced on the edge of her awareness, tantalizing and elusive, like a flame in the wind.

With a start, Emily's eyes snapped open, her breath coming in ragged gasps as she struggled to make sense of her profound experience. Priscilla watched her with a knowing smile and a gleam in her eyes.

"You felt it, didn't you?" Priscilla asked with a knowing look in her eyes. "The power within you, waiting to be unleashed."

Emily nodded, a tremor coursing through her as she realized the weight of what she had experienced. She knew that she had glimpsed something beyond the veil of reality, something both exhilarating and terrifying in its scope.

***

In the days that followed, Emily delved deeper into the mysteries of the occult, her thirst for knowledge bordering on obsession. But with each revelation came a mounting sense of dread, a recognition of the forces she was tampering with and the consequences that could ensue. She had unlocked a power that transcended the boundaries of the known world, and now stood on the precipice of a darkness that threatened to consume her whole.

As Emily continued her studies under Priscilla's guidance, the shadows of the unknown grew ever darker, stretching their tendrils into the recesses of her mind. With each session, she felt herself slipping further into the abyss, drawn inexorably towards a fate she could scarcely comprehend.

One night, as she sat alone in her room, she felt a chill wind blow through the air that raised the hairs on the back of her neck. She glanced up from her book as the world around her dissolved into nothingness before a scene from a nightmare unfolded in front of her.

In the vision, she stood on a desolate street, the air thick with the stench of decay and despair. A little girl stood in the distance, her cries of terror echoing through the empty streets. Immediately, Emily rushed forward, her heart pounding in her chest as she raced to the save the child from whatever horror it was facing.

But as she drew closer, she realized that the girl wasn't alone. A monstrous demonic figure lurked in the darkness, its eyes burning with an unholy fire as it closed in on the child.

As Emily cautiously approached, the dim shadows unveiled a figure that struck terror deep into her heart—its form a twisted amalgamation of flesh and flame cloaked in an ever-shifting aura of infernal fire. Its eyes were twin pools of molten lava that radiated with a searing intensity, and its jagged maw was curled into a cruel smirk. From its smoldering form, tentacles of smoke billowed, twisting and writhing like serpents of pure darkness.

The air grew thick with an acrid scent as the demon drew nearer, its presence sending shivers down Emily's spine. She could feel the unrelenting heat washing over her, threatening to consume her.

With a primal instinct born of desperation, Emily threw herself between the girl and the approaching terror, ready to sacrifice everything to protect her.

And then, in a blinding flash, the vision shattered, leaving Emily gasping for breath. She was sure that what she had just seen wasn't just a dream. It was a premonition into what was coming—a test of her bravery. And she had a feeling that a time would arrive when she would need to stand firm in the face of darkness, ready to make the ultimate sacrifice to protect those she loved.

CHAPTER 20

As twilight enveloped their small town, Andrew and Priscilla strolled along the streets, their hands intertwined until they stumbled on a forgotten park nestled across from an abandoned school, its swings creaking eerily in the gentle breeze. Drawn by an inexplicable curiosity, they ventured into the deserted playground, their footsteps muffled by the overgrown grass.

Andrew watched as Priscilla approached a rusted carousel, its once vibrant colors faded by time and neglect. With a glint in her eye, she reached out and gave the carousel a gentle push, sending it into a slow, mournful spin, before jumping onboard.

With a wide smile, Andrew joined Priscilla on the carousel, their laughter mingling with the haunting melody of a distant ice cream truck.

As they spun around and around, Andrew found himself opening up to Priscilla in ways he never thought possible. He told her about his childhood fears, his dreams for the future, and the demons that had haunted him for as long as he could remember.

Priscilla listened intently, her eyes full of compassion. Then she shared her own stories, each one a piece of the puzzle that was slowly forming between them. Although the nightmare she had endured regarding her sister's betrayal, which had led to her mother's death, that secret she kept buried. The pain of reliving that tragedy, even for the slightest moment, was more than she could bear.

As they continued to spin around and around, Priscilla's attention was suddenly drawn to the edge of the park, where a shadowy figure stood beneath a flickering streetlamp. A moment later, a gathering of spectral figures emerged from the shadows to join the other, their forms all flickering in and out of existence like phantoms summoned from the depths of despair.

Each ghastly figure was a young child, their face frozen in an expression of horror, their ghostly eyes pleading for understanding. They all bore the same unmistakable marks of a horrific tragedy—flesh and clothes covered in blood and ash, an indication of a terrible fire that had swept through the nearby school in a savage act of nature's fury.

Priscilla's heart shuddered as she looked at the haunting assembly. *So many young souls lost,* she thought sadly.

As they spun, Priscilla couldn't shake the feeling that the carousel was not just a relic of forgotten amusement, but a grim monument to a darker history—a place where the echoes of unspeakable tragedy lingered, trapped in a perpetual cycle of despair. She looked sadly at the ghostly figures standing nearby, their silent pleas for salvation echoing through the empty night.

As the carousel slowed to a halt, Priscilla stole one last glance over her shoulder, the images of the dead children burned into her mind's eye. But the park was empty now. The only remnant of the episode was the lingering chill that clung to Priscilla's skin like a shroud.

* * *

***

Emily sat cross-legged in her living room on a plush rug with her eyes closed as she attempted to practice her meditation. Beside her, Trixie lay curled up, her soft snores a comforting backdrop to the rhythmic pattern of Emily's breathing.

As Emily tried to relax, she found it challenging to quiet her mind. Thoughts flitted about like restless birds, refusing to settle. She struggled to focus on her breath, feeling a sense of frustration creeping in.

Just as Emily felt her mind starting to ease, a sudden noise shattered the peace, causing her to startle and open her eyes. Trixie lifted her head, ears perked, as she looked around the room for the source.

"What's wrong, girl?" Emily murmured as she reached out to stroke Trixie's fur.

Emily's heart raced as she scanned the room, her senses on high alert. A jolt of apprehension suddenly shot through her, but she forced herself to stay calm, her mind racing as she tried to make sense of what she was seeing. Was it just a trick of the light, or something more sinister?

Taking a deep breath, Emily shook off the feeling of unease and focused her attention on Trixie for a minute. As the tension in the room eased, Emily decided to turn her focus to something more grounding—her Tarot cards. With trembling hands, she shuffled the cards clumsily, her inexperience evident in her fumbling movements.

As she turned over the first card, a sense of recognition washed over her—the High Priestess, a symbol of intuition and inner wisdom. The second card revealed the Tower, a harbinger of sudden upheaval and unexpected change. And the third card—the Knight of Cups, a messenger of emotional growth and new beginnings.

Emily looked at the cards spread out before her, their vibrant images shimmering in the light. But as she studied them, a wave of dizziness washed over her, the world spinning in circles around her.

Frantically, Emily reached out to steady herself, her vision swimming as the cards blurred into a kaleidoscope of colors and shapes. And then, with a soft gasp, darkness descended, enveloping her in its stiff embrace as she slipped into unconsciousness.

***

The room was no longer the familiar space she had occupied moments ago. Instead, she found herself standing in the midst of a vast, ethereal landscape that seemed to stretch endlessly in all directions. The sky above shimmered with hues of purple and gold, casting an otherworldly glow upon the land below.

Before her stood three figures, their forms shifting and morphing like wisps of smoke, while they emanated a palpable aura of power.

The High Priestess appeared first, her presence commanding yet serene. She stood tall, cloaked in flowing robes that billowed around her like clouds. Her eyes, pools of deep wisdom, bore into Emily's soul, and without a word, she beckoned her forward.

Next came the Tower, a gigantic figure cloaked in crackling energy. Its form was jagged and chaotic, reminiscent of lightning frozen in time. As it loomed over Emily, she felt a surge of fear and awe coursing through her veins, the sheer magnitude of its presence overwhelming.

Finally, the Knight of Cups emerged, galloping gracefully

across the landscape on a majestic steed. His armor gleamed in the surreal light, and his eyes sparkled with an otherworldly charm. With a gentle smile, he extended a hand towards Emily.

Stunned and bewildered, Emily could only watch as the three figures circled around her, their movements fluid and mesmerizing. It was as if they were performing a silent dance, weaving together the threads of fate in intricate patterns that only they could decipher.

And then, as suddenly as they had appeared, the figures began to fade, their forms dissipating like smoke in the wind. With a final, mysterious glance, they vanished into the ether, leaving Emily standing alone in the surreal landscape once more.

***

When Emily finally awoke, she found herself lying on the floor, her head spinning and her heart pounding in her chest. Trixie hovered over her, her concerned whines a comforting presence in the darkness.

She struggled to sit up and felt a sense of disorientation wash over her, her mind still reeling from the experience. She glanced at the tarot cards scattered around her, their enigmatic images staring back at her with silent intensity.

As she blinked away the remnants of the vision, she felt a profound sense of clarity wash over her. Though she couldn't fully comprehend the experience she had just undergone, she knew one thing for certain—the Tarot cards were more than mere symbols on paper. They were conduits of ancient wisdom, gateways to another realm.

Try as she might, Emily couldn't shake the feeling that she had stumbled onto something beyond her understanding, something powerful and ancient that had imbued the cards with a life of their own. And as she gazed at the symbols, which seemed to glow softly, a sense of foreboding gripped her heart, a silent warning of the trials that lay ahead.

With a trembling hand, Emily gathered up the cards, their weight heavy in her palm, and took a deep breath to steady herself as she battled with the urge yet again to run away from the secrets that called to her.

CHAPTER 21

The morning sun cast long shadows across the city streets as Mary made her way to her OBGYN appointment, a cloud of worry covering her like a thick blanket. The weight of her pregnancy seemed to hang heavier with each passing day, a constant reminder of the life growing within her and the dangers that lurked in the shadows.

As she stepped into the sterile confines of the doctor's office, the familiar scent of antiseptic assaulted her senses, mingling with the subtle undertone of fear that seemed to permeate the air. She took a deep breath, trying to steel herself against the rising tide of anxiety that threatened to overwhelm her.

The waiting room was empty except for a few scattered chairs, and the only sound was the soft hum of fluorescent lights overhead. Mary took a seat, her hands folded tightly in her lap as she waited.

Minutes stretched into eternity as she sat there, the ticking of the clock on the wall echoing in her ears like the beat of a distant drum. And then, finally, the door swung open and a nurse appeared, her expression unreadable behind her surgical mask.

"Mary?" she said, her voice muffled by the fabric. "Dr. Roberts will see you now."

Mary rose from her seat, her stomach churning as she followed the nurse into the examination room. Dr. Roberts was waiting for her, her expression somber as she gestured for her to take a seat on the examination table.

"Good morning, Mary," she said, her voice gentle but tinged with concern. "How have you been feeling?"

Mary tried to force a smile, but it felt like a lie on her lips. "I've been okay, I guess," she replied, her voice barely above a whisper. "Just... worried, I guess."

Dr. Roberts nodded, her brow furrowing as she began the examination. After applying a series of sensors to Mary's stomach and chest, the steady rhythm of her baby's heartbeat matched the cadence of hers on the nearby monitor.

And then, suddenly, it happened—the sound of the baby's monitor flatlining, followed immediately by the sharp breath from the doctor as she frantically tried to stabilize the situation.

Mary's world spun out of control as she felt a wave of dizziness wash over her. The edges of her vision blurred as she fought to stay conscious. Panic clawed at her throat, threatening to suffocate her as she struggled to make sense of what was happening.

And then, just as suddenly as it had begun, it was over— the monitor beeped back to life, the sound echoing in the silence of the room like a death knell. Dr. Roberts breathed a sigh of relief, her expression one of grim determination as she turned to face Mary.

"I'm sorry, Mary," she said. "But it seems that some complications have developed with your pregnancy. We're going to need to run some tests to determine the cause, but for now, I want you to try to remain calm."

Calm was nearly impossible as Mary sat there, struggling to come to terms with the reality of what had just happened. The darkness seemed to loom closer now, casting a shadow over her as she braced herself for the storm that lay ahead.

Dr. Roberts stepped closer to Mary, her demeanor compassionate yet grave. "Mary, I understand this is alarming, but it's crucial that we act swiftly to ensure both your well-being and that of your baby. I'll need to perform a thorough examination and order additional tests to assess the situation."

Mary nodded, her voice barely a whisper. "Do whatever you need to do. I just want my baby to be okay."

The doctor offered her a reassuring smile before diving into the examination, her movements precise and methodical as she continued to check Mary's vital signs and monitor the baby's heartbeat. Each moment felt like an eternity, pressing down on Mary's soul.

As the examination progressed, Mary couldn't shake the haunting feeling that hung heavy in the air. The memory of the monitor flatlining plagued her, a chilling reminder of the fragility of life and the darkness that lurked on the edges of her reality.

Finally, Dr. Roberts finished her examination and stepped back, her expression grave. "I should have the test results back in a couple days and I'll call you to go over them. In the meantime, I want you to rest as much as possible and avoid any unnecessary stress."

Mary nodded, her throat tight and her mouth dry. "Thank you, doctor."

As she left the examination room, Mary felt a sense of dread settle over her like a shroud. The darkness seemed to loom closer with each passing moment. Soon, it would swallow her completely.

* * *

***

The days blurred together for Mary as she navigated the treacherous waters of her difficult pregnancy. Somehow, though, amidst the fear and the darkness, there were brief glimmers of hope—moments of joy and anticipation that kept her going even in the darkest of times.

Yet, as the weeks wore on, Mary's condition deteriorated, her body weakened by the relentless onslaught of sickness and fatigue. Every day felt like a battle against an invisible foe, a struggle to hold on to her own life while protecting the precious one growing inside her.

And then, one fateful night, the darkness descended in full force, wrapping its icy tentacles around Mary's fragile form and threatening to drag her down into the abyss. She awoke in the dead of night, her body wracked with fever and her mind clouded with delirium.

Terrified and alone, Mary reached for her phone, her fingers trembling as she dialed for help.

The voice on the other end was a lifeline in the darkness, "911, what's your emergency?"

Mary's voice was barely a whisper as she struggled to form coherent words. "Please... help me... something's wrong..."

Within moments, the sound of sirens filled the air as paramedics rushed to Mary's aid, their voices firm and steady as they worked to stabilize her condition. The journey to the hospital was a blur of flashing lights and muffled sounds, each moment a desperate race against time.

As they arrived at the emergency room, Mary was whisked away into the chaos of the hospital, her world spinning out of control as doctors and nurses swarmed around her like guardian angels. She was dimly aware of the frantic activity, the urgent whispers of medical jargon that filled the air like a cacophony of voices from another world.

And then, suddenly, everything went dark.

For a moment, Mary felt as though she were floating in a void, a disembodied spirit adrift in the vast expanse of nothingness. But then, slowly, the darkness began to recede, replaced by a blinding light that pierced through the shadows and enveloped her in its warm embrace.

When Mary awoke, she found herself surrounded by the soft glow of hospital lights, the steady beeping of monitors serving as a reassuring reminder of her fragile existence. She felt a sense of peace wash over her.

And then, like a miracle unfolding before her eyes, Mary heard it—the sound of a tiny heartbeat, strong and steady, echoing in the silence. Tears welled in her eyes as she reached out to cradle her swollen belly.

In that moment, as Mary basked in the warmth of the hospital room, she knew that she'd been given a second chance—a chance to embrace the light and banish the darkness once and for all.

CHAPTER 22

Andrew and Priscilla walked hand-in-hand along a dirt path, its winding course leading them towards the outskirts of the town. The distant silhouette of a grand cathedral atop a moonlit hill beckoned, its presence looming like a forgotten deity against the night sky. But it was the ancient woods bordering the city that whispered to their souls, their dark secrets carried on the evening breeze.

Underneath the twisted branches, a canopy of moonlit shadows embraced the couple, blending them seamlessly into the night's tapestry. The air carried an intoxicating perfume of earth and moss, stirring the senses. In a secluded clearing where light filtered through the foliage like ethereal stardust, Andrew and Priscilla stumbled upon a secret sanctuary where the ordinary world surrendered to the mystical.

In the embrace of an ancient oak, bathed in the moon's silver glow, Priscilla spread a cloth out on the ground, her smile illuminating the darkness as she arranged her cards. Each symbol whispered its secrets to her, weaving a narrative of her and Andrew's intertwined destinies.

But as Priscilla delved deeper into the reading, an eerie silence descended upon the woods, thick and suffocating.

The moon's bright glow suddenly shifted to an unsettling crimson hue, while unseen forces stirred beneath the twisted branches, their presence palpable in the charged air.

Suddenly, the shadows unfurled, revealing spectral figures that emerged from the darkness, their forms ethereal and sinuous, moving with a grace that defied mortal understanding. Translucent tendrils wove through their corporeal frames, bridging the gap between worlds, while wisps of shadow danced around them.

The air hummed with ancient energy as the spirits circled Andrew and Priscilla. Their distorted faces were etched with the burden of untold secrets, while their voices were a haunting chorus that resonated throughout the forest with a chilling note.

One spirit leaned in, fixing its gaze on the couple. "We give our blessing to this union being forged under the watchful eyes of Fate, but know that there is darkness gathering on the horizon, a storm that will push you to your limits."

Andrew's eyes widened as he questioned the spirit, "What kind of darkness?"

The spirits, their forms shifting like smoke, answered in unison, "The threads of fate have bound you together, but within the tapestry of your love lies the shadow of adversity. Embrace the trials that come, for through darkness, true strength is forged."

Priscilla asked, "How can we escape this darkness?"

Another spirit, its voice a gentle whisper in the night, responded, "The path ahead is fraught with peril, but within the shadows, lies the promise of greatness. Embrace the unknown, for it is in facing our fears that we discover our truest selves."

The spirits then retreated into the shadows, leaving Andrew and Priscilla to ponder the weight of their words.

Andrew's heart pounded as he clung to Priscilla's hand, their fingers intertwined like a lifeline amidst the encroaching shadows. "What do we do now?" he whispered in a voice barely audible over the haunting sounds that echoed through the woods.

Priscilla's eyes searched his, a flicker of uncertainty dancing in their depths. "We face it," she said, her voice steady despite the fear that gnawed at her insides. "Whatever darkness awaits us, we confront it head-on."

Andrew shook his head. "I don't know, Priscilla? What were those things? And how did they know about us?"

"I don't know exactly who or what they were... just that they were some ancient elemental force, probably here before mankind even existed."

"Why would something like that be concerned with us?" Andrew asked as he tried to make sense of what he'd just witnessed.

Priscilla was at a loss for words. She was almost as confused as Andrew was. Her only saving grace was that she had grown up in a family full of magic and witchcraft, which had paved the way for unexplained encounters with the supernatural. Although this particular encounter was greater by far than anything she had ever experienced before.

Priscilla finally said, "My ancestors may be part of the reason they appeared to us."

Andrew looked at her blankly.

"My entire history is full of individuals who existed bearing the weight of being labeled an outcast because of their unique abilities," she continued. "From what I've learned, they all held a deep connection with nature and could commune with spirits. I imagine that's why they showed themselves to us. Because that same blood flows through me."

For a moment, Andrew was silent as he tried to understand. "So, it goes a lot deeper than tarot cards and meditation?"

Priscilla looked at him with a hint of worry creeping into her eyes. Her worst fears were starting to surface that she would yet again be rejected for being different. She nodded slowly. "Yes, it does." A tiny tear crept into the corner of her eyes, "I wanted to tell you everything but I was afraid I'd lose you."

Andrew reached forward and ran his hand along her cheek. "I'd be a fool to let you go just because you're different. That the reason I love you."

Priscilla's lips trembled as she replied, "You do?"

Andrew smiled and nodded.

Immediately, Priscilla threw herself at Andrew, pressing her lips hard to his. "I love you too," she said through forced breaths as her passion ignited a firestorm within them. Together, they made love under the canopy of the trees and in the presence of the unseen ancient spirits that walked the forest for eternity, proclaiming to the world that their bond was forever sacred.

Later, as they lay there under the soft light of the moon, Priscilla said, "We can't let fear consume us." She recited the last words the spirits had said before vanishing, "For it is in facing our fears that we discover our truest selves."

***

Unknown to the couple, a grotesque figure emerged from the darkness, its form a twisted amalgamation of sinew and shadow. Its presence defied the laws of nature, filling the air with a palpable sense of dread. With hollow eyes that drank in the light, it watched from the shadows, its grotesque form pulsating with dark energy.

As the events unfolded before it, the creature emitted an eerie symphony of whispers and hisses, feeding on the fear and uncertainty that surrounded the couple. And as quickly as it had appeared, it vanished into the night, leaving behind only a haunting whisper on the breeze.

CHAPTER 23

Gideon stood hunched over an ancient tome, its crumbling pages whispering secrets of unspeakable power. The room was pitch black except for an array of flickering candles that cast grotesque shadows upon the walls, dancing like spectral phantoms in the darkness. His voice resonated with a low and thick cadence as he recited the arcane spells carefully.

In the midst of his incantations, Gideon was abruptly startled by a strange presence that filled the room. As he felt the tendrils of darkness writhe against his skin like the warm caress of a secret lover, a smile spread across his face. Before him materialized a figure from the darkest recesses of nightmare, its form twisted and contorted, a grotesque mockery of humanity.

"Gideon," the creature's voice, a guttural rasp that seemed to claw at the very fabric of reality, echoed through the chamber. "I have information that would prove useful to you."

Gideon regarded the dark spirit for a moment, taking in its magnificence, power unheard of radiating from the creature. Inside his brain, the darkness that he had merged with rejoiced at the presence of the entity, urging him to accept whatever aid it may bring. "Welcome, spirit," he said. "What may I call you?"

The dark figure replied, "I go by many names, Soul Renderer, The Abyssal Harbinger of Fate, Shadow Bearer. You may call me what you wish. It matters not."

"Very well, then, Shadow Bearer, what dark providence do you bring?"

The demonic figure regarded him with eyes that burned like embers in the darkness, a grin stretching across its twisted features. "I come to offer insight into unfolding events," it declared, its words dripping with venom.

Gideon's heart hammered in his chest as he eagerly awaited the creature's revelations, his mind racing with visions of unspeakable power. "Tell me what you know."

Dark tentacles flew from the shadowy mass and embedded themselves into Gideon's skull, releasing a scream of terror from his mouth. His body began to shake uncontrollably, and a stream of bile dripped down his chin. A second later, the shaking stopped and the terror withdrew from his eyes, replaced by a look of surprise as the demonic figure recounted the meeting between Priscilla, Andrew, and the ancient beings.

It took a moment for Gideon to regain his composure after the demon withdrew his power. "Excellent," he finally murmured, his voice a hollow echo that reverberated through the chamber like the tolling of a funeral bell. "Their fear shall serve as the foundation upon which our ascent to power is built."

The demon nodded in agreement, its presence pulsating with energy. "Their bond may be strong, but it is fragile in the face of the darkness that looms ahead," it hissed, its words like poison dripping from its tongue.

Gideon's lips curled into a macabre smile as he

contemplated the creature's words, his mind consumed by visions of unspeakable power and glory. "Thank you, Soul Renderer," he acknowledged with a nod, "Your help will not be forgotten."

With those words, the demonic figure dissolved back into the shadows, leaving Gideon alone in the darkness. His heart pounded with the thrill of impending power; his ambition stoked to a fever pitch by the whispered promises of the abyss.

"We need to keep a close eye on these two so we'll be ready to capitalize on the situation when the appropriate moment presents itself. Go do what you do best, my friend."

Gideon felt the shadow demon writhing inside him, a force of darkness in all its glory. A moment later, the demon disengaged its hold on Gideon and disappeared into the ether in search of its targets.

Unknown to the unsuspecting town, their priest stood on the precipice of a dark and twisted destiny, his soul ensnared by forces beyond comprehension. And as the echoes of the creature's whispers faded, Gideon vowed to stop at nothing to claim the power that awaited him, even if it meant unleashing unspeakable horrors upon the world.

CHAPTER 24

As the seasons changed in an intricate, spinning dance, the ancient woods evolved into a sanctuary—a hallowed ground where time itself seemed to bow to the growing passion of Andrew and Priscilla. Beneath the twisted branches, their romantic odyssey unfolded like a fiery fantasy, each moment etching deeper into the very fabric of their being. Moonlit walks became a communion beneath a celestial tapestry where starlight weaved through the leaves like ethereal strands of fate. Secluded clearings transformed into altars for their private rites, where the air crackled with the power of their unbridled love.

Beneath the sprawling canopy of the ancient oak, where they had once laid in the embrace of moonlight following the prophecy of the Ancient Ones—whose presence were always felt but never seen again—Andrew felt the fullness of their love encompassing them. He had accepted the cosmic symphony of their destinies, an orchestration foretold by the mystic cards and the silent guardians of the night.

Yet, amidst the serenity, a shiver danced down Andrew's spine—a whisper of unease that stirred the shadows, hinting at secrets lurking just beyond their perception. It was as though the very essence of the forest held its breath, waiting for the darkness to reveal its twisted truths.

He pushed the feeling down, attributing it to nerves, as he drew in a breath, his pulse thundering in his ears. Kneeling in front of Priscilla, he held his hand out to her, presenting her with a ring that glimmered with the promise of forever.

In that sacred moment, guided by the unseen forces that bound their souls, Andrew posed the question that would seal their fate. "Priscilla," his voice trembled, "will you marry me?"

The moonlit shadows danced around them, as if celebrating the climax of their love story. Overwhelmed with emotion, Priscilla quietly murmured her answer, "Yes," tears streaming down her face.

And, so, amidst the ancient, mystical woods, the couple sealed their promise with a passionate embrace—a testament to the dawn of a new chapter in their extraordinary story.

****

The morning light filtered through the curtains, casting a gentle glow on Priscilla's face as she sat at the vanity, dressed in her flowing green lace gown, with her hair streaming around her shoulders like waves of black silk. Anticipation hung in the air as she delicately ran her fingers over the intricate details of her wedding dress, adjusting the fit to make sure everything was perfect.

Her hands trembled ever so slightly, betraying the nervous energy that hummed within her. Just as she reached for the jade earrings on the table, her fingers slipped, and one of them slid off the edge.

"Shit!" she exclaimed as the earring landed with a soft chime on the hardwood floor.

A grunt escaped Priscilla's lips as she crouched to retrieve the runaway jewelry and banged her shoulder on the edge of the vanity, nearly ripping her dress. In that moment, the vulnerability draping around her intensified, as if the slight incident had punctuated the significance of the day. Yet, as she held the earring in her hand, she couldn't help but smile, realizing that, even in the midst of chaos, there was always a touch of enchantment to be found. She just had to look at things from the right perspective.

"I get it," she chuckled as she took a deep breath and looked up toward the ceiling. "I need to calm down."

The scent of Jasmin suddenly wafted through the room, bringing with it sweet memories of times past. Priscilla knew that her mother was there to guide her, and with her at her side, everything would be okay.

As Priscilla took a deep breath to steady herself, a gentle knock at the door interrupted her moment of reflection. With a sigh, she rose from her crouched position and smoothed down her dress before calling out, "Come in."

The door creaked open. "Priscilla, the wedding's about to start!" Emily exclaimed as she stepped into the room wearing a burgundy bridesmaid dress, her eyes sparkling with excitement. "Holy shit! You look absolutely stunning!"

Priscilla couldn't help but smile at her best friend's enthusiasm. "Thank you, Em. I couldn't have done this without you."

Emily grinned; "Of course, you couldn't! Now come on, we don't want to keep everyone waiting. It's time to walk down that aisle and marry the love of your life."

With a last glance in the mirror, Priscilla took a deep breath, steeling herself for the momentous occasion ahead. As she followed Emily out of the room and down the hallway, the scent of jasmine lingered in the air, a silent reminder of the love and support that surrounded her on this special day.

***

The morning sun painted streaks of gold across the sky, casting a warm glow inside Andrew's room. He stood before the mirror, adjusting his tie with meticulous care. His usually steady hands shook ever so slightly, a hint of the nerves that danced beneath his composed exterior.

As he straightened his tie, a sudden knot formed, refusing to cooperate. Frustration crept into Andrew's eyes, and in an attempt to loosen the knot, he pulled a bit too hard. With an unexpected snap, the tie slipped from his hands and landed in a tangled heap on the floor.

"For the love of God!" he grumbled as he bent down to retrieve it.

As his fingers wrapped around the errant cloth, he noticed a slip of paper lying next to it just under the front edge of the dresser. He picked it up and a smile immediately crept onto his face. It was nothing more than a small receipt—a tiny piece of paper from a little restaurant near his home where he had grown up—but it was also a reminder of the last time he had spent together with his father before he died.

"Thank you, Dad," he mumbled softly.

He closed his eyes for a second and took a deep breath before attempting the tie once more time, this time achieving his desired result perfectly. With a smile, he flipped the switch on the wall and walked out of the room, eager to begin his new life with the woman he loved more than he thought could be possible.

***

* * *

Mother Nature herself seemed to join in the celebration, painting the sky with warm hues that cast a golden glow over the park that had been transformed to serve as the perfect backdrop for the union that was about to take place. The pond sparkled next to the small arrangement of white chairs lined up nearby, each adorned with delicate ribbons that fluttered in the gentle breeze.

A hush fell over the crowd as the music started, then, a moment later, Priscilla emerged from the gazebo, a vision of enchantment in her flowing green lace gown, moving as if she was an extension of the land itself. Her bouquet, a tapestry of herbs and flowers, symbolized the union of the earthly and the supernatural. As she walked down a flower-strewn path toward the outdoor altar, the gentle scent of wildflowers wafted through the air, creating a symphony of nature's fragrances.

The aisle, lined with delicate petals, led Priscilla to the arch of vows where Andrew stood handsomely in a classic black suit. His eyes reflected his excitement, along with a touch of nervous anticipation, as he watched her glide across the pathway toward him.

When Priscilla approached, a collective gasp swept through the assemblage as they sat captivated by the beauty and mystery that surrounded the couple. The air was charged with an unseen energy, a manifestation of the mystical love that had blossomed between them. A gentle breeze swept through the park, brushing Priscilla and Andrew's faces with an otherworldly touch as they stood under the arch.

The ceremony unfolded like a tapestry, seamlessly weaving tradition with mysticism. As the minister began to speak, a single butterfly fluttered into the sacred space. It circled the couple, weaving through the petals and hovering near the arch. Priscilla and Andrew shared a knowing glance, their eyes reflecting the recognition of the mystical presence. The insect hovered briefly before gently landing on Priscilla's bouquet, resting there like a tiny, ethereal messenger carrying the blessings of the natural world surrounding them.

As Andrew shared his vows, every word echoed with a profound love. "I vow to be with you in every moment, whether it's the ordinary days or those filled with enchantment," he said, his voice carrying the depth of a promise shaped by the path they'd walked together.

Priscilla, her eyes gleaming, responded with her own sensational vows. "I promise to dance with you under the moonlight and to embrace the mysteries of life with you."

Their oaths hung in the air, creating a sublime melody that resonated in the hearts of the crowd. When the minister pronounced them husband and wife, and the crowd erupted in applause, the butterfly took flight once more, disappearing into the bright blue sky. It was a fleeting moment, a magical interlude that only Priscilla and Andrew fully understood—a symbol of the enchantment woven into their love and the mystical forces that had guided their journey from the very beginning.

CHAPTER 25

A month had passed since Mary's harrowing ordeal at the OBGYN, and even though numerous tests had come back inconclusive, the specter of darkness haunted her every step like a discarded lover consumed by vindictive obsession, determined to inflict chaos on her life, unwilling to release its grip as she struggled to escape its savage clutches.

Then the day finally arrived when the promise of new life would become a reality. As the first pains of labor gripped her, Mary felt a mixture of excitement and trepidation. The whispers of the darkness that had shadowed her pregnancy lingered, casting a chill over what should've been a special occasion.

The living room was bathed in the soft glow of the table lamp, and the air was thick with fearful anticipation. Mary clutched her belly, breathing through each contraction, but a familiar dread gnawed at the edges of her mind as the scourge of complications loomed, threatening to plunge her once again into the abyss.

As the contractions intensified, Mary's breaths quickened, and beads of sweat formed on her forehead. In the midst of her pain, she felt a presence—an ethereal energy that seemed to transcend the boundaries of the physical world. And then, like a whisper in the wind, Nyx materialized beside Mary. Her eyes, filled with ancient wisdom, met Mary's, and a silent understanding passed between them.

"Mary," the witch said, her voice a soothing melody. "Don't be afraid, child, for you are not alone. The forces that once sought to engulf you have been held at bay. Together, we will face this moment, and the light will prevail."

Mary nodded, finding strength in the words of the mysterious figure. The witch's hands hovered above Mary's belly, a dance of unseen energies at play. Mary could feel a warmth, a protective energy enveloping her and the precious life of her son within.

But as the labor progressed, the atmosphere shifted. The room seemed to pulse with an otherworldly energy, and Mary's pain intensified drastically. The witch's brow furrowed, her focus deepening as she sensed a disturbance in the delicate balance between life and the unseen forces that lurked in the shadows.

With a sudden urgency, the witch spoke an incantation, her words ancient and powerful. The room quivered with an unseen force, and Mary felt a surge of energy, both comforting and overwhelming, coursing through her.

Just as the atmosphere reached its peak, the wail of sirens pierced through the air, its presence a beacon of hope.

As the paramedics burst into the apartment, Nyx stepped back. "She needs urgent medical attention," the witch said, her voice a command that brooked no argument. "Take her to the hospital, and do whatever you need to in order to avoid any unnecessary risks. Both her and her son's life lay in the balance right now."

With a seamless transition, the paramedics took charge, guiding Mary onto a stretcher and rushing her out of the room. The witch lingered for a moment, her gaze fixed on the ambulance as it sped away into the night.

"May the light guide you, Mary," Nyx whispered, her words carrying through the air like a gentle breeze. And with that, the mysterious figure faded into the shadows.

In the ambulance, as Mary clutched the talisman the witch had given her, she felt a renewed strength. The journey to the hospital was a race against time, but Mary held onto the hope that the light, strengthened by the ancient magic of the witch, would guide her through the darkness once more.

***

Minutes later, surrounded by the sterile whiteness of the hospital room, Mary clutched at her belly, the pain of her contractions interwoven with the haunting memories of the graveyard nightmares. A steady rain outside beat against the windows in a relentless symphony that mirrored the tumult within her.

The scent of antiseptic hung in the air as Mary lay on the hospital bed, writhing in agony. The medical team moved with a deep sense of urgency, their eyes focused on the monitors that blinked with the vital signs of both her and her baby.

Doctor Johnson, an older man with graying temples and a calm demeanor, looked at her from his perch at the foot of the bed. "Mary, we're facing some unusual complications right now. You need to push through this, okay? We're here for you, but we need your strength."

Mary, with beads of sweat on her forehead, nodded through the pain, an unsettling fear flickering in her eyes. As the rhythmic beeping of the fetal monitor transformed into an ominous symphony, heightening the tension in the delivery room, she saw the shadow demon beside her, its ethereal fingers wedged inside her stomach as it sought out her child.

"Hang in there, Mary," the nurse urged. "You're doing great. We're almost there."

As Mary pushed, an unnatural chill permeated the room. The medical personnel worked with an urgent intensity, unaware of the unnatural presence in the room. But she had seen it—the creature that had stalked her in her dreams—and she was determined that it would not have her child.

Doctor Johnson said urgently, "Mary, we need one more firm push. Come on, you can do this."

With a final, valiant effort, Mary pushed, her strength waning as the room plunged into a heart-stopping silence. The air itself seemed to thicken with an oppressive presence, and the medical team exchanged tense glances.

The newborn, eerily still, lay in the nurse's arms, the room swallowed by a profound hush. Mary, panic clawing at her chest, pleaded with unseen forces for the miracle she so desperately needed, her eyes fixed on the elusive shadow demon attempting to steal her son's soul.

Doctor Johnson, intensity in his every movement as he worked to reel in the baby's fleeting life-force, whispered earnestly, "Come on, little one. Breathe."

Then, as if answering the pleas of a desperate mother, Matthew's tiny chest quivered, and a faint breath escaped his lips. The room erupted into a symphony of relieved gasps and hurried footsteps as the baby, suspended between the realms of life and death, drew another tremulous breath. The shadow demon, momentarily repelled, retreated into the murky corners of the delivery room, its insidious presence lingering.

Tears of relief welled in Mary's eyes as the medical team worked to stabilize her son. The delivery room hummed with a cacophony of medical instruments and the fragile cries of a newborn who had narrowly escaped the clutches of evil.

Doctor Johnson, a mix of exhaustion and wariness in his eyes, said, "Your son's a fighter, Mary, I'll give you that. So are you."

As Mary held her newborn son for the first time, the room became a sanctuary of newfound hope. The echoes of supernatural struggles and the shadows that had threatened to engulf them now yielded, for the moment, to the cries of a miracle reborn.

Then, a second later, the unthinkable happened. A cry erupted from Mary's mouth as a fountain of blood flowed like a river from between her legs to the floor. In the throes of agony, Mary glimpsed the fleeting shadow in the corner of the room, surmising that if the shadow demon couldn't have her son, it would take her instead.

The delivery room once again became a battleground, as the cries of her newborn mingled with Mary's own desperate pleas for survival. Then a burst of ethereal energy suddenly enveloped the room, unnoticed by everyone else. Mary, on the precipice of surrender, felt an unseen force cradle her, as if the spirits themselves were guiding her through the tempest. She knew it was Nyx who come to save her yet again. A moment later, with a low supernatural growl that reverberated through Mary's soul, the shadow demon retreated, its hunger for death unsatisfied.

In the aftermath, once the danger had passed and the medical team had stabilized Mary's condition, the room fell silent. Mary lay exhausted yet triumphant, her newborn nestled snuggly in her arms. As she gazed at her son through tear-stained eyes, truly a miracle of will and divine salvation, she couldn't shake the feeling that the forces that had haunted her dreams were now intertwined with the very fabric of their existence.

CHAPTER 26

The expansive cruise ship hummed with life as Andrew and Priscilla stood hand in hand on the deck of the ship, their hearts still soaring from the ceremony that had bound them together as one. The warm sun kissed their skin as they gazed out at the endless ocean, its surface sparkling like a sea of diamonds under the midday sky.

As they began their honeymoon, surrounded by the hustle and bustle of fellow travelers, Priscilla's laughter echoed through the air like a sweet symphony. She spun gracefully in her flowing white blouse, the delicate lace dancing in the gentle breeze. Every second, Andrew was increasingly captivated by her beauty. Her laughter was a beacon of happiness guiding them through their grand adventure.

Over the next few days, they explored every corner of the ship, from the elegant dining halls adorned with crystal chandeliers, to the cozy lounges where they shared intimate moments over glasses of champagne. Each day brought fresh adventures, from snorkeling in crystal-clear waters to lounging on pristine beaches, hand in hand, lost in their own world of bliss.

On the fourth night of their magnificent journey, as the sun dipped below the horizon, painting the sky in hues of pink and orange, Andrew and Priscilla found themselves on the top deck, wrapped in each other's arms as they watched the stars twinkle overhead. The air was filled with the sweet scent of saltwater and the soft sound of waves lapping against the hull. The night was absolutely perfect.

***

For the first part of the ritual, Gideon retrieved an assortment of jars from a nearby shelf, each one containing a different substance: blood-red ichor, writhing maggots, and foul-smelling entrails. With meticulous care, Gideon poured the contents of each jar into an enormous cauldron, the noxious mixture emitting a sickening stench that permeated the chamber.

Next, he retrieved a series of twisted artifacts from a velvet-lined box. These artifacts were relics of unspeakable horror: a desiccated hand with gnarled fingers, an eye preserved in a jar of murky fluid, and a mummified tongue that twitched with a semblance of life.

With trembling hands, Gideon arranged the artifacts around the cauldron in a sinister pattern. Then, he began to chant in a guttural language, his voice echoing through the darkness like the whisper of ancient evils.

As the ritual reached its climax, Gideon plunged his hands into the cauldron, his fingers sinking into the foul mixture with a sickening squelch. He drew out handfuls of the noxious brew and smeared it across his face and body, the vile concoction seeping into his pores and staining his skin with a sickly hue.

With each motion, Gideon's chanting grew louder and more frenzied, his body contorting with unnatural spasms as he became one with the darkness that surrounded him. The air crackled with energy, and the chamber filled with a chorus of anguished wails and otherworldly screams.

Finally, as the last echoes of his chant faded into silence, Gideon collapsed to the floor, his naked and defiled body wracked with exhaustion and his mind clouded by visions of unspeakable horror as he communed with the darkest depths of his own depravity, reveling in the grotesque ecstasy of his twisted desires.

While he lay there motionless, basking in the aftermath of his descent into the abyss, Gideon felt the familiar fingers of the shadow demon caressing his dark heart like a gentle lover. Its touch brought him back from the madness that had engulfed him, and he sat up in wide-eyed wonder. "The power is incredible!" he said. "So many secrets... so many wonders revealed!"

"This is only the beginning of your journey, my faithful servant," the demon hissed into his ears. "Now that your eyes are open to the truth, the knowledge available to you is endless. And I have one more spell to teach you."

A flurry of images suddenly exploded into Gideon's brain in rapid succession—volcanoes erupting with savage fury, the seas churning and boiling, mountains crumbling to dust, a whirl-wind tempest destroying everything in its path—and all around these scenes, arcane symbols and shapes flew at lightning speed to create an archaic formula that resonated with dark energy. A scream flew out of Gideon's mouth as the spell burned itself into his flesh, glowing bright red before being absorbed into his body.

With a crazed look in his eyes and a wide grin on his face, he rose to his knees. "Do you have a particular target in mind?" he asked the demon.

The demon replied simply, "Look into the mirror."

Gideon shuffled toward the corner of the room where he stood before a large scrying mirror, its surface shimmering with an otherworldly glow. His eyes, dark pools of hatred, were fixed on the image that danced upon its surface—a grand cruise ship sailing serenely across the tranquil waters.

A cruel smile twisted Gideon's lips as he watched the passengers on board, their laughter and happiness a stark contrast to the darkness that lurked within his own heart. Then the scene shifted to focus on the subject of his pursuit—the newlyweds.

"Soon, they will know the true power of the storm," Gideon murmured, his voice dripping with venom.

With a flick of his wrist, he traced the same series of arcane symbols in the air, channeling his new dark magic into the mirror's reflection. "Let's see how strong you really are, witch!" he sneered.

The image wavered and shifted, the once peaceful sky darkening with ominous storm clouds gathering on the horizon. Lightning crackled and thunder rumbled as the winds whipped into a frenzy, lashing out with unbridled fury.

***

As the night wore on, a sense of unease began to creep into Priscilla bones. The sky darkened, clouds gathering ominously on the horizon. The once gentle breeze turned into a fierce wind, whipping through their hair and sending shivers down their spines.

"Do you feel that, Andrew?" Priscilla asked, her voice tinged with concern.

Andrew nodded with a furrowed brow. "It looks like a bad storm's coming."

Priscilla closed her eyes for a moment as she focused her energy toward the oncoming tempest. "This isn't an ordinary storm. I can feel it. There's something evil at its center."

No sooner had she spoken those words, and it was upon them. A sudden clap of thunder echoed through the air, followed by flashes of lightning illuminating the sky in jagged streaks of light. The ship rocked violently as towering waves crashed against its sides, sending passengers stumbling and grasping for support.

Cries of panic filled the air as the crew scrambled to secure the ship against the raging storm. Andrew and Priscilla clung to each other, their hearts pounding as they prayed for safety amidst the chaos.

Andrew's grip tightened on Priscilla's hand as he felt her body tense beside him. But instead of fear, he saw determination in her eyes, a glint of something mysterious and powerful.

As the storm raged on, Priscilla closed her eyes once more and whispered ancient words under her breath, her hands moving in graceful, intricate gestures. A shimmering light enveloped the ship, casting a protective barrier around it like a cocoon.

The wind howled and the waves roared, but miraculously, the ship remained steady, riding out the storm unscathed. Andrew watched in awe as Priscilla's spell worked its magic.

Then, just as suddenly as it had begun, the storm began to subside, the wind losing its ferocity and the waves gradually calming to a gentle swell. Exhausted but relieved, Andrew and Priscilla dropped to their knees.

***

Gideon's lips curled into a cruel smile as he felt the power of the storm respond to his commands. He could sense the fear and panic spreading among the passengers aboard the ship, their desperate cries for help echoing in the night.

With a last flourish of his hands, Gideon unleashed the full force of his spell, directing the fury of the storm toward the unsuspecting vessel. The winds howled and the waves roared, but miraculously, the ship remained steady, riding out the storm unscathed. "It seems she is powerful indeed," Gideon said to the demon writhing inside him. "She should suit our purpose perfectly."

CHAPTER 27

In the hushed tranquility of the early morning, Andrew ventured into the heart of the city toward the local coffee shop, a cherished sanctuary for both him and Priscilla. The air hummed with energy as he crossed the threshold of the bustling establishment, embracing the familiar feeling of warmth that greeted him like an old friend.

Each step carried him deeper into the welcoming allure of the cafe's ambiance, a symphony of subtle sounds and fragrances that wrapped around him like a soft blanket. Approaching the counter, Andrew found himself drawn to the barista, who apparently was a new employee he hadn't met yet. With a gentle smile perched on her lips, she stood poised and ready to fulfill his every caffeine-fueled desire.

"Good morning!" the barista greeted with genuine excitement. "What can I get for you today?"

"Good morning," Andrew replied with a soft smile. "A cappuccino and a latte, please."

The barista nodded, her hands deftly preparing the drinks with practiced ease. The rich scent of freshly ground coffee beans filled the air, mingling with the sweet aroma of steamed milk. As she worked, she struck up a casual conversation with Andrew.

"Busy day ahead?" she asked, pouring the velvety foam over the espresso for the cappuccino.

Andrew chuckled softly. "Not really. My wife and I actually just got back from our honeymoon. Thought I'd start it off right with a heavy dose of caffeine."

The barista's smile widened, almost to where it bordered on lunacy, and there was something unsettling in the glint of her eyes, hidden beneath the warmth. "Oh, that's lovely! Congratulations! Here you go, two drinks for the newlyweds, on the house."

Andrew's eyes lit up as he accepted the drinks. "Thank you very much!"

"Consider it my gift to the two of you, Andrew," the girl replied.

Andrew did a double-take at the mention of his name, and for the briefest of seconds, watched as the girl's eyes turned pitch-black before returning to normal. He tossed it up to a trick of the light, but a shiver traced down his spine as he sensed a subtle shift in the atmosphere, a whisper of something darker lurking behind the cheerful facade. "Thank you," he mumbled again as he backed away from the counter and turned to leave.

With the freshly brewed drinks cradled in his hands, he made his way back home, the memory of the barista's unsettling gaze lingering in his mind like a shadow cast by the morning sun.

***

Priscilla stirred, the remnants of her dreams still clinging to her consciousness like cobwebs in a forgotten corner. Slowly, she slid out of bed, stretching her weary bones awake. The room was dimly lit, the morning sun casting soft shadows that danced along the walls.

"Morning, love," Andrew's voice broke the silence.

Priscilla looked up to see him standing in the doorway with a smile on his face. He had the coffee cups balanced on a tray in one hand and a bouquet of wildflowers in the other.

"Morning," Priscilla smiled, taking the flowers. "They're beautiful," she said as she breathed in the fragrance before embracing him with a long and powerful kiss.

After laying the bouquet down on the bed, nestled between their two pillows in a display of harmony, Priscilla lit an array of fairy lights and scented candles, filling the space with a cozy glow. The room smelled of jasmine and sandalwood, wrapping them in a comforting embrace.

Andrew watched her quietly from the doorway. "You make everything special," he whispered.

Priscilla looked at him with a sparkle in her eyes. "It's not just me, it's us. Together, we make magic."

"Now, I need that coffee," Priscilla said with a smile.

Andrew chuckled as he handed the drink to her before settling on the edge of the bed. "So, caffeine is the true source of your power?"

Priscilla slipped onto his lap with a twinkle in her eye and took a long sip of her latte, "Not a word to anyone, Mr. Henson, or I might have to do some very naughty things to you."

As was all too common for Andrew, he was instantly lost in her magical gaze. "Don't worry. Your secret's safe with me. Although, I'd like to hear a little more about this punishment you had in mind."

Before Priscilla could reply, her world suddenly spun out of control and she fell onto the bed, dropping her drink to the floor. A brief gasp issued from her mouth and then everything went black. A second later, it was over.

"Priscilla!" Andrew cried. "Are you okay?"

Priscilla slowly sat up on the edge of the bed, shaken and disoriented for a moment. "Yeah, I'm okay," she said as she steadied herself. "Just give me a second."

"What happened?"

"I got dizzy suddenly, but it's gone now. It's nothing. I've had bouts of vertigo periodically my whole life. Luckily, it doesn't happen very often."

Andrew looked at her in concern, "Are you sure you're okay?"

"Yeah, I'm fine," Priscilla said as she pulled Andrew onto the bed and straddled him, "Now, about that punishment I was referring to..."

Neither of them noticed the liquid from the spilled drink slithering across the floor like a giant amoeba, disappearing silently into a small crack in the floorboard.

***

The sanctuary of, what was now, Andrew and Priscilla's apartment morphed into a silent witness of the depths of their love. As the days melded into weeks and the weeks into months, their love story unfolded like a fairytale.

One evening, as the sun dipped below the horizon, casting long, ominous shadows across their home, Priscilla felt a soft chill creep up her spine. Though Andrew held her close, she couldn't shake the sensation of being watched. But then again, for Priscilla, the eyes of the dead were always watching her, lurking in the shadows and hiding in the corners.

"Andrew," she murmured, her voice barely above a whisper, "do you ever think about... about starting a family?"

His embrace tightened around her. "All the time," he

admitted, his voice soft and filled with longing. "I can't imagine anything more perfect than raising a child with you, Priscilla."

A flicker of hope ignited within her, dispelling the darkness that had threatened her a minute ago. "I was hoping you'd say that. Everything has been moving so fast lately and I didn't know how to tell you, or how you'd react?"

Andrew's eyes grew wide, "Are you—?"

Before he could finish, Priscilla nodded happily and threw her arms around him, holding him tight as tears streamed down her face. "Yes, we're going to have a baby!"

And in that moment, as they sat together in the fading light, she dared to believe that their love was strong enough to conquer whatever darkness lay ahead.

***

As twilight draped its velvet cloak over the world outside, a soft knock echoed through their apartment. Priscilla ran to the door and threw it open. Barely able to contain her excitement as she ushered Emily inside.

Jinx immediately set upon her, slathering her with kisses. "My God, Pris," Emily exclaimed as she returned Jinx's affection. "What's going on? You look like the cat who swallowed the canary."

Priscilla grinned, a mischievous glint dancing in her eyes that matched the flicker of the candles flames that lined the coffee table nearby. "Grab a seat, Em," she said as she led Emily to the couch. "There's something I... I mean we, need to tell you."

With a nod to Andrew, who stood nearby with a proud grin, she turned back to Emily, excitement bubbling in her veins. "Em... Andrew and I are gonna be parents," she blurted out, unable to contain herself any longer.

Emily's jaw dropped, her eyes wide with disbelief and excitement. "Holy shit, Pris! That's incredible!" she exclaimed as she hugged Priscilla tightly. "I'm so happy for you both!"

"Yeah, can you imagine me a mother?"

Emily replied, "I think you'll make an amazing mom!"

"I agree," Andrew chimed in, his own face beaming.

As they sat in the living room, they shared stories and laughter, the future stretching out before them like an endless, winding road.

None of them saw the face watching them through the candle's flames—a twisted wraith born from the ashes of the fire—which quietly disappeared into the ether, carrying with it a dark secret.

CHAPTER 28

Priscilla lay nestled against Andrew, her eyelids heavy as a peaceful sleep slowly began to take over. Then, the hand of tranquility suddenly morphed into a nightmare's icy grip. Darkness descended like a suffocating shroud, enfolding her in its chilling tendrils as she plunged headlong into the twisted maze of her memories. Within this labyrinth, her childhood home loomed before her like a sinister apparition, its walls throbbing with the discordant pulse of unbearable anguish.

In the dimly lit hallway, Priscilla senses were assaulted by the putrid stench of decay and despair. Shadows writhed along the walls, their sinuous movements taunting her with every step. At the corridor's end stood her sister, Victoria, a swirling vortex of dark energy engulfing her, while her eyes were filled with a hatred that seared into Priscilla's soul.

As if in response to her terror, the walls began to press in on Priscilla, threatening to squeeze the life from her. Panic clawed at her as Victoria's deranged laughter echoed through the hall.

Desperately, Priscilla turned to run, when suddenly their mother materialized before her, a beacon of light amidst the encroaching darkness. With a defiant stance, she pushed back against the engulfing shadows, driving the darkness away.

Then Victoria unleashed all of her savage fury toward their mother, her hands twisted into talons of rage. Priscilla watched in helpless horror as their mother fell, the life draining from her eyes in a silent scream.

The nightmare escalated into a frenzied crescendo as Victoria turned her manic gaze on Priscilla, her visage contorted into a grotesque mask of madness. The air crackled with intensity, sending shockwaves rippling through the house, as Victoria sent a blast of energy hurling toward Priscilla.

Desperately, Priscilla summoned every ounce of her strength, grappling with the maelstrom of dark energy that threatened to consume her. The cacophony of screams and whispers reverberated through her brain, drowning her in a sea of terror.

Blood pooled at her feet, a grim testament to the violence that engulfed them. Priscilla's heart hammered in her chest as she fought to maintain her grip on reality, her very existence hanging by a thread.

Priscilla snapped awake, cold sweat coating her body. Andrew held her tight, his worried eyes cutting through her lingering terror. Desperately struggling to breathe, she held onto him tightly, finding comfort in his comforting presence amid the lingering fear that consumed her.

"Pris, it's okay," Andrew whispered, his voice a soothing comfort against the turmoil raging within her. "You're safe now. It was just a bad dream."

But even as Andrew held her close, Priscilla couldn't shake the lingering sense of dread that clung to her like a second skin. In the cold light of dawn, the echoes of her nightmare still lingered, a haunting reminder of the darkness that lurked within her.

***

Priscilla stood before the bathroom mirror, her fingers tracing the faint curve of her belly beneath her shirt. She stared at her reflection, a mixture of excitement and apprehension swirling inside her. The reality of impending motherhood was sinking in, and she couldn't help but feel a flutter of nerves. The ghost of her mother standing behind her in the mirror did little to ease her apprehension.

As she was lost in thought, the door flew open, and Emily barged in, her eyes gleaming with excitement.

"Pris! I found it!" Emily exclaimed, waving a flowy garment in the air like a triumphant banner.

Priscilla turned with a confusing smile on her face. "Found what?"

Emily grinned and held up a dress. It was a soft, shimmering fabric, flowing gently to the floor with delicate lace detailing along the neckline.

"It's the perfect maternity dress for you!" Emily declared in a bubbly voice.

Priscilla reached out to touch the fabric. "Em, it's beautiful. Thank you."

Emily beamed. "I knew you'd love it! Come on, let's try it on. I bet it'll look amazing on you."

Together, they slipped on the dress, its fabric enveloping Priscilla's burgeoning bump with perfect elegance. As Priscilla stared into the mirror, a tide of emotion surged through her, filling her with a subtle sense of foreboding, as if the reflection was hiding shadows that lurked just beyond the surface. Her mother's death would always be a void in her heart that would never be filled, but the actions she had to take against her sister stirred a dark force that resided inside her, a force that scared her to death. And it was something she hoped she'd never have to use again.

"Em, I don't think I could face this alone," Priscilla murmured softly, with a hint of sadness in her voice.

Emily wrapped her arms around and squeezed tight. "You won't have to. I'll be right here, through every twist and turn that may come."

In that moment, as their eyes met in the mirror's reflection, Priscilla sensed the weight of the future pressing down upon them. Yet, amidst the darkness, there was a flicker of hope—a bond forged in adversity, a friendship that would endure, a beacon to guide them through the looming darkness.

***

As Priscilla stood in the center of the small bedroom that would soon become the nursery, her mind buzzing with ideas, Emily entered behind her, her eyes sparkling with excitement. "This is going to be perfect for little Grace," Emily exclaimed.

Priscilla nodded with a smile, "Yes, it is."

The first piece of business was a trip to the local department store to focus on selecting furniture and decorations—with lots of pink. Together, they chose a cozy crib, a comfortable rocking chair for late-night feedings, and shelves adorned with whimsical decorations and books.

Once home, Priscilla and Andrew busied themselves with assembling the furniture and adding personal touches to the room, while Emily took up the task of painting the walls. Laughter filled the air as they worked, broken occasionally by a choice curse word when one of the many some-assembly-required items refused to cooperate, or a splatter of paint ended up on the floor instead of the wall.

Amidst the cheerful chaos, Andrew was determined to get everything perfect for their little one. As he carefully assembled the crib, he focused intently on following the instructions, his brow furrowed in concentration.

However, disaster struck when Andrew reached for a screwdriver on the nearby shelf. In his haste, he knocked over a box of screws, causing them to scatter across the floor. Reacting quickly, Andrew bent down to retrieve them, but in his rush, he misjudged his footing and stumbled, the palm of his hand falling on an array of the screws that had landed with their sharp points upright like the spikes in the bottom of a deadly animal trap.

A sharp cry of pain erupted from Andrew as he recoiled, blood gushing from his hand, which had three of the screws lodged deep into his flesh. Priscilla's eyes widened in shock as she rushed to him.

"Oh my god, Andrew, are you okay?" Priscilla exclaimed, her voice trembling as she examined the wound.

Andrew gritted his teeth against the pain, his face pale, as he pulled the metal pieces out. "Shit! This hurts like a bitch!" he said through clenched teeth, blood staining his hand and dripping onto the floor.

With Priscilla's help, Andrew carefully got back to his feet, holding his injured hand against his chest. Emily rushed out of the room and quickly returned with a wet cloth and some bandages. A minute later, they had the flow of blood staunched and his hand wrapped up tight.

Despite the pain and the blood, Andrew insisted on finishing the crib, to the dismay of both Priscilla and Emily, determined not to let the accident derail their plans for the nursery.

After carefully arranging the furniture and adding

personal touches to the room, the three of them stepped back, satisfied with their progress. "I think we're almost done," Priscilla declared proudly.

But Emily had a surprise up her sleeve. With a mischievous twinkle in her eye, she gently nudged Priscilla and Andrew toward the doorway. "I still have something special in store for this room. Why don't you two take a break and relax in the living room while I add my own little touch?"

With Priscilla out of sight, Emily wasted no time. She retrieved her paintbrushes and set to work diligently on a corner of the room, adding strokes of color to the wall. She painted with care and precision, infusing the mural with love and creativity.

After what felt like hours, Emily finally put the finishing touches on the mural. Satisfied with her work, she called out to Priscilla and Andrew.

As they stepped back into the room, Priscilla gasped in astonishment. In the corner of the room, a beautiful mural had taken shape, depicting a serene forest scene with woodland creatures frolicking among the trees. Tears welled up in Priscilla's eyes as she took in the scene.

"You painted this?" Priscilla whispered, her voice cracking with disbelief.

Emily nodded, her own eyes shimmering. "I wanted to surprise you," she said softly.

Priscilla embraced Emily tightly. Finally, after hours of meticulous planning and hard work, the nursery had been transformed into a magical haven, brimming with love, warmth, and the promise of new beginnings.

But a slight chill ran through Emily as she gazed at her handiwork once more. In the lowest corner of the mural, barely perceptible, was a tiny figure, only an inch or two tall, that resembled a mysterious creature. Its form was humanoid but ethereal, with slender limbs and delicate features. Its skin seemed to shimmer with an iridescent glow, and long, flowing tendrils cascaded from its head like wisps of mist. Its eyes, two pools of deep, mesmerizing blue, seemed to pierce through the mural, locking gazes with anyone who dared to look upon it.

Baffled, Emily furrowed her brow, certain that she hadn't painted the figure herself. She couldn't shake the tension that washed over her as she studied the creature, its presence seeming to radiate a strange energy that set her nerves on edge.

Glancing at Priscilla, who was still admiring the mural with a radiant smile, Emily hesitated. Should she mention the strange figure? Or was it simply a trick of the light, a figment of her imagination?

Emily forced a smile and joined Priscilla's side. "It's perfect, isn't it?" she said, hoped to hide her growing sense of unease.

Priscilla nodded enthusiastically, her eyes sparkling with joy. "Absolutely perfect," she agreed, unaware of the strange creature lurking in the corner of their sanctuary.

As they turned to leave, for the briefest of seconds, Emily swore she saw the image move, ever so slightly.

CHAPTER 29

Andrew's hands gripped the steering wheel tightly as he sped through town. The air inside the car was charged with a mix of excitement and anxiety. Priscilla, in the throes of labor, tried to steady her breathing while Andrew navigated the streets nervously.

"Hang in there, Pris," Andrew said. "We're almost there."

The roads blurred past as Andrew weaved through traffic with a recklessness born out of nerves and desperation.

Priscilla gritted her teeth, "Andrew, slow down. We'll get there. Just calm down!"

But Andrew ignored her plea as he maneuvered the car in and out of traffic, narrowly avoiding collisions and sending the occasional honk from other drivers. The tension in the car grew palpable as they approached a busy intersection.

"Andrew, seriously! Slow down!" Priscilla cried.

"Sorry, Pris. I just... I want to get there as fast as we can so there aren't any complications."

"Well, there's going to be a lot of complications if we end up in an accident along the way."

As they approached the intersection, the traffic light turned red. Andrew, too close to stop safely, slammed on the brakes, causing the car to screech to a halt just inches from the car in front.

Priscilla screamed, "Andrew!"

Andrew, his heart beating rapidly and his eyes wide with fright, took a deep breath. "I'm sorry. I guess I got a little carried away."

Priscilla placed a hand on Andrew's shoulder. "We'll be fine. Let's just get to the hospital safely, okay?"

As Andrew and Priscilla breathed a sigh of relief, flashing red and blue lights suddenly illuminated the interior of the car. Andrew's heart skipped a beat as he glanced nervously at Priscilla, whose grip on his hand tightened.

The officer approached the vehicle, his silhouette imposing against the backdrop of the evening sky, his face obscured by the darkness.

"Sir, do you know why I pulled you over?" the officer asked in a stern tone as he bent down low so they could get a glimpse of him. With a long nose, pointed chin, and beady eyes, the man resembled a real-life Joker anxious to spread his chaos throughout the world.

Andrew stammered, "I... I'm sorry, officer. We're rushing to the hospital. My wife is in labor."

The officer's gaze shifted from Andrew to Priscilla, who was visibly in discomfort. His lips curled into a wide smile that sent a shiver down Andrew's spine.

"Well, isn't that just precious," the officer said, his voice dripping with contempt. "But you can't just go around endangering lives, now, can you?"

Andrew's heart sank as he realized the severity of the situation. He pleaded with the officer, explaining their urgent need to reach the hospital.

The officer's smile widened even further, but there was something predatory in his expression. "I'll tell you what," he said, leaning closer to the window. "I'll let you off with a warning. But only if I escort you to the hospital myself."

Andrew exchanged a wary glance with Priscilla, but with no other choice, he reluctantly agreed.

As the officer climbed back into his car and motioned for Andrew to follow—his long, crooked fingers resembling talons on a bird of prey—a chill ran down Andrew's spine. There was definitely something off about the officer, something dark and creepy that made him his skin crawl.

Minutes later, Andrew finally breathed a sigh of relief when he saw the entrance to the hospital come into view. After Andrew pulled up to the front, the officer parked his car nearby and approached Andrew's vehicle once more.

"Ah, the anticipation of what's to come," the officer whispered with an unsettling grin. "It's thrilling, isn't it? The unknown, the darkness... It's all part of the grand design."

Andrew's eyes widened in alarm, while Priscilla's hand tightened around his as they exchanged a nervous glance.

"Excuse me?" Andrew managed to stammer, his voice trembling.

But the officer merely chuckled darkly, his eyes gleaming with a twisted delight. "Enjoy the calm while it lasts," he said, his words dripping with a sinister promise. "For soon, the storm will descend, and oh, what a spectacle it will be."

With that, the officer turned away, his laughter echoing hauntingly in the night as he climbed back into his vehicle and disappeared into the darkness.

***

The atmosphere in the delivery room buzzed with the frenetic energy associated with childbirth. Priscilla, surrounded by the sharp smell of antiseptics and the various sounds of medical apparatus, navigated a desperate dance with fate, as each contraction felt like she was being pummeled by a heavyweight fighter.

With her eyes closed tight, Priscilla sought to ease her body and mind from the relentless torment, hoping to call upon her years of experience to enter a meditative state that would block out the pain. In the brief moments between contractions, while Andrew held her hand firmly in a show of support, Priscilla whispered soft words of encouragement to both herself and her unborn daughter.

But as the minutes passed and her labor intensified, she felt a jarring snap inside her, like a fishing line that wasn't strong enough to hold on to its prized catch.

Priscilla looked up at Andrew in fear. "Something's wrong!" she cried.

Andrew held Priscilla's hand tight, trying to offer any form of comfort that might guide her through the turmoil, but he saw the look in her eyes and instantly felt the terror rising inside his own soul.

The doctor quickly stepped in; his movements urgent but precise. "I need you to push, Priscilla."

As Priscilla strained against the crushing weight of her fear, her heart pounded in sync with the ominous silence that enveloped the room. The relentless beeping of the baby's heartbeat monitor, once a beacon of hope, now echoed only absence. Panic seized every breath as Grace emerged, a fragile wisp of life, silent and still.

A chilling hush descended on the room like a suffocating fog, freezing time itself in its merciless grip. The medical team moved in a frantic dance against the encroaching darkness, with urgent commands slicing sharply through the air.

Andrew's grip on Priscilla's hand tightened, a desperate

anchor in the tempest that threatened to consume them. Together, they stood on the edge of the abyss, their hearts gathered in a desperate, silent plea to the heavens above.

"Please, God, not our baby," Priscilla's voice wavered, tears carving rivers of anguish down her trembling cheeks.

Amidst the chaos, Andrew's voice pierced through the tumult like a beacon of unwavering hope, "Hold on, Priscilla. She'll make it. She has to."

Time stretched thin, each second a cruel eternity as the medical team battled to restore life to the child. And then, in a heartbeat that seemed to linger on the precipice of oblivion, Grace drew in a shuddering breath.

Relief surged like a tidal wave, crashing over the room in a deluge of raw emotion as the medical team scrambled to stabilize her fragile form. And then, amidst the cacophony of chaos, the doctor's reassuring words pierced through the haze of fear like a ray of golden light. "Her heartbeat is strong. Grace is with us."

Once she was stabilized, the head nurse presented their baby to them. With tears streaming down their faces, Priscilla and Andrew embraced their daughter. Against all odds, Grace had weathered the storm, her spirit unbroken by the darkness.

But little did they know, as they held her close in that moment of triumph, that fate had already begun to weave its cruel tapestry once more. For as the medical team celebrated their hard-won victory, the room around Priscilla suddenly stopped, everyone but her caught in frozen animation.

She turned her head towards the entrance of the room, where a shadowy figure stood. A shiver ran down Priscilla's spine as the shadow approached her in a coiling and shifting gait until it stood beside her.

Shrouded in a cloak of writhing black energy, the figure

bent its head down low so that it was only inches from hers. And then, in a chilling whisper that froze the blood in her veins, the being spoke, its words dripping with malice. "You may have saved her for now," it hissed, "but the darkness will always find a way back."

With those ominous words hanging in the air like a curse, the shadow disappeared and time returned to normal once more, leaving Priscilla shaking under the threat of a future filled with darkness and fear.

CHAPTER 30

To say that Matthew had a strange childhood would be a vast understatement. Quite often, normal, everyday things seemed spooky to him. While other kids went through life without noticing anything odd, Matthew saw things differently. He felt like he could see things others couldn't, like there were secrets all around him. As his early years unfurled in shadowy hues, the ordinary moments of his childhood took on a sinister tone dripping with whispers and hidden mysteries.

Matthew's laughter seemed to hint at mysterious things beyond what an ordinary person could see. With each passing day, Mary's anxiety grew as her son's unusual abilities flourished. She knew firsthand how the darkness could infest a person's mind and destroy their life, and she dreaded the thought of her son going through the same torture as his father.

At night, when everything was dark, his nightlight made strange shadows on the walls, and Mary watched in silent trepidation as Matthew talked to imaginary friends who seemed so real to him. He believed in them as much as he believed in the shadows on the walls, and they whispered

153

secrets that pulled him into their world.

As the days wore on, and the air in Matthew's room grew heavy with the weight of an unseen presence, Mary could no longer ignore the ominous whispers that echoed through the darkness. One evening, she overheard her son engaged in a hushed conversation that sent a chill coursing down her spine.

"The Nice Lady says she's been watching over us for a long time, Mommy," Matthew murmured, his voice barely more than a whisper.

Mary's blood ran cold, her mind racing with thoughts of evil spirits and hidden agendas as she sought to subdue the terror that was slowly rising inside her.

***

Mary, bathed in the soft glow of her computer screen, delved into the abyss of the supernatural, her fingers dancing across the keyboard desperately in search of answers to the questions that lurked in the shadows of her mind. As she scoured the corridors of online forums and occult websites, her unease grew like a gathering storm on the horizon. She grappled with the presence of her son's world and the haunting memories of her own brushes with the supernatural.

Meanwhile, Matthew, oblivious to his mother's inner turmoil, reveled in the companionship of his unseen playmates. His laughter echoed through the apartment, a discordant melody that clashed with Mary's silent turmoil. The "nice lady," a spectral presence that had inserted itself into their lives, blurred the lines between reality and the unseen, leaving Mary teetering between curiosity and dread.

One evening, as twilight draped the living room in a

shroud of shadows, Mary found Matthew engaged in a whispered conversation. The hairs on the back of her neck stood on end as she listened to her son's words.

"She says the old man wants to talk to me, Mommy. She said he's really sad," Matthew murmured.

Mary attempted to quell the rising panic that threatened to engulf her, but her voice trembled ever so slightly, betraying her fear. "Okay, sweetie, it's getting late. Let's say goodnight to the Nice Lady and get ready for bed."

As she tucked Matthew into bed, the shadows flickered ominously in the moon's soft light streaming through the window. Mary wrestled with the internal turmoil winding through her brain, torn between shielding her son from the darkness that was twisting its way into their lives, and confronting the unearthly reality that swirled around him.

***

She found herself standing in the dimly lit living room of her apartment, the air around her thick and heavy. The familiar sound of Matthew's laughter echoed in the distance, but there was something off about it, something twisted and unsettling.

As she moved through the apartment, each step felt like wading through a dense fog. She rounded the corner and froze in terror as she came face to face with the "Nice Lady." Her ethereal form was twisted and contorted; her features warped into a grotesque mask of evil. Long, jagged claws extended from her fingers, dripping with an oily black substance that splattered onto the floor at her feet.

"Mary," the spectral figure hissed, her voice a chilling whisper laced with venom. "You can't protect him. He's ours now."

Then she saw Matthew huddled in the corner of his room,

his face buried in his arms as he wrapped himself tight in defense against the deadly spirit.

Mary rushed forward but the deadly phantom quickly blocked her way. She darted to her left and skirted around its lashing claws, her momentum sending her tumbling to the floor. Frantically, she scurried on her hands and knees toward Matthew.

As she held her arms out to him, he lifted his face and glared at her, his eyes burning with hatred. Sharp fangs jutted from the corners of his mouth, and a dark mist surrounded him. "As usual, Mother, you failed again," he hissed. "You're too late."

Mary's blood ran cold as she tried to scream, but no sound escaped her lips. She stumbled backward, her heart racing as she sought to escape from the nightmare. But as she turned to flee, another figure materialized from the shadows—the "Old Man."

His presence was suffocating, his features twisted into a grotesque caricature of violence and despair. His eyes gleamed with an unholy light, their depths filled with the torment of centuries trapped in the limbo between life and death. A tattered cloak hung from his emaciated frame, billowing around him like the tattered remnants of a shroud.

"He belongs to us," the Old Man growled. "And now it's time for you to join us, Mary. Welcome to Hell!"

Desperation clawed at Mary as she fought against the suffocating grip of the darkness. And then, just as the madness threatened to consume her entirely, Mary jerked awake, her body drenched in a cold sweat. Gasping for breath, she pulled the blanket to her chin for a moment, seeking an escape from the lingering nightmare.

With her body still trembling from the tendrils of her dream, Mary slowly slipped out of bed. Each creak of the floorboards echoed a discordant symphony in the night. With hands that shook as if possessed by unseen forces, she reached for the doorknob of Matthew's room. But before she dared to turn the handle, she pressed her ear to the door, straining to catch any whisper that might escape the room beyond.

The silence was deafening, broken only by the erratic thudding of her own heart. With a shaky breath, she steeled herself and slowly turned the knob, the metal groaning in protest as if aware of the horrors that may lurk on the other side.

A soft exhale slipped past her lips as she cracked the door open, revealing Matthew nestled comfortably in his bed, sound asleep. His peaceful and innocent face was a stark contrast to the nightmare visage she had just experienced. But even as she gazed at her sleeping son, a chill crept up her spine, the result of her imagination running rampant with the terrors that lurked in the shadows.

CHAPTER 31

As twilight painted the nursery in eerie hues, Grace's cries shattered the quiet, reverberating against the encroaching darkness. A moment later, Priscilla bolted into the room, her breath catching in her throat at the sight of her daughter's trembling form.

Grace's wide eyes darted around the room, as if they could see things beyond the veil of reality. Then, Priscilla saw it too —a small, enigmatic shadow in the corner of the room slithering through the mural on the wall like it was the serpent in the Garden of Eden. A chill ran down her spine as she picked up her daughter, trying desperately to calm her down.

"Shhh, Grace, it's okay," Priscilla whispered as she held her tight. "Mommy's here now."

With her eyes fixed on the mural, trying to ascertain the nature of the threat, as the tendrils of fear crept into her soul, she reached deep within, tapping into the ancient wellspring of power that flowed through her veins. With a trembling voice, she spoke words that resonated with the very fabric of reality, "By the moon's silver light and the stars' celestial might, I invoke the guardians of the night."

But Grace's cries only seemed to escalate, each one a fresh stab of panic, as the walls themselves came alive, twisting into grotesque shapes to mock their terror.

Priscilla's voice escalated as she fought to banish the sinister presence, "Let the spirits of the departed stand as sentinels, warding off the darkness that seeks to consume."

As the words spilled from her lips, the tension in the air thickened, suffocating them. Then a surge of energy pulsed through the room. The shadows retreated, overwhelmed by the power of her invocation, and a sense of peace settled over them.

As Grace's cries gave way to a blissful silence, she knew that their sanctuary had been secured, guarded by forces unseen but ever vigilant.

Suddenly, a loud scratching sound issued from the corner of the room. With a worried look in her eyes, Priscilla inched her way toward the site of the noise—the mural Emily had painted only a short time ago. As she drew closer, the noise stopped. Initially believing the sound to be a rodent of some sort, she was surprised to see a small hole in the plaster about two inches in diameter. When she crouched down to inspect the opening closer, she felt like she was gazing into a miniature gateway to the Underworld.

***

While the sinister entity never showed its presence again, Priscilla was ever vigilant against the darkness, saying a silent prayer to the gods each time she opened the nursery door.

In the months that followed, Grace's presence filled the home with a palpable warmth that seemed to deepen with each passing day. As an infant, she was a picture of serenity, her tiny form cradled in Priscilla's arms as she rocked her gently to sleep.

In the soft glow of twilight, Priscilla would often sit by Grace's crib, watching as her daughter slumbered peacefully, her chest rising and falling in a rhythm as gentle as a lullaby. With each breath, it seemed as though Grace was inhaling the very essence of the world around her, absorbing its wonders with the innocence of a newborn.

As the weeks turned into months, Grace's gaze began to sharpen, her eyes brightening with newfound curiosity. No longer content to simply observe the world from the confines of her crib, she reached out with chubby fingers, grasping at the air as if trying to snatch onto the secrets that lay just beyond her reach.

Priscilla marveled at her daughter's growing awareness, delighting in each new milestone as Grace embarked on her journey of discovery. From her first tentative attempts at crawling, to the joyous triumph of taking her first steps, all the way past her toddler years, Grace's progress was a testament to the boundless energy that lay within her.

As Grace grew older it became increasingly evident that they were quickly outgrowing their small apartment. And so, the search for a new home began in earnest.

One day Priscilla and Andrew found themselves drawn to the outskirts of town. Their search led them to a weathered structure with timeworn charm that stood as a solitary silhouette against the canvas of the afternoon sky.

"That's the house I saw in my dream, Mommy!" Grace exclaimed as soon as they pulled to the curb alongside the property.

Priscilla wasted no time, dialing the realtor's number displayed on the for-sale sign. Moments later, a young woman pulled up behind their car and eagerly approached them.

The dwelling exuded a strange allure, embraced by hills that seemed to slumber like ancient guardians and forests whispering secrets to the wind. The air crackled with an eerie energy, as if the land held secrets too profound for mortal understanding.

Crossing the threshold, Priscilla felt an echo of something ancient and powerful. Immediately, she thought of the ancient beings that had confronted her and Andrew years ago. It was as though the house had been waiting, aware of the unique energies coursing through their family.

Within those weathered walls, they found a living, breathing entity, each room pulsating with a history steeped in mystic energies. Even the backyard seemed alive, the foliage whispering secrets to those who dared to listen.

It was clear to Priscilla and Andrew that this house was meant for them, a nexus where the ordinary and the supernatural converged. Moving in marked a turning point, especially for Andrew, who found himself embracing beliefs he once scoffed at.

As they settled into their new abode, a sense of anticipation hung heavy in the air. The house, with its enigmatic charm, became a vessel for the mysteries that awaited, promising a journey into the unknown.

While the family embraced the mystic energies that surrounded their new home, they remained blissfully unaware of the shadowy entity that lingered just beyond the reach of perception. The night air, thick with the weight of unseen forces, held its breath, knowing that the moment of reckoning approached—a moment when the dark force hiding in the shadows would seize the chance to unleash its chaos upon the unsuspecting family.

CHAPTER 32

While Grace, slept soundly in her room, blissfully unaware of the spiritual dance about to unfold, Priscilla, dressed in a flowing robe that trailed behind her like a ghostly apparition, moved with an almost ethereal grace. As she entered the dimly lit room, a single, flickering candle illuminated her intense gaze, casting eerie shadows that seemed to dance in tandem with the unseen forces at play.

A few minutes later, Andrew entered the room with Emily in tow, whose face bore a mixture of excitement and apprehension as she took in the atmosphere. The evening held a peculiar weight, an intangible heaviness that lingered in the air like a haunting melody. Emily couldn't shake the uneasiness that clung to the shadows.

Priscilla sensed Emily's hesitation and offered her a reassuring smile. "Don't worry, Em. I know this is your first time doing something like this, but I'll guide you every step of the way."

Emily nodded as she glanced around the room, taking in the flickering candlelight and the mysterious symbols etched into the walls. "I trust you, Pris," she said nervously. "But I have to admit, I'm feeling a little out of my depth here."

Priscilla laid a comforting hand on Emily's shoulder, her touch grounding and reassured. "That's completely normal. Just focus on your breathing and let the energy of the room flow through you. You'll find your footing soon enough."

Priscilla sensed that the boundary separating the tangible and the intangible had become fragile. "The veil is especially thin tonight," she murmured in a soft hush. "Just be prepared."

As the supernatural energy intensified, the room seemed to resonate with a power that transcended the natural order.

Andrew's gaze remained fixed on the flickering candle, "You know I've always supported your rituals, Priscilla, but this... tonight seems different. Something feels wrong. Do you know what's going on?"

Priscilla whispered, "I can't say, but there's an energy, an ancient force, trying to make itself known."

Andrew's eyes grew nervous, "I don't know about this, Pris? Maybe we should stop before something bad happens?"

Suddenly, the candle's flame swayed violently. The temperature plummeted, and ghostly laughter echoed through the darkness. Emily, now visibly shaken, pleaded, "Priscilla, I'm getting a little freaked out here!"

Priscilla ignored their pleas as the candle's flame swayed to the will of unseen whispers. Taking a deep breath, she expanded her consciousness until visions of a shadowy figure cloaked in darkness filled her mind. The room suddenly echoed with spectral voices speaking in a long-forgotten language.

Priscilla's voice cut through the discord, "We can't back down now. There's something here that demands our attention. I need to know what it wants."

The volume of the ghostly voices grew into a tempest surrounding them. Priscilla continued, determined to call out the source of the energy, "Who are you? What do you want?" she commanded.

The response came as guttural whispers that seemed to emanate from the room's very walls. Andrew, his eyes wide with terror, strained to understand the cryptic messages. "Priscilla, what's it saying?"

Priscilla, her eyes still closed, absorbed the chilling revelation. "It speaks of darkness. A darkness that will test us and change us."

Suddenly, Priscilla's eyes snapped open. The candle extinguished, plunging the room into darkness. A foreboding chill settled over the house, and the wind outside howled like a mournful symphony. The atmosphere weighed heavy as an unseen presence lingered in the shadows.

Andrew reached for the matches to relight the candle, but before he could strike a flame, ghostly laughter echoed from nowhere and everywhere simultaneously.

Then, as quickly as it had begun, the disturbance subsided. The candle suddenly flickered back to life on its own, and the room returned to normal, yet an ominous aura remained.

Priscilla met Andrew and Emily's gazes with a look of fear and regret. She had sensed the power circulating throughout the room and knew the danger they were facing, but in that brief moment of overzealousness, she hadn't been able to pull back before it was too late. Tears misted up in her eyes, "I'm sorry. I couldn't stop in time. Now I fear there's no way to escape this. Whatever has been set in motion, we're a part of it."

Andrew and Emily rushed to Priscilla's side, enveloping her in a comforting embrace.

"Then we face it together," Emily said defiantly.

***

* * *

In the depths of the night, while the rest of the world slept under the watchful eye of the moon, Grace lay sound asleep in her innocent dreams, blissfully unaware of the darkness that lurked nearby. The wind whispered through the cracks in the window, carrying with it a sinister melody.

The darkness outside Grace's room seemed to come alive, a deadly entity taking shape as it slinked into her bedroom like a shadow. Its presence distorted the air, causing a subtle ripple in the fabric of reality.

Grace stirred in her sleep, a faint frown marring her otherwise peaceful expression. Unseen hands, cold and insidious, caressed her forehead, leaving a chill that seemed to penetrate her very soul. The room's temperature dropped, and the moonlight flickered ominously, casting fleeting glimpses of a grotesque silhouette standing beside Grace's bed.

The shadow demon whispered unholy secrets in the deepest recesses of Grace's dreams, filling her innocent mind with nightmarish visions that danced in the shadows. Grace tossed and turned in her bed, caught in a macabre dance orchestrated by forces beyond comprehension. She twitched back and forth fitfully, the sanctity of her sleep shattered by the darkness that now clung to her like a curse.

Outside the room, the wind intensified into a haunting wail, matching the intensity of the unseen presence. As the shadow demon completed its dark ritual, it melted back into the ether, leaving no trace of its violation. The dark being lurked there in the shadows, biding its time for the next move in its sinister game.

CHAPTER 33

Matthew's childhood was a dance where the lines between the real and the unseen blurred like watercolors on a rainy windowpane. From his earliest days, he showed signs of something more, a connection to the realms beyond our own, babbling not just to toys but to whispered entities only he could hear.

As the years unfurled like some dark, twisted flower, Mary's worry deepened. Matthew's gift—or curse, depending on how you looked at it—grew stronger, weaving a tangled web around their lives. Bedtime became a stage for spectral dialogues, where unseen voices whispered secrets from the shadows. Mary could only watch nervously as her son danced on the precipice between worlds.

With school on the horizon, she faced a dilemma. Should she shield him from a world that might fear or reject him, or toss him into the lion's den of public education? But with bills to pay, homeschooling was a luxury she couldn't afford.

And so, with a heavy heart, Matthew stepped into Elmwood Elementary, a lone figure in a sea of cruelty. It didn't take long for the whispers to start, for the shadows to stir with unseen menace. The monsters that had lurked in the corners of his reality now crept into the light, eager to test the limits of his abilities.

***

In the dimly lit classroom, Mrs. Lawson's voice droned on like a broken record. Her monotonous tone was like a funeral dirge played on a kazoo.

While she carried on aimlessly, for the majority of her students the lesson became less about first grade biology and more about trying not to nod off. Meanwhile, Matthew sat among his oblivious classmates, his spectral companions fluttering around him hungrily, like a flock of pigeons.

As Matthew battled to maintain focus, a sensation like icy fingers crawling up his spine seized him. A touch, colder than the kiss of death itself, settled heavily on his shoulder. Startled, he turned to confront the shadowy specter looming at his side, its features lost to an otherworldly gloom that devoured all light.

"Matthew," a voice whispered, a chilling echo that seemed to emanate from the very depths of the void. "Help me."

His gaze followed the ghostly figure's spectral stare, leading him to a neglected bookshelf nestled in the darkest recesses of the room. Meanwhile, his classmates toiled on, blissfully ignorant of the supernatural drama unfolding in their midst.

Approaching the ominous shelves, the apparition pointed a translucent finger towards a weathered tome, its ancient cover adorned with cryptic symbols that writhed and twisted as if imbued with a sinister life force. With trembling hands, Matthew reached for the cursed volume, feeling an electric surge course through him as his fingertips brushed its aged spine.

Simultaneously, the classroom lights flickered erratically, casting shadows that danced like spirits along the walls. Whispers filled the air, intertwining with the palpable unease that settled over the room. It was as though reality itself trembled in response to the arcane forces at play.

Mrs. Lawson's sharp words cut through the eerie silence like a blade. "Matthew, what are you doing?"

Beside him, the ghostly figure cried out, "Release me from this prison!"

The ancient book suddenly flew open on its own, its pages filled with mystical symbols and disturbing illustrations. Unearthly winds, as cold as the breath of the abyss, began to swirl around the classroom, as the overhead fluorescent lights flickered and then went dark one by one.

Among the unsettling illustrations within the book were scenes that seemed to transcend nightmares. Grotesque creatures with twisted limbs and sinister grins leered from the pages, while nightmarish landscapes shrouded in darkness and despair filled the rest. One illustration, etched in painstaking detail, depicted a horde of creatures emerging from the depths of a shadowy forest. Their bodies were contorted and misshapen, with jagged teeth and claws gleaming in the eerie light. Each creature's eyes glowed with a sickly green hue.

In the foreground of this disturbing scene, a lone figure cowered in terror, its features twisted in a silent scream of horror. The creatures loomed menacingly over it, their grotesque forms casting twisted shadows upon the ground.

As the unsettling illustrations seemed to come alive before Matthew's eyes, whispers thick with despair slithered through the air like serpents, coiling around him. Fear, raw and primal, oozed from the very walls, wrapping the classroom in a suffocating blanket of dread.

Frantically, Matthew grappled with the ancient tome, his efforts to close it blocked by some unseen force. Beside him, the ghostly apparition quivered. "Release me!" it howled, its voice a tortured lament that pierced the darkness.

In an instant, the room plunged into absolute blackness, a vacuum that devoured sound and sight alike. A scream, laden with the anguish of the damned, tore through the silence, reverberating from the bowels of the earth itself. When the lights flickered back to life, the ancient tome slammed shut, the ghostly figure evaporating into the shadows like mist. Alone once more, Matthew stood trembling, the spectral encounter clinging to him like a second skin.

Mrs. Lawson, oblivious to the supernatural episode, fixed Matthew with a stern glare. "Focus, Matthew. We have work to do," she admonished.

Meanwhile, his classmates carried on, their pencils scratching against paper in blissful ignorance. For them, it was business as usual, the chilling encounter confined to Matthew's shaken mind.

As Mrs. Lawson resumed her lesson, Matthew's eyes darted nervously to the bookshelf, half-expecting the ghostly figure to reappear, but the apparition and the book were gone.

The bell sounded, its harsh chime slicing through the classroom like a rusty blade. Matthew gathered his things, chancing one last wary glance at the bookshelf. The shadows, now thick with secrets, trailed behind him as he exited.

Outside, the chatter of his classmates taunted Matthew like unseen demons. Mockery followed him, as his peers, ignorant of the spectral world that lurked just beyond their sight, jeered at his "imaginary friends," their laughter a cruel symphony that echoed through the air.

The weight of isolation hung heavy on Matthew as he trudged to his mother's car. Ghostly whispers mingled with the taunts, intensifying his sense of loneliness. Mary, witnessing her son's anguish, felt a pang in her chest, familiar echoes of her own past trauma resurfacing.

The haunted look in Matthew's eyes as he slumped into the car cut through Mary like a razor. She knew the pain he carried. She knew all too well the cruelty of the schoolyard.

"How was school today?" she asked, her voice a feeble attempt to bridge the chasm of silence between them.

Matthew just shrugged.

"Did you learn anything interesting?" Mary asked, her concern etched into every line of her face.

But Matthew remained silent.

"What about friends? Did you make any new ones?"

"I don't want to talk about it," Matthew whispered, his voice a fragile thread barely holding back the flood of emotions within.

With tears stinging her own eyes, Mary shifted the car into gear and drove away, the weight of her son's struggles pressing down on her like a suffocating shroud.

CHAPTER 34

Slowly, Grace underwent a haunting transformation. The once vibrant hues of her surroundings dulled into muted shades, and the air in her room took on a stale, oppressive quality. Her room became a symphony of unsettling sounds. Whispers, too faint for human ears to perceive, slithered through the air like serpents. A cacophony of eerie creaks and ominous rustlings echoed, painting a chilling backdrop to her fitful sleep. The cough that began to resonate from her frail form seemed to carry a deep undertone, as if the very essence of darkness permeated each convulsive hack.

When Priscilla entered with a tray of steaming soup, the temperature in the room dropped noticeably. The scent of the broth clashed with an underlying odor of decay that seemed to come from Grace herself. Priscilla recoiled, sensing an unnatural chill that had settled within the very fabric of the room.

"Grace, sweetheart, you need to eat something," Priscilla urged desperately, her breath visible in the frigid air. Grace, just met her gaze with vacant eyes that reflected the encroaching darkness within.

As days passed by, the darkness within Grace deepened,

manifesting in ways that defied all rational explanation. Her once sparkling eyes now held a murky depth, as if a sinister force had settled behind the gaze of the innocent child. The delicate whispers that escaped her lips in the dead of night spoke of terrors that eluded the grasp of the waking world, haunting her every slumber.

Desperation drove Priscilla and Andrew to seek medical help, but the doctors were baffled. No physical ailment could account for the drastic decline in their daughter's health. The couple felt the tendrils of fear tightening around their hearts as the sinister force continued its insidious grip on Grace's fragile existence.

One afternoon, as Priscilla sat by Grace's bedside, the room was suddenly plunged into an inky abyss, and the air thickened with an oppressive weight, sending a foreboding chill creeping through the house.

Grace's eyes fluttered open. In that unsettling moment, the emptiness that now resided within the child's gaze sent shivers racing down her mother's spine. The room seemed to hold its breath as Grace spoke, her voice a haunting echo of her former self.

"I see them, Mommy," Grace whispered, her words hanging in the air like a spectral mist. "The shadows talk to me, and they're getting louder."

A surge of panic gripped Priscilla, and she reached for Andrew, who had hurried into the room just in time to witness the encroaching darkness. An otherworldly laughter, laden with evil, reverberated through the air, penetrating the very core of the couple's souls. The sinister echoes sent tremors through the room, as if the laughter itself were an entity dancing on the fringes of reality.

In that chilling moment, the once-joyful sanctuary of their home was transformed into a spiritual battleground. Priscilla and Andrew stood in the void, clinging to one another as the laughter echoed through the darkness, carving its mark into the soul of their daughter.

The room slowly surrendered back to the afternoon light. Grace now lay on her bed, her eyes transformed into vacant orbs. A cold silence settled through the room as the aftermath of the supernatural onslaught unfolded.

From the depths of Grace's slight frame, a guttural voice erupted. The words it uttered were a macabre symphony that reverberated through the air, chilling the bones of her horrified parents.

"Leave this vessel!" Priscilla demanded, her voice a shaky plea to the demon that had ensnared her daughter's soul.

Grace smirked, the wickedness in her gaze amplifying the darkness that now surrounded her. The voice, dripping with malice, responded with a hiss that sent shockwaves through the room.

"She's mine now, bitch!" the voice declared, the words hanging in the air like a dark incantation.

Priscilla and Andrew watched in horror as Grace's body contorted in unnatural ways, her limbs moving in jagged angles, as if manipulated by unseen hands. As Grace writhed on the bed, her voice echoed through the room in a grotesque harmony of guttural growls and unearthly shrieks. Then, with a sudden, violent convulsion, Grace levitated off the bed.

Priscilla and Andrew stumbled backward, their terrified screams drowned out by the sinister laughter emanating from their daughter's twisted form.

Then, for a brief moment, recognition returned to Grace's eyes as she fought the demon inside her. "Mommy... Daddy..." she pleaded weakly, "help me!"

A moment later, Grace's innocence was gone once more,

her soft words replaced by the voice of the demon. "On second thought," it spat, "go fuck yourselves!"

With tears streaming down her face, Priscilla fumbled for the Bible on the nightstand. Her hands trembled as she began reciting prayers, her voice fighting against the cacophony of demonic laughter and unearthly growls.

Andrew joined the battle for Grace's soul, reciting his own prayers with the ferocity of a desperate father. As their combined love cut through the demon's power, Grace's body plummeted back to the bed.

In a moment of eerie calm, Priscilla, sweat-soaked and breathless, faced the evil force within Grace. Her eyes locked onto the void in her daughter's gaze as she whispered ancient words of power passed on from those who came before her.

The demonic voice hissed in defiance, but Priscilla's persistence began to chip away at its control. The room trembled as the struggle reached its zenith and a faint light began to pierce the darkness. Grace's contorted form gradually relaxed, the evil dissipating like fog in the morning sun.

With a final, guttural roar, the demonic entity released its hold on Grace, retreating into the shadows. The room returned to an eerie stillness. Grace, now peacefully asleep, seemed freed from the nightmarish clutches that had gripped her.

Priscilla, exhausted and drained, collapsed beside Grace's bed. Andrew joined his wife in a silent embrace as the weight of the ordeal lifted, yet the aftermath of their daughter's possession echoed in the hushed quiet.

***

After a last check to make sure Grace was okay, Priscilla and

Andrew walked slowly to their own bedroom, both of their hearts numb with the weight of the recent ordeal. Tears stung Priscilla's eyes when they reached the doorway to their room and she turned to Andrew, her voice choked with emotion. "I... I need to be alone for a bit," she whispered.

Andrew's brow furrowed as he reached out to gently cup Priscilla's cheek. "Are you sure? I can stay with you."

Priscilla shook her head, a single tear escaping down her cheek. "I just... I need some time to process everything. Please, Andrew."

Andrew looked at her gently for a moment and nodded. "Okay," he said softly, pressing a tender kiss to her forehead. "I'll be here if you need me."

With a grateful smile, Priscilla watched as Andrew quietly left the room, leaving her alone with her thoughts and the overwhelming sense of grief that threatened to consume her. It didn't take long for the torrent of emotions to release, flowing from her like a tidal wave.

After the tears had dried, she took a deep breath, knowing that she needed her best friend now more than ever. Priscilla's trembling hands reached for her phone. With a deep sigh, she dialed Emily's number, her fingers hovering over the screen for a moment before pressing the call button.

After a few rings, Emily's voice came through the line, filled with concern. "Priscilla? Is everything okay?"

Priscilla's voice wavered as she struggled to find the right words. "Emily, can you come over? It's about Grace. Something terrible happened."

A heavy silence hung between them for a moment before Emily responded, "I'll be right there."

True to her word, Emily arrived at Priscilla's doorstep a few minutes later, her eyes filled with worry as she took in the haunted look on Priscilla's face.

As they settled into the living room, Priscilla recounted the horror of Grace's possession, her voice quivering as she relived the hellish ordeal.

Emily listened in silence, her heart breaking for her friend as she witnessed the raw anguish etched across Priscilla's face. Tears glistened in her eyes as she reached out, enveloping Priscilla in a tight embrace.

"I can't shake this feeling of guilt, Em," Priscilla confessed, her voice barely above a whisper. "I should've been able to protect her... to keep her safe."

Emily held Priscilla tighter, her own tears mingling with Priscilla's as she whispered words of comfort. "You did everything you could, Pris. None of us could have predicted what happened. Grace is safe now, and that's all that matters."

"I should've known," Priscilla said as she buried her face in Emily's shoulder.

CHAPTER 35

A man out of place and out of time, Solomon sat in the dimly lit chamber, his tie-dye T-shirt and ponytail a stark juxtaposition to the room's ancient and mystical ambiance. The stone walls were adorned with arcane symbols, their intricate patterns seemingly alive in the flickering candlelight. Ancient texts lay scattered around, their worn pages whispering secrets of long-forgotten eras. At the center of the room, a crystal ball rested on a small table, its surface glowing with an eerie light.

Solomon leaned forward, whispering incantations in a language that predated civilization, his voice a mere murmur resonating with the hidden energies of the universe. As he channeled his focus, the crystal ball responded, its mists swirling and clearing to reveal a terrible scene before him. Solomon's breath hitched as he was pulled into the depths of the prophecy.

The world around him was plunged into chaos. Cities lay in ruins, their structures twisted and broken like the bones of some great, fallen beast. Fires raged unchecked, consuming everything in their path with a voracious hunger. Shadows moved ominously, the air thick with despair and the stench of death. At the heart of this devastation stood a figure shrouded in darkness.

This being, cloaked in evil, emanated an aura so vile that it seemed to taint the very fabric of reality. His eyes, void of humanity, surveyed the destruction with cold satisfaction. Armies of followers, twisted by his influence, marched under his banner, spreading terror and death in their wake. The skies themselves seemed to weep blood, casting a crimson pall over the ruined landscape.

Solomon's heart pounded in his chest, each beat echoing like a drum of war. He had seen darkness before, but this was different. This was a vision of utter annihilation, a future where hope was a distant memory.

But amidst the darkness, a glimmer of light appeared. The scene shifted, pulling Solomon's consciousness to a stark, sterile hospital room. The harsh fluorescent lights flickered ominously, casting long, eerie shadows. Machines beeped and hummed, their sounds blending into a discordant symphony of tension and urgency.

In the center of the room, a woman lay on a hospital bed, her face contorted in pain and fear. Sweat matted her hair to her forehead, and her breaths came in ragged, desperate gasps. Nurses and doctors moved frantically around her, their expressions grim. Something was wrong.

The mother's screams pierced the air, a raw, primal sound that seemed to resonate with the very foundations of the earth. Blood stained the sheets beneath her, and the monitors flashed warnings in red and yellow. Solomon watched, his heart aching with a helplessness he hadn't felt in centuries. He knew he was witnessing a pivotal moment, but he was powerless to intervene.

With one final, excruciating push, the woman brought her child into the world. The room fell silent, the tension hanging thick in the air, as everyone waited for the sound of life to escape his lips. But there was none.

Finally, Death's grasp was released and the baby's first cry rang out, resonating with an ancient, mystical energy that seemed to cut through the chaos like a blade of light. The doctors worked quickly, their movements a blur as they tended to both mother and child.

Solomon's breath caught in his throat. This child was no ordinary infant. As he watched, the air around the baby shimmered with a divine glow. Matthew. The name came to Solomon as if whispered by the universe itself. Then, the name of the mother. Mary.

The vision began to fade, leaving Solomon back in his chamber, his heart still racing. He closed his eyes, whispering a prayer of gratitude and resolve. He now understood his purpose more clearly than ever before. Matthew was the key to preventing the dark future he had seen, and Solomon had to ensure the boy was prepared for the monumental task ahead.

Solomon sat in his chamber, the echoes of the vision still reverberating in his mind. The crystal ball's glow had faded, but the images it had revealed were seared into his consciousness. He knew he couldn't waste any time. The darkness was growing, and the world was teetering on the edge of an abyss. But there was hope.

Solomon rose from his seat, his mind racing with plans and possibilities. He had to find Mary and Matthew, to guide and protect them. He gathered a few essential items—ancient texts, talismans of protection, and a small, intricately carved box containing powerful charms. These would be crucial in the battles to come.

As he prepared to leave, Solomon took a moment to center himself. He closed his eyes and whispered another incantation, seeking guidance and strength from the divine forces that had always been his allies. The surrounding air shimmered briefly, a comforting presence affirming his resolve.

He opened his eyes, a new determination burning within them. He had faced many challenges in his long life, but this felt different. This was a pivotal moment in the eternal struggle between good and evil. The stakes were higher than they had ever been. A plan began to formulate in his mind—a plan that must not fail.

Solomon stepped out of his chamber, the ancient door creaking ominously as it closed behind him. As he walked through the corridors of his hidden sanctuary, the memories of his vision played out in his mind. He saw again the desolation wrought by the uprising darkness and the hopelessness in the eyes of those suffering. But he also saw the light in Matthew's eyes, the promise of a new dawn.

With a final glance back at his sanctuary, Solomon set off towards the future. The world might be unaware of the battles being fought in the shadows, but he knew. And he would fight with every ounce of his strength to ensure that the light would prevail.

CHAPTER 36

Solomon sat in a dimly lit hotel room surrounded by arcane symbols and ancient texts. A soft glow emanated from a small table where candles flickered, as he focused his gaze on a crystal ball placed at the center of the table.

He calmly whispered incantations in an ancient language, channeling his energies beyond the veil of time and space. The crystal ball shimmered, and as the mists cleared, Solomon glimpsed Mary and her son, Matthew, browsing in a small bookstore.

Closing his eyes, Solomon envisioned the bookstore, focusing on the details of the surroundings. With a gesture of his hand, he muttered an incantation to project his presence into that moment. In an instant, he stood amidst the shelves, his colorful clothing blending oddly with the unique ambiance of the establishment.

Solomon approached Mary and Matthew, his face lit up with a warm, friendly smile. His eyes, however, held the intensity of a man on a mission.

Solomon, feigning surprise as he pretended to bump into Mary, exclaimed, "Oh, sorry, I didn't mean to bump into you. I get a bit lost in the sea of books sometimes." He extended his hand to her. "I'm Solomon, by the way."

Mary took his hand, smiled politely, and replied, "I'm Mary. No problem. It happens. I guess I was lost in my own little world too."

Solomon, glanced at Matthew. "He seems to be having a good time."

Mary, chuckled. "Yeah, he's my little bookworm."

Solomon, crouching down to Matthew's eye level, said, "Hey there, buddy. What's your name?"

Matthew replied shyly, "I'm Matthew. I like stories about dragons."

Solomon let out an exaggerated gasp. "Dragons? No way! They're my favorite too. Did you know they can see things others can't?"

Matthew's eyes grew wide. "Really?"

"Absolutely. They see the magic in the world that others might miss. You've got a bit of dragon magic in you too, I can tell."

Mary, exchanging a bemused look with Solomon. "Dragon magic, huh?"

Solomon grinned at Mary and then looked back down at Matthew. "It's the most special kind of magic there is. But shh, it's our little secret."

As they continued to chat about dragons, books, and the adventures that awaited within the pages, Mary couldn't help but notice the genuine connection Solomon seemed to share with Matthew. There was an unspoken understanding that danced in the air, a recognition of something beyond the surface.

As Solomon moved his hands around while they talked, Matthew saw the enormous gold ring on his finger and his eyes grew wide. "Wow, thanks a cool ring!" he exclaimed.

Solomon looked down at the ring and then back up at

Matthew. "Yes, it is. It's a very special ring, with very special powers. Would you like to try it on?"

Matthew looked at Solomon in disbelief, and then at his mom. "Can I?"

Mary looked uncomfortable at the thought of a complete stranger offering something so bizarre, but then again, her life had been one strange moment after another. "I don't know?"

"Please?" Matthew begged.

After a second, Mary nodded, giving in to another moment of high strangeness.

Unheard by either, Solomon uttered a soft syllable before removing the ring from his finger and placing it on Matthew's. For a brief second, undetectable by everyone else, the air shimmered with an unseen energy. Solomon looked at Matthew and smiled. "It looks perfect on you. Maybe one day you'll have one just like it?"

Matthew's eyes grew even wider as he looked at the ring, which had shrunk mysteriously so that it fit Matthew's finger perfectly. "This is so cool! Don't you think, Mom?"

Mary nodded in agreement, although her voice was tinged with concern, "Yes, it's lovely, Sweetie. Now, it's time to give the nice man his ring back."

A slight pout covered Matthew's lips before he pulled the ring from his finger and handed it back to Solomon.

After placing the ring back on his finger, Solomon stood up, and with a playful wink, said, "Well, it was great meeting you both. If you ever want to chat more about dragons or anything else, I guess you know where to find me."

As Solomon strolled away, Mary couldn't shake the feeling that their chance encounter was more than mere coincidence. The mystical possibilities that hovered in the hazy corridors of her life had just become a bit more tangible, and she wondered if this laid-back hippie might hold the key to unlocking some of the mysteries surrounding her son.

Days passed, and Mary found herself revisiting the bookstore, drawn by an inexplicable force. As she wandered through the narrow aisles, she couldn't shake the memories of her encounter with Solomon.

Just as Mary was immersed in a sea of books, Solomon emerged from the shadows with a gentle smile on his face and a knowing glint in his eyes. "Fancy meeting you here again. This bookstore certainly has a way of calling you back, doesn't it?"

Mary was slightly taken aback, but intrigued. "It's true. I can't seem to stay away. What brings you back?"

"Sometimes, books have a way of finding their readers," Solomon replied. "Or maybe it's the readers who find the books? It's a dance between destiny and choice, wouldn't you say?"

Mary nodded, sensing that Solomon was talking about more than just books and bookstores.

Solomon looked at Matthew who was engrossed in a picture book nearby and said "Your son, Matthew, he has a special connection with the world beyond that which meets the eye."

Mary stood with her arms crossed, trying to shield herself from the direction the conversation was going. "What do you mean?"

Solomon smiled a warm and genuine smile, hoping to put Mary at ease. "I'm simply stating that there are forces at play throughout this world, some ancient and powerful. I can sense them. And I think Matthew can too, in his own way. I'm here to offer guidance, to help you understand and navigate the mystical currents that flow through his life."

Mary carried a measure of uncertainty in her eyes.

"Guidance? What kind of guidance?"

Solomon replied, "The kind that helps you both embrace the extraordinary journey ahead. Trust me, Mary, I'm here to help."

As Solomon spoke of mystical forces and destiny, Mary's gaze shifted uneasily toward Matthew, who was still immersed in his world of colorful illustrations. She couldn't shake the truth she'd been avoiding—that her son was special. The encounters had become more frequent, and Mary, torn between denial and concern, hoped to shield Matthew from the potential dangers that accompanied his gift; the same dangers that had torn Michael from her.

Her voice tinged with a mix of uncertainty and fear, Mary finally said, "Look, I appreciate your offer, but Matthew is just a little boy. I don't want him getting tangled up in anything... otherworldly."

Solomon nodded empathetically. "I understand your concern, Mary. It's a natural instinct for a parent to want to protect their child. But sometimes, denying the truth can be more perilous than facing it. Matthew's gift is a part of who he is, and embracing it can open doors to understanding and control."

"I just want him to have a normal childhood. No visions, no spirits, just a normal, happy life."

"I don't propose to take away his normalcy, Mary. Instead, I offer guidance to ensure that his extraordinary abilities become tools for growth and enlightenment rather than sources of fear."

Mary hesitated, torn between her desire for Matthew's safety and the realization that denying his gifts might not be the right solution.

Solomon replied gently, "I've walked the paths of magic and mysticism for a long time. Let me help you and Matthew navigate this journey. There are ways to protect him without stifling his true nature."

But Mary, despite Solomon's assurances and the undeniable truth of Matthew's abilities, clung to her reluctance. She looked at Solomon with a mix of fear and defiance. "I appreciate your offer, Solomon, but the answer is no"

Solomon, his gaze compassionate yet persistent, replied, "Mary, I understand your concerns. But denying his gifts won't make them disappear. It's crucial to guide him so that he can navigate this path safely. There are ways to protect him, to help him control and understand his abilities without letting them overwhelm him."

Mary shook her head as tears started forming in the corners of her eyes. "I can't, Solomon. I've already walked down this road with his father."

Solomon, with a hint of disappointment in his eyes, replied, "I respect your decision, Mary. But if you ever change your mind, you know where to find me."

As Solomon gracefully retreated into the shelves of the bookstore, Mary couldn't shake the lingering uncertainty that filled the air. She grabbed Matthew's hand as they left the store, determined to shield him from the unseen forces that Solomon spoke of. The mysteries of the supernatural world would remain unexplored, at least for now, in the hope that her son could have the ordinary, safe childhood she so desperately needed for him.

CHAPTER 37

It wasn't over.

Priscilla could feel its presence lingering in the corners of their house, just out of sight, waiting for the chance to snatch onto Grace once more, that's if it had actually relinquished its hold on her in the first place. She feared that a part of the demon still clutched onto her, like a splinter sunk deep into the flesh that's nearly impossible to remove. And it was all her fault.

Her eyes misted over as the scene replayed itself in her mind. Both Andrew and Emily had sensed it, the power of the encroaching darkness, and tried to warn her, but her arrogance got in the way and her daughter paid the price. Now, the only choice she had was to fight like hell and free her from this nightmare.

For a short time, Grace almost seemed normal, smiling periodically as she sat at the dining table munching on a snack or coloring in one of her coloring books. The rosiness in her cheeks began to slowly return, and her eyes held their innocence once more.

It didn't last long, though. The dark force, having found a home within the walls of their once-peaceful abode, reveled in the chaos it had sown. Its tendrils slithered through the very fabric of their lives, leaving behind an insidious mark that tainted the air they breathed and the walls that sheltered them. In the silent hours of the night, the house echoed with the whispers of unseen entities that permeating every nook and cranny, weaving a sinister tapestry of despair.

Priscilla and Andrew found themselves entangled in a web of supernatural horror that threatened to consume them all. Sleep became an elusive ally, for the night was no longer a sanctuary but a battlefield where the forces of light clashed with the darkness that had claimed their daughter. The very air became charged with an oppressive energy, as if time itself had warped under the weight of the unholy presence that loomed over them.

In the waning twilight of hope, the couple witnessed the gradual erosion of Grace's humanity. Her laughter, once a melody that echoed through the halls, now morphed into an eerie resonance that sent shivers down their spines. Her once-rosy cheeks now carried the pallor of poison flowing through her veins, while the light in her eyes dimmed with each passing day, harboring secrets that only the shadows could whisper.

As Grace moved through the hallways, her steps echoed with an unsettling resonance, as though the very floor protested the presence of an otherworldly force. The pictures on the walls, once capturing moments of joy and happiness, now seemed to contort into grotesque shapes, mirroring the distorted reality that gripped the household.

***

The air was thick with an unsettling tension that seemed to seep through the cracks of the dimly lit living room. Priscilla and Andrew held each other tight on the couch as they sought each other's strength to fight the encroaching darkness.

A faint knock suddenly echoed through the room. Priscilla looked at Andrew nervously before she cautiously approached the front door, her hand trembling as she turned the handle.

She was shocked to see Emily standing there, her face clouded in fear and worry. "Something told me you were in trouble, so I came over," she said softly, her voice barely audible above the whispering shadows. "What's going on?"

Priscilla's heart clenched as she embraced Emily tightly. "Emily, you shouldn't be here. It's too dangerous."

Abruptly, the air rippled with an unnatural force, and Grace materialized in the doorway. The creaking floorboards announced her presence, and her eyes, once innocent orbs, now gleamed with evil. The very essence of her being seemed tainted, a vessel for an unrelenting darkness that clawed at the fraying edges of her sanity.

Emily looked at Grace, who stood in the doorway, her tiny figure shaking and twitching, and let out a gasp. The sight of Priscilla's daughter bathed in the oppressive darkness that surrounded her sent a shiver down Emily's spine.

"Grace..." Emily whispered, her voice barely a breath. "Oh, my God..."

Priscilla nodded solemnly, her lips trembling, "We need to save her."

"You're all so blind," Grace hissed, her voice a chorus of ominous whispers that hung in the air like a sinister melody. The words clawed at the very souls of her grief-stricken parents, sending a shiver down their spines. The room itself seemed to recoil, as if unable to contain the weight of the dark energy that emanated from the possessed child.

Priscilla, her eyes filled with tears, pleaded, "Grace, please, we love you. Fight this. We won't give up on you." Her voice trembled weakly, a desperate plea that echoed through the house.

Grace responded with a haunting laugh, a sound that reverberated through the very foundation like a demonic echo. "Love? What the fuck do you know of love? You're both pathetic. Your so-called love is nothing compared to the power that courses through me. I can see your weaknesses. I can smell your fears." The words hung in the air like an ancient curse.

As the room grew colder, shadows slithered and coiled around Grace like serpents responding to the dark force that now manipulated her every move. An icy wind whispered through the cracks in the walls, carrying with it the anguished cries of a realm touched by darkness.

The three of them clutched each other as they faced the demonic entity that wore Grace's face. The room became a battlefield, a nexus of conflicting energies that clashed and collided.

Grace walked towards them, her movements deliberate and haunting, an eerie grace that defied the innocence of a child. The room seemed to warp around her, the very fabric of reality bending to accommodate the unholy presence that now dominated her.

"You're fools to resist. Embrace the inevitable, because your suffering has just begun," she said, her voice a chilling blend of her own and the guttural resonance of the demon that held her in its thrall.

With a wave of her hand, unseen forces erupted, sending objects flying through the air and crashing to the floor. The explosion of wood and glass echoed like the wails of tortured souls. The three of them recoiled, desperately shielding themselves from the onslaught.

Amidst the chaos, a dark figure materialized behind Grace, its presence casting a suffocating aura that rippled through the air. The demon, now partially visible, grinned through Grace's contorted visage.

"You truly are amusing little piss-ants! Know that the darkness is inevitable, and I am its champion." The words echoed through the room, each syllable dripping with venom. "Now, it's time for you to die!"

Priscilla, trembling with fear, locked eyes with her daughter, desperately seeking a glimmer of the Grace she once knew. The possessed child, now a mere puppet manipulated by the demonic force, responded with a mocking laughter that reverberated through the room.

As the chaos unfolded around them, Priscilla's mind raced with the realization that they weren't strong enough to defeat the evil presence gripping their daughter. They needed help fast!

"Emily, go!" Priscilla cried. "The church! Find help, someone who knows how to fight this!"

Emily hesitated, torn between her desire to help and the understanding that Priscilla was right. They weren't strong enough. She nodded as she turned and bolted from the room, leaving Priscilla and Andrew to face the demon.

With a deep breath, Priscilla centered herself, drawing upon the wellspring of ancient psychic energy within her. She extended her senses, reaching out to the tumultuous energy swirling around Grace, seeking a foothold amidst the chaos.

Priscilla locked eyes with her daughter, her psychic presence intertwining with the evil force that held her daughter captive, "Grace, I know you're in there somewhere. Don't let it control you."

Andrew added his own energy to the battle by reciting every word of scripture his mind could grasp to combat the chaos surrounding them.

As Grace, or what remained of her, struggled against the demonic influence that gripped her, Priscilla saw a flicker of recognition in her daughter's eyes. It was a brief moment of hope amidst the chaos, a glimmer of the child they once knew fighting to break free from the darkness that consumed her.

"Grace, listen to me!" Priscilla cried out, her voice trembling with fear and desperation. "You have to fight it! We're here with you, we won't let it take you!"

For a moment, the room seemed to still, the oppressive atmosphere easing as Grace's struggles against the demonic influence intensified. Priscilla felt a surge of hope, a flicker of light amidst the suffocating darkness.

But the demon, sensing its hold slipping, redoubled its efforts, unleashing a torrent of supernatural fury that threatened to destroy them. Priscilla gritted her teeth, her psychic barriers straining against the onslaught as she poured every ounce of her strength into protecting Grace.

Priscilla knew that time was running out, but she refused to yield. She was the last line of defense against the forces that sought to destroy everything she held dear.

CHAPTER 38

Emily's desperation reached a fevered pitch as she ran through the stone corridors of the old church. The walls, adorned with faded religious murals, seemed to absorb the echoes of her hurried footsteps. The scent of aged wood and burning incense hung in the air, intertwining with the lingering echoes of centuries-old prayers.

As she entered the dimly lit nave, the soft glow of votive candles bathed the altar in an ethereal light. The polished pews, each a testament to years of devout worship, led Emily toward the heart of the church.

Father Matthias emerged from the shadows that clung to the corners of the nave. His gaze, weathered and wise, met Emily's anxious eyes, and a knowing silence passed between them. "What brings you to this sacred place, my daughter?"

Emily's voice trembled as she began to recount the horrifying events that had unfolded. She spoke of Grace's possession, the malevolent force that gripped her, and the relentless nightmare that had consumed their lives. Father Matthias listened in solemn silence, his expression reflecting a deep understanding of the supernatural battle at play.

"We didn't know where else to turn," Emily said, her plea

filled with desperation. "We need help, Father. Fast! Or a little girl is going to die!"

Father Matthias sighed as he contemplated the gravity of the situation. "Under normal circumstances, a full inquiry would need to be processed by the church to undertake an exorcism. But given the dire nature of the situation, and the direct threat that it poses, I can override the need for such formalities. Unfortunately, my body can no longer handle the strain of such an encounter, but I believe Father Gideon may be of service."

"Where can I find Gideon?" Emily asked desperately.

Father Matthias pointed toward the shadowy alcove at the far end of the nave. The flickering candles cast wavering light on the old books and scrolls that lined the shelves. "He often lingers in the corners where the ancient texts are kept."

As Emily neared the alcove, the flickering candles cast fleeting glimpses of Gideon's features, revealing a face etched with the scars of a man who had traversed the realms between light and shadow. The air in the alcove carried the musty scent of aged parchment, mingling with the lingering aroma of incense.

Gideon, sensing Emily's presence, turned with a fluid grace. His eyes, a shade darker than the shadows that embraced him, pierced through the dim light. "You seek help for something that troubles you, child," he stated, a knowing smile playing on his lips.

"Father Gideon," Emily began, her voice trembling slightly. "I... we need your help right away! A young girl, Grace, she... she's possessed by something terrible."

Gideon's eyes narrowed as he listened intently, his expression unreadable. "Possession is a grave matter indeed," he replied in a voice like gravel. "But why do you seek my help, child? Surely Father Matthias—"

"Father Matthias said he's not physically able to help. He sent me to find you," Emily interjected, her voice rising in urgency.

A flicker of something passed over Gideon's face, too quick for Emily to discern. "And what makes you think I would help?" he asked, his tone feigning reluctance.

"We have no one else to turn to," Emily pleaded, her eyes searching his. "Please, Father. Grace's life is at stake."

For a long moment, Gideon said nothing, his gaze fixed on Emily as if he was having an internal dialogue with someone else who was judging her worth. Finally, he sighed, his features softening slightly. "Very well," he said, his voice tinged with resignation. "I can offer you what you desire—a chance to free the child from the clutches of the demon that haunts her. But know this: delving into matters of the supernatural carries its own risks. Are you prepared to face them?"

Emily nodded, her determination unwavering. "I'll do whatever it takes to save Grace."

"Then follow me," Gideon said, turning away and disappearing into the shadows of the alcove. "But be warned, the path ahead is fraught with peril."

As Emily trailed behind Gideon, she couldn't shake the feeling that there was more to him than met the eye. The darkness seemed to cling to him like a cloak, whispering secrets that chilled her to the bone. But Grace's life was at stake, and she was willing to follow Gideon into the abyss if it meant saving her. Little did she know the true depths of darkness that awaited her.

***

Deep within the heart of the church, concealed behind

hallowed walls, the clandestine chamber lurked in the shroud of darkness. Bathed in the ghastly glow of ritual candles, Gideon's chanting reverberated in the chamber, his form warped by the flickering flames.

The air within his secret sanctum hung heavy with a sinister weight, an ominous presence that seemed to pulse with the very essence of evil. Gideon's voice, a guttural undertone, reverberated off the ancient stone, resonating with the forbidden lore he sought to command.

As his incantations swelled to a crescendo, the atmosphere quivered with an otherworldly anticipation. The chamber's entrance, veiled by heavy drapes adorned with cryptic symbols, trembled as shadowy figures slithered forth from the abyss beyond.

The hooded figures, their visages swallowed by darkness, encircled Gideon in silent reverence. The air itself seemed to thrum with energy, as if the very fabric of reality strained under the weight of their presence.

With a twisted dagger raised high, its blade oozing with a vile, black ichor, Gideon addressed his congregation. "Brothers and sisters of the Abyss, tonight heralds the convergence of our might. Tonight, we offer the ultimate sacrifice to usher in our dominion upon the world."

The hooded figures, their voices a chilling chorus, intoned in unison. "As above, so below. Our allegiance to the shadows binds us to this accursed pact."

Gideon lowered his gaze to the altar, where Emily's naked and trembling body lay bound with thick ropes to large iron rings attached at each corner. Desperate whimpers escaped her muffled lips as he bent down close to her. "Just know that your sacrifice will serve a higher purpose."

The hooded figures, their eyes gleaming with malice, encircled the altar like vultures awaiting a feast as the obsidian dagger descended, glinting in the candlelight's dance.

"Tonight, we offer this vessel as a conduit to the abyss," Gideon declared, his voice laced with perverse ecstasy. "May her blood satiate the shadows' hunger, and may her essence fuel their infernal desires."

As the dagger met flesh, a primal scream pierced the chamber's veil. The dark blade drank deep, and the chamber trembled with an unholy rapture as Emily's blood poured out like a fountain. The hooded figures chanted in fervent unison, their voices merging with the ritual's eerie symphony.

The sacrificial blood cascaded upon the altar, forming grotesque sigils that seemed to writhe with a sinister life. The air itself drank in the essence, and the chamber resonated with malevolent energy, as if reality itself quivered in response.

With Emily's final breath, shadows coalesced in the chamber, swirling around Gideon and his acolytes in a malefic dance. The air, thick with death's stench and dark magic, bore witness to the grotesque ritual's climax—a blood-soaked covenant promising unspeakable horrors upon the world's unsuspecting soul.

CHAPTER 39

Matthew's journey through elementary school was marked by countless struggles, both seen and unseen. From the moment he stepped foot into the bustling corridors on his first day, he felt a sense of unease that seemed to linger like a shadow over his every move. While other children laughed and played, Matthew often found himself isolated; shunned and teased for being different.

The whispers began almost immediately, like distant echoes in the wind. As the days turned into weeks and the weeks into months, the voices grew louder and more insistent, their spectral voices taunting him relentlessly.

No corner of the school seemed safe from the torment that followed him like a dark cloud. The playground became a battleground where he was forced to confront the cruel taunts of his peers, while the cafeteria was turned into a minefield of ridicule and humiliation.

And yet, in the middle of all the darkness, there were moments of fleeting hope—small acts of kindness from unexpected sources that served as a beacon of light to guide him while the storm raged on. A smile from a passing teacher, a kind word from a classmate—these were the moments that kept Matthew going, letting him know that he was not alone in his struggles.

Still, as the years passed, Matthew found himself sinking deeper into despair as the shadows lengthened and the whispers grew more urgent.

Each day brought with it a chorus of spectral murmurs, their whispers growing louder, more insistent, until they became an inescapable cacophony that echoed within the corridors of his soul. In the stillness of the night, the walls of his room seemed to close in, their shadows twisting into grotesque shapes that loomed over him like specters of his own fears.

Yet amidst the suffocating weight of his turmoil, there persisted a fragile glimmer—a flicker of resilience that refused to be snuffed out. In the fleeting moments between dusk and dawn, Matthew would steal away to the sanctuary of his bedroom, where the moon cast its silvery light upon the worn floorboards. There, surrounded by the comforting embrace of stuffed animals and worn-out blankets, he clung to the belief that somewhere, beyond the veil of darkness, lay a path to salvation.

But with each passing day, the whispers grew louder, their words laden with an ominous warning that sent shivers down Matthew's spine. And as he braced himself for the trials that lay ahead, he couldn't shake the unsettling feeling that the shadows were not merely a product of his imagination, but harbingers of something far more sinister.

*****

Stepping into the unfamiliar halls of middle school, Matthew hoped for a fresh start—a chance to leave behind the torment of his elementary years. However, the transition proved to be anything but smooth. The whispers that had haunted him in his previous school seemed to follow him like a malevolent shadow, clinging to him with a tenacity that refused to be shaken.

In this new environment, Matthew found himself struggling even more to navigate the complexities of adolescent social dynamics. The whispers of the spirits that had tormented him since childhood seemed to grow louder with each passing day, their spectral voices mingling with the mocking laughter of his new classmates.

Matthew found himself adrift in a sea of unfamiliar faces and unfamiliar surroundings. And the darkness that had plagued him for so long seemed to follow him wherever he went, casting a shadow over his every move.

As the days turned into weeks and the weeks into months, Matthew struggled to find his place in this new world. The whispers of the spirits that followed him grew louder and more insistent, their taunts and jeers echoing through the crowded hallways.

One day, as the sun hung low in the sky, casting long, twisted shadows that seemed to slither across the pavement like serpents, Matthew trudged home from school through the empty streets, the echo of his footsteps a hollow drumbeat in the silence. A chill wind whispered through the trees, carrying with it a sense of foreboding that prickled at the back of his neck.

As he turned onto his street, a sudden movement at the edge of his vision caught his eye. Something darted across the road, a shadowy shape that moved with an unnatural fluidity. Then, from the depths of the shadows, it crawled. A creature unlike anything he had ever seen, a grotesque abomination of sinew and bone that seemed to defy all logic and reason. Its eyes burned with evil, its jagged teeth dripping with viscous saliva, as it slunk toward him on twisted, gnarled limbs.

Panic surged through Matthew as he stumbled backwards, his mind struggling to comprehend the nightmare unfolding before him. With a scream, he turned to flee, but it was too late. The creature was on him in an instant, its clawed hands closing around his throat with a vice-like grip.

He gasped for air, his vision swimming as darkness threatened to engulf him. With a desperate surge of adrenaline, he fought back, clawing at the creature's face with all his strength. But it was like fighting against a force of nature itself, each blow met with only cold, unyielding flesh.

Just when he thought all hope was lost, a blinding light pierced the sky. The figure of a man emerged from the shadows, his black skin melding with the encroaching darkness as he wielded a weapon forged of silver and steel. With a fierce battle cry, he lunged at the creature, driving it back with a flurry of blows.

The creature shrieked in agony, its unearthly wails echoing through the night as it stumbled backwards, its form flickering and distorting like a mirage in the desert. With one final, desperate lunge, the mysterious warrior delivered a killing blow, driving their weapon deep into the creature's chest.

As the creature collapsed to the ground, its form dissolving into a cloud of noxious smoke, Matthew collapsed to his knees, gasping for breath. The warrior kneeled beside him, his features obscured by the dim light, and offered a hand to help him up.

"Thank you," Matthew whispered, his voice hoarse with exhaustion and fear. "Who are you?"

The man merely smiled, his eyes glinting with a knowing light. "Just a friend," he replied. A pair of wings then sprung from his back. "The name's Lucas," he said before he leaped into the sky and disappeared into the night.

Matthew watched him go, his heart still racing with adrenaline. But as he made his way home, the image of the creature lingered in his mind like a festering wound, a reminder of the horrors that lurked in the shadows, waiting for him.

CHAPTER 40

A sardonic smile played on Gideon's lips as he surveyed the gravity of the situation, tasting the malevolence that hung heavy in the air. An otherworldly anticipation thickened the atmosphere as the couple ushered him inside. Priscilla looked around worriedly, "Where's Emily?"

Gideon replied, ". I told her that it would be best to stay away. The ritual will be too dangerous and she could've been compromised."

Priscilla's lips quivered, "But, we need all the help we can get, Father. This being is stronger than anything I've seen before."

"I've danced this dance with darker entities before," Gideon declared. His confidence bordered on arrogance, yet Priscilla and Andrew clung to his words as if they were threads of hope in a tapestry of despair. "Leave it to me. I'll do what's needed to free your daughter from this unholy grip."

A wicked laugh erupted from Grace's mouth, who sat perched on the edge of the couch like some unholy creature of the night whose name is uttered to frighten young children who don't behave. "I'm not so sure you have it in you,

Father," she cackled. "Let's see if you can still get it up?"

As Gideon prepared his ritual, a distant howl echoed through the night, a lament for souls lost to the abyss. His deep voice filled the room with a spectral chill, each syllable dripping with ancient power; the Latin incantations spilling from his lips like poison.

"Exorcizo te, omnis spiritus immunde, in nomine Dei omnipotentis," Gideon intoned, his hands tracing arcane symbols that shimmered with forbidden energy. Shadows danced in response to his words, twisting and writhing in a grotesque pantomime of agony.

A scream flew from Grace's lips as her body convulsed from the force of the supernatural struggle, her essence caught in the crossfire. "Ergo, draco maledicte et omnis legio diabolica," Gideon pressed on.

A frigid wind suddenly swept through the room, yet Gideon remained persistent, his powerful voice rising above the chaos. "Ecclesiam tuam securi tibi facias libertate servire, te rogamus, audi nos!"

As Gideon called upon ancient names and symbols, the evil force coiled within Grace responded with a chorus of unearthly growls and sinister whispers. The room throbbed with the clash of supernatural energies, each pulse creating a disquieting symphony that reverberated through every section of the house.

Gideon, growing weak and exhausted from the onslaught, pushed on with a relentless determination bordering on madness. Beads of perspiration glinted like sinister jewels on his brow. "Ut inimicos sanctae Ecclesiae humiliare digneris, te rogamus, audi nos!"

Guided by an eerie grace, his hands wove intricate patterns in the air, as though sculpting unseen forces into submission. The fluid movements conjured ethereal sigils that hung in the air, pulsing with an arcane power that reverberated through the very essence of the room.

Priscilla and Andrew watched the unfolding spectacle with faces etched in a mixture of terror and hope. The air crackled with anticipation, as they desperately prayed that the ritual would finally free their daughter of her possession and return the sanctity of their home.

Gideon's eyes, once harboring a glint of darkness, blazed with a deep intensity as he confronted the evil entity lurking within Grace. His gaze pierced through the shadows, seeking the heart of the demon that had ensnared her.

As the ritual neared its climax, Gideon's voice thundered to a crescendo. "Ut inimicos sanctae Ecclesiae proterantur, te rogamus, audi nos!"

Yet, just as victory seemed within reach, Gideon's demeanor twisted into something sinister. Seizing the opportune moment, the malevolent force within Grace unleashed a chilling laughter, merging with Gideon's own voice. "You thought you could banish me?" his guttural voice sneered.

The room plunged into an inky darkness, as shadows coalesced around Gideon, shaping an unholy silhouette that mirrored the demonic entity they sought to expel. Priscilla and Andrew were paralyzed for a moment as the ritual spiraled toward eternal darkness.

Priscilla immediately sensed that something dark and sinister was at work within Gideon and exchanged a nervous glance with Andrew. "What's going on, Gideon?" she asked, her voice betraying a mixture of fear and suspicion.

Gideon's lips curled into a sly smile, his eyes glinting with something unsettling. He didn't respond immediately, letting the silence stretch between them like a taut wire. When he finally spoke, his voice sent shivers down their spines.

"Trust the process," he said in an ominous tone. "The ritual is reaching its climax."

As the rite intensified, Priscilla and Andrew could feel a tangible force drawing strength from their fear and desperation. But beneath the surface, there was something more sinister at play.

Unknown to them, Gideon's motives were not what they seemed. The forces within him, thought to be at odds with the demonic entity attached to Grace, now conspired in a union of darkness. Instead of banishing the demon, the ritual seemed to feed it, amplifying its power with each passing moment. Shadows clung to Gideon like loyal companions, their allegiance sealed in an unholy covenant.

As the ritual neared its conclusion, the convergence of dark forces threatened to consume them all. Gideon's eyes gleamed with a twisted satisfaction. The exorcism, meant to liberate Grace, had become a catalyst for a darkness far more insidious than the family could have ever imagined.

Priscilla and Andrew, still clutching to the diminishing hope that Gideon would save their daughter from the demonic clutches, watched the ritual with a mixture of fear and desperation. Shadows danced to the rhythm of Gideon's incantations, casting grotesque silhouettes that twisted with the cosmic struggle.

Suddenly, a surge of light erupted from the cross that Priscilla and Andrew clung to as their beacon of salvation—an elegant and weathered talisman inscribed with the prayer of St. Michael that had been handed down through the generations of Priscilla's ancestors. The sacred power clashed head-on with the evil force, creating an explosion that shook the room to its core.

Gideon, surprised by the unforeseen event, found himself caught in a tempest of warring energies, desperately trying to maintain control over the maelstrom he had unleashed.

As Grace convulsed on the floor, the demon within her wailing in agony, a volley of blood-laced mucus shot like a cannon from her mouth, engulfing the room in gore.

Priscilla and Andrew's voices wavered at the sight of the terrifying spectacle as they fought desperately to drive the demon from their daughter. The room had transformed into a scene of writhing shadows, divine light, and the anguished contortions of the possessed.

As the battle reached its harrowing peak, the deceptive veil concealing Gideon's true intentions began to unravel, revealing the poisonous tapestry woven beneath. The dark force within him, now weakened and infuriated by the unexpected resistance, fought with a desperate fervor to regain control.

In a calculated and deadly move, Gideon, with a wave of his hand, redirected the force within Grace towards himself. In a macabre dance of shadows, the demonic entity seized a chance to survive by merging with Gideon, resulting in a horrifying fusion that challenged the distinction between man and demon. The room quaked in terror as Gideon's once-human features were twisted and warped by the unholy power, creating a grotesque and otherworldly sight.

Gideon, now a vessel for both the demonic entity and his own darkness, grinned with a sinister satisfaction, the very embodiment of a conjured nightmare. "You fools think you can avoid the inevitable?" his voice, a guttural fusion of man and demon, echoed with a haunting resonance. "I am the harbinger of this darkness, and it is time to embrace the true power that awaits."

The battle, once a desperate struggle for their daughter's salvation, had suddenly taken a dangerous turn toward the abyss. Priscilla and Andrew found themselves facing the grim reality that the true power of its darkness was yet to be revealed.

In a final act of desperation, Priscilla and Andrew summoned every ounce of strength remaining. The ancestral relic, clutched tightly in their trembling hands, glowed brightly with an intensity that nearly blinded them.

Grace, as if emerging from a nightmarish slumber, suddenly gasped for air. Her eyes, once vacant and hollow, now held a glimmer of recognition. The sacred power surging through her pushed back against the darkness that sought to consume her.

With a guttural scream that echoed through the room, Gideon convulsed. The demonic entity, now weakened and overwhelmed by the onslaught, began to unravel. The shadows recoiled and the unholy fusion crumbled, leaving Gideon writhing on the floor.

The room fell silent, the echoes of the struggle lingering like haunting whispers. Priscilla and Andrew rushed to Grace's side. Her eyes fluttered open for a second and a soft smile crossed her lips before she collapsed in her parents' arms, freed from the demonic grip.

Gideon, weakened and defeated, lay on the floor, his power diminished by the unexpected turn of events. As the family embraced in the aftermath of the ordeal, he feigned defeat, whispered an ominous vow, "You may have won this battle, but the darkness never truly fades. It merely bides its time, waiting for the opportune moment to return."

Another spasm tore through Gideon as he played the role of a tortured victim, concealing the darkness that still lurked within him. A moment later he rose to his knees gasping, and looked at the family through deceptive eyes. "It's over," he said softly.

CHAPTER 41

Days passed and Grace slowly returned to a semblance of normal, the color of her cheeks regaining their rosy hue, while her eyes began to dance with childish delight once more. With the strength of Priscilla's magic and the power of her love to protect her daughter from the darkest of threats, the memory of the nightmare that had threatened to destroy her was now locked away in the deepest recesses of Grace's mind.

Even though Grace had virtually no recollection of the horrors she had endured, a heavy weight hung over their family like a dense fog. Priscilla was haunted by a deep sense of regret, her mind weighed by thoughts of what could have been. She retreated inward, lost in a maze of self-blame and remorse, while Andrew struggled to make sense of the rift that had formed between them.

As the months flew by, the gap between Priscilla and Andrew widened, swallowing the warmth and affection that once defined their home. Where joy and laughter had once echoed, now only the hollow echoes of their fractured love remained.

Tensions simmered beneath the surface, each breath thick

with unspoken regrets. Priscilla and Andrew, who were once inseparable, now found themselves lost in a sea of despair, their bond weakening under the weight of their torment.

One fateful afternoon, the unspoken rift between Priscilla and Andrew reached a crescendo, the air filled with an oppressive weight. Shadows danced on the walls, seeming to twist into grotesque shapes that mirrored the fractured state of their relationship. Beneath their feet, the very foundation of their home groaned, as if it was a harbinger of impending doom.

****

An icy wind swept through the room, carrying with it a mournful wail that echoed through the cracks in the floor. Ghostly apparitions materialized in the darkness, their anguished forms reaching out with spectral fingers, clawing at the edges of reality.

Priscilla's heart pounded in her chest as the shadows enveloped her, dragging her into a bottomless abyss. Desperation clawed at her mind as she struggled to find a hold amidst the suffocating darkness. She tried to scream but her voice was drowned out by the cacophony of despair that echoed through the void.

As she sank deeper, Priscilla could hear the whispers of her past echoing through the darkness, a chorus of regrets and unspoken grievances. The spectral figures closed in, their faces twisted in anguish, their touch like ice against Priscilla's skin.

With a final, agonized cry, the darkness consumed her, and as the shadows closed in around her, the room bore witness to the tragic demise of a family torn apart by the darkness that lurked within.

When Priscilla opened her eyes, a soft tear streamed down her cheek as she realized that the love they once shared was lost forever. Careful not to wake Andrew, she reached for her phone on the bedside table. What she needed now most of all was a friend.

She checked her voicemail for messages. Nothing. Then she looked for text messages, and even opened her email. Still nothing. It's as if Emily had disappeared from the face of the earth, running away as fast as she could to escape the madness that seemed to follow Priscilla wherever she went. And she couldn't blame her. Still, a deep feeling of dread coursed through Priscilla's bones that suggested that something terrible had happened. If that was true, and it was because of her, she didn't know if she could live with herself.

***

Andrew woke from the nightmare with tears in his eyes and sorrow in his heart. The images of his dream had brought forward all the deepest emotions he had sought to suppress. Now he knew he couldn't hold them back any longer. He felt everything that he had held dear slipping away from him.

As Priscilla slept soundly next to him, he slipped out of bed and quietly shuffled from the room, hoping a bit of fresh air would quiet the tempest brewing inside him.

Minutes later, Andrew trudged along the dirt road, the distant silhouette of the church looming like a specter against the early dawn sky. Sorrow draped over him like a heavy cloak, each step a weary march through the quagmire of his own despair.

Within him, a storm raged, a whirlwind of regret and heartache tearing at his soul. What had once been a journey of wonder shared with the love of his life now felt like a solitary descent into despair.

His mind churned with the echoes of his own accusatory words, each syllable a dagger that pierced his conscience. He knew, deep down, that Priscilla wasn't to blame for the darkness that now enveloped them. It was his own anger, his own mistrust, that had set them on this path of destruction.

As the sun dipped below the horizon, casting long shadows across the landscape, Andrew's heart grew heavier with each passing moment. The church, a beacon of hope in the encroaching darkness, offered little solace as Andrew approached its weathered doors. With a creak, they swung open, inviting him into the dimly lit sanctuary within.

Alone in the confessional booth, Andrew bared his soul to the unseen presence on the other side. His words hung heavy in the air, a desperate plea for absolution in a world tainted by sin and sorrow. But as he confessed his sins, he felt a chill creep into his bones, a sense of unease that gnawed at the edges of his consciousness.

Gideon, the supposed vessel of divine mercy, listened with a predatory patience, and when he spoke, his words dripping with honeyed deceit.

As Andrew emerged from the confessional, the weight on his shoulders felt heavier than ever. The road stretched out before him, a path filled with peril and uncertainty, and he knew that the journey ahead would test not only his faith but his very sanity.

CHAPTER 42

The drone of the teacher's voice filled the classroom, a monotonous hum that seemed to seep into Matthew's very bones. He struggled to keep his eyes open, the heavy weight of exhaustion pressing down on him like a leaden cloak. With each passing moment, his eyelids grew heavier, until finally, he succumbed to the irresistible pull of sleep.

In the darkness behind closed eyes, nightmares lurked, waiting to pounce on his vulnerable mind. Images of death and destruction danced before him, vivid and horrifying in their intensity. He saw streets choked with rubble, buildings ablaze with fire, and faces contorted with fear and anguish.

Then, in the middle of the chaos, he saw his mother lying broken and bloodied on the ground, her lifeless eyes staring into the abyss. A scream tore from Matthew's throat as he jolted awake, his heart pounding in his chest.

Blood pounded in his ears as he looked around the classroom, disoriented and panicked. The teacher's voice droned on, oblivious to the terror that gripped him. With trembling hands, Matthew pushed himself upright, his breath coming in ragged gasps.

But as he scanned the room, his eyes fell on the clock, and

his blood ran cold. Hours had passed in the blink of an eye, and the once bustling classroom now lay silent and empty except for the teacher. Fear gripped Matthew as he stumbled to his feet, his mind racing with thoughts of his mother.

"You won't be able to save her," the teacher said.

Frantic, Matthew rushed from the classroom, the echo of his footsteps the only sound in the empty halls. With each step, the weight of his vision bore down on him like a physical force, driving him forward with a desperate urgency.

As he burst through the doors and into the daylight, he saw it. Their school, once a bustling hub of activity, now lay in ruins. Smoke billowed from shattered windows, and the air was thick with the stench of blood and death.

With a sinking feeling in the pit of his stomach, Matthew stumbled forward, his heart pounding in his chest. And then, he saw her, exactly like the picture he had seen moments before, his mother lying broken and bloodied on the ground, her lifeless eyes staring into the abyss. Tears streamed down Matthew's face as he fell to his knees beside her, his hands trembling as he reached out to touch her cold, lifeless skin.

But as he did, a voice echoed in his mind, cold and mocking.

"You couldn't save her," it whispered, a cruel reminder of his powerlessness in the face of fate.

With an anguished scream, Matthew collapsed beside his mother's body, the weight of her death crushing him like a vise. In that moment, he knew that nothing would ever be the same again.

***

Matthew's eyes snapped open, his body drenched in cold

sweat. He found himself sitting at his desk in his dimly lit bedroom, the remnants of his nightmare still clinging to his mind like cobwebs. The digital clock on his nightstand blinked 3:13 AM in red, ominous digits.

Heart still racing, Matthew struggled to catch his breath. He ran a hand through his tousled hair, trying to shake off the remnants of the horrific vision that had gripped him. With trembling hands, he reached for the lamp beside his bed and flooded the room with light, banishing the shadows that seemed to linger in the corners.

Mom! The thought consumed him. He needed to find her, to make sure she was safe. Swallowing hard against the lump in his throat, Matthew pushed himself up from his chair and stumbled out of his room.

The hallway stretched before him like a tunnel, the silence heavy and oppressive. Every creak of the floorboards echoed loudly in his ears, amplifying the fear that coiled in his stomach. He called out for his mother, his voice a shaky whisper that seemed to dissipate into the darkness.

Panic clawed at him as he checked each room of their small house, his heart sinking with every empty space he encountered. Finally, after what felt like an eternity of searching, Matthew found her in the kitchen, her back to him as she stood at the sink, washing dishes in the pale light filtering in from the window.

Relief washed over him as he approached, but as she turned around, horror seized him like icy claws sinking into his flesh. Her face was a grotesque mask of torn flesh and dripping blood, her once gentle features twisted into a nightmarish visage. A strangled cry escaped Matthew's lips as he stumbled backward.

"Matthew, what are you doing up so late?" she asked, her voice gurgling as a stream of blood dripped down her chin.

"Did you come to give mommy a hand?"

Mary opened her arms wide and shuffled toward Matthew with a twisted gait.

The air seemed to thicken around Matthew as his mind struggled to comprehend the horror unfolding before him. He blinked, desperate to dispel the nightmare that held him captive, but when he opened his eyes again, the gruesome image remained unchanged.

With a sudden gasp, Matthew jolted awake once more, his body drenched in sweat as he sat up in bed, panting heavily. His heart raced like a runaway train as he tried to shake off the lingering terror of his dream.

Determined to banish the nightmare once and for all, Matthew swung his legs over the edge of the bed and pushed himself upright. He stumbled out of his room, his pulse pounding in his ears as he made his way through the silent house.

Finally, he reached his mother's room and pushed open the door with trembling hands. Relief flooded through him as he saw her lying sound asleep in her bed, her chest rising and falling rhythmically with each breath.

Tears pricked at Matthew's eyes as he crossed the room and kneeled beside her bed, his hand reaching out to gently brush the hair from her face. She stirred slightly, a faint smile tugging at the corners of her lips as she slept on, unaware of the terror that had gripped her son.

As Matthew leaned in to kiss his mother's forehead, her eyelids fluttered open slowly, revealing warm, hazel eyes that gazed up at him with concern.

"Matthew?" she murmured in a thick voice. "What are you doing up?"

Matthew pulled back slightly, a deep frown tugging at his lips. "I had another nightmare," he admitted, his voice barely above a whisper.

Mary reached out to gently stroke his cheek. "Oh, sweetheart," she said. "Do you want to talk about it?"

Matthew's throat tightened. "It was... it was horrible," he confessed, his voice trembling. "I saw you... but you were hurt, Mom. I thought..."

As tears threatened to cascade down Matthew's face, Mary pulled him close, holding him tightly against her. "It was just a dream, Matthew," she reassured him, her voice gentle but firm. "I'm right here, safe and sound. You have nothing to worry about."

Matthew clung to her, the tension slowly draining from his body as he took comfort in her embrace. "I know," he whispered, his voice muffled against her shoulder. "But it felt so real."

Mary pulled back slightly, cupping his face in her hands and meeting his gaze with unwavering certainty. "Sometimes our minds can play tricks on us, especially when we're feeling scared or anxious," she said softly. "But you're safe now, Matthew. And I'm right here with you."

A sense of peace washed over Matthew as he looked into his mother's eyes, feeling the weight of his fear slowly lifting from his shoulders.

Mary pressed a kiss to his forehead. "Now, why don't you try to get some more sleep? Everything will look better in the morning, I promise."

As Matthew reluctantly pulled away from his mother's embrace, a sense of calm settled over him. He nodded, reassured by her words, and made his way back to his room.

Entering his dimly lit bedroom, Matthew took a deep breath, trying to shake off the remnants of his nightmare once more. He glanced around the room, the familiar sights offering a sense of comfort and safety.

But as he turned towards his bed, something caught his eye. A flicker of movement in the corner of the room, barely noticeable in the darkness.

Heart pounding in his chest, Matthew squinted into the shadows, his mind racing with fear. He took a hesitant step forward, the floorboards creaking beneath his feet.

And then he saw it. A figure standing in the corner, its form shrouded in darkness. For a moment, Matthew's breath caught in his throat as another surge of panic washed over him.

But as his eyes adjusted to the darkness, he realized it was just his coat hanging on the back of his desk chair, swaying gently in the breeze from the open window.

With a shaky laugh, Matthew ran a hand through his hair, feeling foolish for letting his imagination run wild. He closed the window and drew the curtains, expelling the shadows from his room.

Feeling completely drained, Matthew crawled into bed and pulled the covers up to his chin, his eyelids growing heavy. As he drifted off to sleep, he said a silent prayer, hoping to banish the lingering echoes of his nightmare once and for all.

CHAPTER 43

A dark and heavy gloom hung in the air as Priscilla perched anxiously on the edge of the sofa, while Andrew, a storm brewing in his eyes, paced the room restlessly. Priscilla, her voice quivering, dared to break the suffocating silence. "Andrew, we can't keep pretending. Something's got to give."

Andrew stopped his pacing and spun around, holding Priscilla with an angry glare. "Give? You think that's the answer? After everything we've gone through? I don't know if I have anything left to give?"

Priscilla looked at Andrew sadly. "I don't even recognize us anymore," Priscilla confessed, tears welling in her eyes. "Every word feels like a knife ready to strike."

Andrew scoffed, his bitterness slicing through the heavy atmosphere. "You're the one who shattered us, Priscilla. With your damned mysteries and secrets."

Priscilla shot back, "Secrets? You think I asked for this? You don't know what it's like, living with a past that claws at you every damn day; seeing things I don't want to see; feeling things I don't want to feel."

The tension in the room tightened, the ticking clock on the wall sounding like a countdown to the end. Priscilla's shoulders sagged as a gust of wind rattled the windowpane, heralding an approaching storm outside that mirrored the storm raging within. "I never wanted any of this," she whispered.

For a moment, Andrew's anger wavered, and he drew closer. "Maybe it's time we face the truth," he uttered, the word "truth" echoing like a death knell.

Priscilla gripped the edge of the sofa, her knuckles turning white from the tension. "I can't lose her, Andrew. I can't lose everything," she pleaded, tears carving paths down her cheeks.

A heavy silence blanketed the room, broken only by the distant rumble of thunder. Andrew, wrestling with his own demons, turned away.

"Maybe this is the only way," he said sadly.

Outside, the storm mirrored the turmoil within both of their hearts, with Grace caught in the turbulence of their fractured love.

***

The divorce proceedings unfolded with an eerie swiftness, as if even the universe itself wanted to expedite the unraveling of their once-unbreakable bond. Three months had passed since their initial separation, and now, within the somber confines of the lawyer's office, their decision pressed down on them like a leaden sky.

An oppressive tension hung in the air, thick as fog, each passing moment weighed down by the undeniable finality of their failed relationship. Priscilla and Andrew sat across from each other, the gulf between them a gaping chasm of emotional desolation.

The lawyer moved with a solemn grace, each motion

deliberate, knowing that what was being unraveled before him was not just a legal contract but the tearing apart of souls bound together by what was believed to be an unbreakable bond.

The lawyer's voice shattered the silence in the room as he addressed Priscilla, "You seek joint custody, correct?"

Priscilla nodded sadly. "Yes, joint custody. Grace needs both of us."

Andrew's eyes mirrored her sentiment. "Absolutely. Grace deserves to have us both."

A solemn nod from the lawyer, and the conversation veered toward the division of assets. "What about the house and other shared belongings?"

Priscilla's voice was tinged with uncertainty. "I'd like to keep the house, if that's possible. I want her to have a little sense of stability."

Andrew's gaze softened, a flicker of tenderness in the storm. "Of course. I want Grace to feel safe and secure."

As the legal proceedings unfolded, Priscilla and Andrew found themselves navigating the treacherous waters of untangling a life once woven together with threads of love and devotion. The division of assets became a cruel reminder of their shattered dreams, each possession a relic of a past now irretrievably lost. Their once-shared home, a sanctuary of their love, now stood as a stark testament to the wreckage of their broken vows.

"And spousal support?" the lawyer inquired, his voice a solemn echo in the dimness.

Priscilla's gaze flickered toward Andrew, a silent plea for understanding passing between them. "No spousal support. I don't want to burden Andrew any further."

Andrew's hand reached across the table. "I don't need anything, Priscilla. Just joint custody. We'll figure out the rest as we go."

As the lawyer meticulously finalized the details, a silent pact passed between Priscilla and Andrew, binding them in an unspoken understanding. The room, instead of being tainted by bitterness, exuded an unexpected sense of closure.

The room echoed with the rustle of papers and the groan of the lawyer's chair as the final signatures were etched into the parchment. The divorce decree, now a binding contract, marked the grim conclusion of one chapter and the hesitant dawn of another. When it was all over, Priscilla and Andrew rose from their seats, and even though the weight of the moment lay heavy on their shoulders, an eerie calm settling over them like a shroud.

CHAPTER 44

Even though nearly a year had passed since the successful exorcism that had liberated Grace from the clutches of the demonic entity, the weight of the ordeal and its aftermath still bore heavy on Andrew's heart.

One evening, as the sun dipped below the horizon, Andrew sat quietly in the living room of his small apartment holding a picture tightly in his hands. He remembered the day it had been taken all too clearly—a trip to the local zoo on Grace's second birthday. The morning had started out perfectly, the sun shining brightly as Grace embraced the sights and sounds of nature all around her. And then, even when a thunderstorm had sprung up unexpectedly cutting their trip short, her playful innocence still exuded from her as she watched the rain fall and the lightning strike. The sound of her laughter had filled the air around them, bringing cheer amidst the clouds—a sound he hadn't heard for a long time.

With a sigh, Andrew reached for his coat, needing the solace of the night to clear his thoughts. As he wandered through the familiar streets, he found himself drawn to the church that had played a pivotal role in the tumultuous events that had unfolded in his life.

Gideon greeted him as he entered the dimly lit sanctuary. "Andrew!" he said with mock surprise. "It's been some time since you've entered these doors. I've missed you and Priscilla at morning mass. What brings you to this holy place this evening?"

"To be honest, Father, I feel like I've lost everything. After the divorce, my life doesn't seem to hold any direction anymore."

As Andrew entered the sacred space, he found a comforting refuge within the hallowed walls. Gideon guided Andrew to a pew, and they began to talk in hushed tones.

"I'm sorry to hear that you and Priscilla are no longer together. It's a shame that such a strong bond has been broken. How's little Grace doing?"

Andrew was silent for a second before answering. "Grace is doing good. She seems to have blocked out the entire experience, which is probably for the best. It just hurts to have her jostled back and forth between me and Priscilla like she's some kind of material object instead of a human being."

"I understand your pain, friend. Luckily, Grace is strong and resilient. In the end, I'm sure everything will work out according to God's plan. But, tell me Andrew, what drove you and Priscilla apart?"

Andrew swallowed hard for a second as he searched for the right words. "It wasn't just the horror that Grace went through that caused the separation. Deep down inside me, I felt like I had been betrayed."

"How so?"

"The night before... when everything changed, Priscilla was performing a seance. Emily was there with us, and we both sensed that something dark and evil was nearby. We tried to get her to stop, but she wouldn't listen. If she had, maybe none of this would've happened?"

"It's easy to look at the past and see what could've been done differently. Hindsight is twenty-twenty, after all. But remember that everything that happens is part of God's plan."

Andrew sighed. "I'm sorry, Father, but I'm having a hard time understanding how almost causing our daughter's death is part of some kind of master plan?"

Gideon smiled warmly, knowing that he was starting to pull the threads apart that would let him inside and gain Andrew's trust. "Maybe the plan was for you to be here in front of me at this moment? Aren't we always exactly where we're supposed to be at each moment in time?"

"But there's been so much pain leading to this moment... pain that shouldn't have happened?"

"Unfortunately, pain is a necessary part of everyone's growth."

Andrew leaned back in the pew; exhaustion plastered on his face. "At one time, I thought the future was going to be beautiful, perfect even. Now all I see is sorrow. Part of me knows it wasn't Priscilla's fault for what happened, but another part of me blames her."

Gideon's eyes widened just a little as he sensed an opportunity. "Tell me more about this seance. Is that something Priscilla performed often?"

Andrew nodded. "It had become a weekly ritual, her communing with the dead. Apparently, she's always had this ability. She even said once that it was something passed down to her from her ancestors. Until then, it had never been anything major, a little sound here or there; sometimes a small voice, like a whisper, would say something barely audible. But that night was completely different... It changed everything."

Gideon patted his hand on Andrew's shoulder to offer a

sense of comfort and support, and as he did, a small jolt of electricity jolted through Andrew's shoulder and down his spine. "I can sense a great deal of turmoil wrestling inside you. The road you've traveled has been fraught with challenges, my friend. But it's also a path that can lead to strength and enlightenment."

Andrew gave Gideon an inquisitive look, "Enlightenment?"

"Your journey didn't end with the exorcism," Gideon said with his piercing gaze. "There is much you have yet to learn, and the darkness that once threatened you may manifest again. You, my son, have the potential to be a guardian against such evil in the future."

Andrew, captivated by Gideon's words, felt a newfound sense of purpose awakening within him. The idea of becoming a protector against the supernatural forces that lurked in the shadows resonated with him.

Gideon, sensing a tiny spark growing in Andrew's eyes, continued, "I can offer you guidance, a mentorship, if you will, that will give you the knowledge to face whatever darkness may come your way if you're willing to let me?"

Andrew nodded, his eyes filled with a mixture of determination and uncertainty. "I need to understand as much as I can so that I can help to protect others from the kind of horror we faced. If there's a way I can make a difference, I'm willing to learn."

A fleeting smirk danced across Gideon's lips, a shadow of something darker lurking beneath his façade. With a subtle wave towards the altar, he beckoned Andrew forward. "Then kneel, Andrew, and let the sacred power that resides within this sanctuary guide you. Your journey as a defender against the darkness begins now."

Nervously, Andrew kneeled before the ancient altar,

unaware of the sinister undercurrents swirling around him. Gideon conducted a brief ceremony, blending age-old rituals with mysterious incantations, each word spoken echoing sharply in the dimly lit chamber.

As the ritual approached its climax, Andrew felt a surge of energy coursing through him, electrifying his senses with a tingling anticipation. It was as if the very air crackled with an unseen power, binding him to a destiny he could scarcely comprehend. Gideon laid a hand on Andrew's shoulder once more, sealing his fate with a single touch.

"You are no longer just a witness to the supernatural; now, you are a guardian, a warrior against the shadows," Gideon intoned, his words carrying a weight that settled like a stone in the pit of Andrew's stomach.

With the ceremony concluded, Andrew rose, his mind swirling with a tornado of emotions. The path ahead was shrouded in darkness, yet, with Gideon as his mentor, Andrew stood ready to confront the horrors that lurked in the shadows, unaware of the true depths of the darkness that awaited him.

CHAPTER 45

Mary sat in her small, cluttered living room, the flickering light of the floor lamp casting long, eerie shadows on the walls. She stared blankly at the stack of overdue bills on the coffee table, her mind miles away. Outside, the wind howled like a wounded animal, and the distant hum of traffic seemed more like a ghostly whisper than the normal sounds of the night. Her heart pounded with a relentless rhythm, each beat underscored by a gnawing dread she couldn't shake.

Matthew's connection with the supernatural had grown darker and more intense over the years. What had begun as innocent conversations with friendly spirits had transformed into a relentless torment by malevolent entities. Mary had hoped, against all evidence, that ignoring the problem would make it disappear. But now, denial seemed as foolish as it was futile. The shadows had grown longer, and along with it, the darkness deeper.

Her phone buzzed on the table, shattering the heavy silence. The screen displayed a message from Matthew:

"Mom, I'm at the old warehouse on Cook Street. Can you pick me up? Please, hurry."

A cold sweat broke out on her forehead. Cook Street. The

old warehouse was a haven for troublemakers, drug addicts, and the lost souls of the city. Mary's pulse quickened as fear twisted in her gut. She knew Matthew had been struggling, but she hadn't realized just how far he had fallen. She grabbed her keys and bolted out the door, her thoughts a whirlwind of guilt and desperation. She had failed him, failed to protect him from the dark forces that had been encroaching on his life.

The drive through the dark streets felt like a journey into another world, each turn taking her deeper into the heart of her own fears. The city's familiar landmarks seemed sinister, cloaked in shadows that danced and writhed as if alive. When she arrived at the warehouse, the sight that greeted her was worse than she had imagined. The building loomed in the darkness, its windows broken and the walls covered in layers of graffiti that seemed to shift and shimmer in the dim light. She hesitated for a moment, her fear threatening to overwhelm her, but then she heard a faint, almost imperceptible cry for help.

"Matthew!" she called, her voice echoing in the empty space. She ran toward the sound, her heart hammering in her chest.

The inside of the warehouse was a nightmare of twisted metal and crumbling concrete. The air was thick with an oppressive darkness. Her breathing quickened as she realized the full extent of the danger. Matthew was nowhere to be seen, but she could feel his presence, his fear, and his despair.

"Matthew," she whispered, tears streaming down her face. "Where are you?"

The surrounding shadows began to move, coalescing into dark, menacing shapes. They seemed to feed off her fear, growing stronger with each passing moment. Mary felt a cold chill run down her spine as a sudden, oppressive silence fell over the room, broken only by a low, sinister whisper that seemed to come from everywhere and nowhere at once.

"Mary," the voice hissed, dripping with malice. "We're so happy you could join us!"

Mary's heart pounded harder as she backed away, her instincts screaming at her to run. But before she could turn, the shadows surged forward, enveloping her in a suffocating grip. The air grew thick, and she struggled to breathe, her vision blurring as the darkness closed in.

"Matthew!" she screamed, her voice cracking with desperation. "Help me!"

But there was no answer, only the oppressive darkness pressing in on all sides. Mary fought against the shadows, but they were too strong, their icy tendrils wrapping around her, squeezing the life out of her. She could feel her strength ebbing away, her hope slipping through her fingers like sand.

Just as she thought she might succumb to the darkness, a brilliant light exploded in the room, blinding her. She shielded her eyes, and when she looked again, she saw Michael standing between her and the shadows, his presence a radiant beacon of hope and power.

"Mary," he said in a voice that pushed back the encroaching darkness. "You need to leave this place. It's not safe."

"Michael!" she stammered, her eyes wide and her voice trembling. "I can't leave Matthew. He's in danger."

"Mary, listen to me," Michael replied urgently. "Matthew isn't here. He never was. This was a trap."

The realization hit her like a punch to the gut. She suddenly felt the ground sway beneath her feet. "A trap? But... the text..."

"The darkness deceived you, Mary," Michael explained. "You must leave now, for both your sakes."

Mary felt a surge of emotions rushing through her. She had lost Michael once, and now he was there in front of her again, but instead of the strong embrace she had longed so desperately for, he was telling her to leave. Although every fiber of her being wanted to stay with him, if only for a short time, the determination in his eyes made her realize that he was right. The shadows had played her, using her desperation to lure her into their lair. And that meant that Matthew was all alone!

"Please, Michael," she begged. "Help me. I can't do this by myself."

Michael stepped closer, his presence growing stronger, pushing the shadows back further. "You are never alone, Mary. I am always with you. Trust in the love we share, and you will find the strength you need."

With a final, sorrowful glance at the darkness, Mary turned and bolted out of the warehouse. The cool night air hit her like a wave. She ran to her car, her breath coming in ragged gasps. Her hands trembled as she fumbled with the keys, finally getting the door open and collapsing into the driver's seat.

As she sped away, her mind was a maelstrom of fear and determination. The warehouse receded in her rearview mirror, but the terror it housed still clawed at her. She had to find Matthew and make sure he was safe.

Her phone buzzed again, but this time she didn't check it. She couldn't afford to fall into another trap. Instead, she drove with single-minded focus, praying silently that her son was home safe, waiting for her.

In the distance, a faint glow lingered in the sky, a reminder that even in the darkest of times, there was always a light to guide her. With Michael watching over them, Mary knew they would find a way to overcome the shadows and reclaim their lives. She gripped the steering wheel tighter, the resolve solidifying within her.

Her phone buzzed yet again. This time, she chanced a glance at the screen, hoping to see Matthew's name as the source of the call. Instead, it just read UNKNOWN CALLER. She quickly reached over and rejected the call.

A second later, chaos ensued inside her vehicle as her car came to a screeching halt in the middle of the road. The windshield wipers turned on, her headlights flashed sporadically, the door locks popped up and down repeatedly, and the radio squelched on. Before she could turn the radio off, the same sinister voice sounded through the speakers, "We're coming for you, Mary! You and your son!"

Then everything went silent as the chaos withdrew and her car returned to normal. For a long moment, Mary sat slumped over the steering wheel crying hysterically.

A sharp rap on the window jolted her. She looked up, blinking through tears, to see a police officer peering in, concern etched on his face. He was tall and lanky, with a face that seemed to stretch unnaturally in the dim light. His eyes glinted with an odd, almost feral curiosity.

She rolled down the window, trying to compose herself. "Ma'am, are you alright?" the officer asked, his voice gruff but not unkind.

Mary wiped her tears with the back of her hand. "I... I'm fine. Just a little shaken up."

The officer nodded, glancing around the interior of her car. "Mind if I ask what happened? You were stopped in the middle of the road."

"I... my car just went haywire," Mary stammered. "The lights, the locks, the radio... everything went crazy for a moment."

He raised an eyebrow, his expression skeptical but intrigued. "Sounds like you might have an electrical problem. Are you sure you're okay to drive?"

Mary nodded quickly. "Yes, I just need to get to my son. He... he needs my help."

The officer's gaze sharpened. "Do you need any assistance? I can call for backup if you're in danger."

"No," Mary said, shaking her head vigorously. "I just need to go. Thank you, but I have to go."

The officer lingered for a moment, his eyes narrowing slightly as he studied her. "Alright, ma'am. Just be careful. And if you need help, don't hesitate to call 911."

As he spoke, Mary noticed something odd. The officer's badge number seemed to shift slightly, almost as if it were changing before her eyes. She blinked, and it was back to normal. Her heart raced with a sudden surge of paranoia.

"Thank you, Officer..." she glanced at his name tag, but the letters seemed to blur together.

He smiled, a slow, almost predatory grin. "Just doing my job, ma'am. Take care now."

With that, he gave a curt nod and stepped back, watching as she rolled up the window and restarted the car. Her hands trembled as she gripped the steering wheel, her mind racing. Why did she feel like she had just brushed against something dark and dangerous?

Mary shook off the feeling and pressed down on the accelerator, her car moving forward with a steady hum. The sinister encounter with the officer left a chill in her bones, but she forced herself to focus on the road ahead. Every second counted.

As she sped through the empty streets, she whispered a silent prayer. *Michael, keep us safe.*

CHAPTER 46

The weeks that followed blurred into a surreal haze of spiritual training and shadowy guidance from Gideon. The church transformed into Andrew's haven, a sanctuary where he delved deeper into the ancient tomes and whispered incantations, each word a step closer to understanding the darkness that lurked just beyond the flickering candlelight. Unknown to Andrew, Gideon's true intentions remained carefully concealed beneath a carefully crafted façade of mentorship and guidance.

As Andrew immersed himself further, Gideon's subtle influence steered him toward darker forbidden knowledge, the kind that danced on the edge of sanity. Texts meant for those who have undergone a lifetime of training became weapons in Gideon's arsenal, each page a thread in the tapestry of his dark manipulation.

One fateful evening, after hours of grueling practice, Gideon's expression turned grave. "Andrew," he said, his voice a low rumble that seemed to echo off the ancient stones, "you've made great strides, but there are depths yet uncharted. Tonight, we will unveil a ritual that will bind you closer to the divine forces and give you the strength you need to fight the darkness that lurks around every corner."

Innocent and eager, Andrew nodded, unaware of the darkness that lay beneath Gideon's words. The ritual unfolded in the church's gloomy embrace, a dance of light and shadow that pulsed with an otherworldly energy. Gideon's guidance led Andrew deeper into the abyss, each incantation bringing him unknowingly a step closer to the heart of the darkness.

As the ritual reached its apex, a surge of power coursed through Andrew. A sinister force slithered from the darkness and wormed its way around him—gently mingling clandestinely with the divine power—that seemed to breathe life into the surrounding shadows themselves. Gideon, with a glint in his eyes, reveled in the success of his dark machinations.

Gideon's gaze held a calculated intensity, a harbinger of the sinister plot unfolding beneath his kindhearted facade. Shadows clung to him like loyal companions, and the malicious force within him grew in conjunction with Andrew's newfound strength.

When the ritual was done, Andrew stood before the altar lost in silent contemplation. Gideon materialized behind him, "The path you walk is not without sacrifice," he said. "But remember, Andrew, with great sacrifice comes great power."

***

With Gideon's influence tightening its grip, Andrew found himself ensnared in a web of darkness, his journey hurtling toward a precipice of unspeakable peril. In the depths of the church, where shadows danced and secrets whispered, Andrew and Gideon huddled together, their faces illuminated by the feeble glow of wavering candles.

"There are powers beyond our understanding," Gideon hissed, his eyes gleaming with a hunger that sent shivers down Andrew's spine. "Secrets that lurk in the darkest corners of the universe, waiting to claim those foolish enough to seek them."

Andrew's voice wavered as he spoke, memories of past horrors clawing at his mind. "My wife... my ex-wife... she dabbled in things she shouldn't have. It tore our family apart. You were there, Father. You saw what she was responsible for. I'm just eternally grateful that you saved my daughter."

Gideon's eyes glinted with a cold, calculating light. "Perhaps she was simply not strong enough to face the power of true darkness?" he mused.

As the weight of his past sins bore down on him, Andrew felt Gideon's hand on his shoulder, a cold comfort in the face of impending darkness. "Don't dwell on the past, my friend," Gideon said. "Instead, focus on your studies, and know that you possess the strength to succeed where Priscilla once failed."

***

The moon hung low in the sky, its soft glow casting a veil over the gnarled oaks that loomed like silent sentinels around the churchyard. Andrew stepped out into the night, feeling the air thicken with an unnatural chill, tendrils of unseen darkness wrapping around him like icy fingers.

Beside him, Gideon moved with a sinister purpose, his presence stretching beyond the church's walls like spreading shadows. The whispers grew louder, their ancient tongues weaving a tapestry of forgotten truths that tugged at Andrew's soul. The air crackled with energy, guiding him toward a path shrouded in darkness.

Gideon's voice, a chilling murmur, slithered through the night. "Embrace it, Andrew. The shadows hold secrets the daylight dare not reveal. Walk with me into the abyss."

The spectral voices heightened, a chorus of sorrow compelling Andrew forward. An otherworldly ballet unfolded amidst the gravestones, as shadows intertwined and moved in eerie harmony.

Caught between the safety of the church and the allure of the shadows, Andrew wavered, the whispers clawing at his nerves. The ancient oaks, guardians of forgotten secrets, swayed in a haunting rhythm—a harbinger of the night's impending descent into madness.

A sinuous tendril of darkness slithered forward, encircling Andrew like a serpent's embrace, before the visage of a woman materialized before him. Her smile, a beacon in the darkness, seduced him with its unearthly beauty. But behind the facade, Gideon saw the truth—an abomination born of Hell's darkest depths, poised to ensnare its unwitting prey.

As the spectral voices grew louder, Andrew felt a chill race down his spine. "What do you want from me?" he whispered, his voice barely audible above the haunting melody that filled the air.

The female spirit, her form translucent and ethereal, drifted closer to Andrew, her voice a melodic echo from beyond the grave. "Release," she murmured, her words carrying the weight of centuries. "Release from this eternal torment, this purgatory of shadows."

Gideon's eyes narrowed as he portrayed a facade of concern. "Don't listen to her, Andrew," he interjected. "She's just trying to ensnare you in her web of deceit."

But Andrew was captivated by the allure of the spirit before him. "How can I help you?" he asked in a soft voice tinged with uncertainty.

The spirit's smile widened, her features twisting into a pained mask of desperate longing. "Break the chains that bind us," she implored, her voice growing stronger with each word. "Free us from this cursed existence and we shall grant you the power to banish the darkness that threatens to consume you."

Gideon's hand tightened subtly on Andrew's arm. "She speaks lies, Andrew," he insisted. "Do not be swayed by her promises. She seeks only to manipulate you, to lead you astray."

But Andrew couldn't tear his gaze away from the spectral figure before him, her beauty a stark contrast to the darkness that surrounded them. "I want to help you," he declared. "Whatever it takes, I'll find a way to set you free."

With a triumphant smile, the female spirit nodded, her form dissolving into wisps of smoke that vanished into the night. And as Andrew watched her fade into the darkness, he couldn't shake the feeling that he had just made a deal with something far more sinister than he had ever imagined.

***

Driven by a sense of duty and a gnawing curiosity, Andrew returned to the graveyard alone, his footsteps echoing off the weathered tombstones. The night air was thick with anticipation as he approached the spot where he had first encountered the spectral woman.

From the shadows, Gideon observed Andrew's actions with a twisted satisfaction. His plan had unfolded flawlessly, each step orchestrated to lead Andrew further down the path of darkness.

"Show yourself," Andrew called out into the darkness, his voice trembling. "I've come to set you free."

For a moment, there was only silence, broken only by the distant howl of the wind. Then, slowly, the figure materialized before him, her form flickering like a candle in the night.

"You've returned," she said, her voice a melodic whisper that sent shivers down Andrew's spine. "Are you prepared to fulfill your promise?"

Andrew nodded. "I am," he declared. "Tell me what I need to do."

The woman smiled widely, her features twisting and warping as if she were caught in reality's gravitational pull. "You must break the seal that binds us," she said urgently, gesturing toward a crumbling mausoleum nearby. "Within lies the key to our freedom."

Andrew approached the decrepit structure slowly, his heart pounding in his chest with each step. The ancient doors creaked loudly, grating through the silence, as he pushed them aside. The air inside was cold and damp, accentuating the bitterness overshadowing him already. Shadows danced on the walls, and the scent of decay was overwhelming.

Steeling himself, Andrew stepped inside, the darkness swallowing him whole. He could feel the oppressive weight of centuries pressing down on him as he made his way deeper into the crypt.

Suddenly, the shadows seemed to come alive, writhing and twisting as they coalesced into a monstrous form that barred his path. The creature's eyes glowed with hatred, and its angry growl echoed through the chamber, reverberating off the stone walls.

As Andrew trembled in terror at the foot of the beast, he fought against the nearly irresistible impulse to turn and run. Then, the memories of Grace's torment flooded his mind—the piercing screams, the relentless darkness—and he felt a renewed determination to rise above his current self and confront the unholy force that stood before him.

Drawing on the strength he had gained from his training, Andrew faced the creature head-on. He recited the incantations Gideon had taught him; his voice unwavering despite the fear that threatened to consume him. With each word, he felt a surge of power coursing through him, and the creature recoiled, its form flickering like a dying flame.

Finally, with one last incantation, the creature disintegrated into a cloud of dark mist, dissipating into the shadows. Andrew, breathless and shaken, continued his journey deeper into the mausoleum, wondering what diabolical horror waited for him next.

At last, he reached the inner sanctum, where an ancient seal lay embedded in the floor, its surface etched with arcane symbols. With trembling hands, Andrew reached out and touched the seal, feeling a rush of energy as it began to crack and splinter beneath his fingers.

As the seal shattered, a blinding light erupted from within the mausoleum, illuminating the graveyard with an otherworldly glow. And in that moment, Andrew knew that he had done something irreversible—that he had unleashed forces beyond his control.

But as he turned to face the spectral woman once more, he saw only gratitude in her eyes. "Thank you," she whispered, her voice fading into the night. "You have freed us from our prison, and for that, we are eternally grateful."

As the last traces of the spectral woman vanished into the darkness, Andrew couldn't shake the feeling that he had just taken another step toward a destiny from which there could be no turning back.

As Andrew shattered the seal and freed the spectral woman, a cruel smile tugged at the corners of Gideon's lips while he watched from the shadows. "Well done, Andrew," he whispered to himself. "You have proven yourself worthy of the power that awaits you."

But even as he watched Andrew's triumph, Gideon knew that this was only the beginning. With each act of defiance against the forces of light, Andrew grew closer to embracing the darkness that lurked within him—a darkness that Gideon would take pleasure nurturing and then exploiting.

Putting on the mask of a teacher confronting his pupil after a hard-fought lesson, Gideon approached Andrew from the corner of the courtyard, his strides long and measured.

As the spectral voices faded into the night, leaving behind an eerie silence, Andrew's heart raced with uncertainty and he turned toward Gideon. "What have I done?" he murmured, his voice barely a whisper above the rustle of the wind through the ancient oaks.

Gideon's expression remained impassive, but a flicker of satisfaction danced in his eyes. "You've made the right choice, Andrew," he said, his voice smooth like honey but carrying a hidden venom. "You've chosen the path of power, the path that will lead you to greatness."

But Andrew couldn't shake the feeling that had settled in the pit of his stomach. He had freed a bound entity from a prison sentence without even inquiring who, or what, it was, and the reason for its imprisonment. "Was it the right choice?" he wondered aloud, his voice tinged with doubt.

Gideon's smile widened, a predatory gleam in his eyes. "Of course," he assured Andrew, his tone dripping with false sincerity. "You've taken the first step toward embracing your true potential. Together, we will unlock powers beyond your wildest dreams."

"Do you know who she was?" Andrew asked.

"I know a little of the legend. Her name was Isobel, and

she and her lover, Elias, were accused of witchcraft centuries ago. The townspeople believed they were responsible for a number of tragedies in the village and tried to destroy them. After Elias died at their hands, Isobel fled to the mausoleum where she tried to cast one last spell to save them both, but instead was trapped inside and cursed to remain imprisoned for all eternity."

Andrew was stunned. "I... I just freed her."

Gideon bent down and retrieved an ancient dark grimoire from the floor near the broken seal, its mere presence casting off an ominous energy. "And here is the power she promised you."

As they made their way back to the church, Andrew couldn't shake the feeling that he had just stepped into a trap —one carefully laid by the very man he had trusted most. And as the shadows lengthened around them, he couldn't help but wonder what darkness awaited him on the path he had chosen.

CHAPTER 47

The hallways of Fairview High School were a labyrinth of social dynamics and unspoken rules. Under the harsh glare of fluorescent lights, the students moved in synchronized chaos, a cacophony of laughter, whispers, and the slamming of locker doors. Unfortunately, her quiet demeanor and air of mystery turned Grace into a prime target for the cruelty of those around her.

It started with snide comments and mocking laughter, subtle enough to go unnoticed by teachers but sharp enough to wound. They would whispered behind her back, calling her "Ghost Girl" and spreading rumors about her family's strange practices. Grace endured their cruelty in silence, her thoughts often drifting to the protective charms and incantations she had learned from her parents.

Yet, as the days passed, the boundaries between Grace's two worlds began to blur in unsettling ways. Her encounters with the otherworldly became more frequent and more intense.

One afternoon, while sitting alone in the dimly lit library after school, desperate to finish another research paper that she had put off until the last minute, Grace felt a cold draft brush the back of her neck. The temperature dropped suddenly, the air growing dense and heavy. She shivered and glanced around, looking for the source of the chill. The pages of her book fluttered as if caught in an invisible breeze, and the overhead lights flickered, casting eerie shadows on the walls.

She felt a prickling sensation run up her spine, as if eyes were watching her from the shadows. Then, soft unintelligible murmurs seemed to drift from the very walls themselves. Grace's heart pounded in her chest as she felt the protective charms in her pocket getting hot against her skin. Quickly, she snatched up her things and ran out of the library, the feeling of unseen eyes following her each step of the way.

On her way home, with darkness quickly approaching, she took her usual route past the old, decrepit house at the edge of town, its broken windows and sagging roof a testament to years of neglect. That night, the house seemed to hold a deep, hopeless presence, the air around it heavy and oppressive. As she hurried by, she heard a faint, eerie whisper carried on the wind, a sound like distant, mournful cries.

She glanced up and glimpsed a shadowy figure in one of the broken windows. Its eyes glowed faintly, an unnatural, sickly green, and it watched her with an intensity that made her blood run cold. The figure moved, its form shifting like smoke, and the window shattered with a sudden, violent crash. A gasp escaped her lips before she turned and ran.

Grace sprinted home, her breath coming in ragged gasps as she navigated the familiar streets. The shadows seemed to lengthen and reach out for her as she fled, her heart pounding in her ears. By the time she reached her front door, the sky was a deep, inky black, and the oppressive feeling from the old house still clung to her like a shroud.

She burst through the door, the familiar warmth of her home greeting her. The scent of lavender and the soft glow of candlelight from the living room instantly contrasted with the darkness outside. Grace leaned against the door, closing her eyes and trying to steady her breathing.

"Grace?" Priscilla's voice was a soothing balm to her frayed nerves. Her mother appeared from the kitchen, concern etched on her face. "What happened, sweetie? You look terrified."

Grace opened her eyes, tears welling up. She crossed the room and collapsed into her mother's arms. Priscilla held her tightly, stroking her hair and murmuring reassurances.

"It's okay, Grace. You're safe now," Priscilla said softly, leading her to the couch. They sat down, and Priscilla held her daughter's hands, feeling the warmth returning to them. "Tell me what happened."

Through choked sobs, Grace recounted her day—the relentless bullying, the eerie events in the library, and the terrifying encounter with the shadowy figure at the old house. Priscilla listened intently, her face a mask of calm concern. When Grace finished, Priscilla gently wiped the tears from her cheeks.

"First things first," Priscilla said, her voice steady and reassured. "We'll place stronger protective charms around you, and I'll speak to your father about this. But right now, I need you to breathe with me."

They sat in silence for a few moments, breathed deeply in unison. Grace felt the tightness in her chest begin to ease, the oppressive weight lifting slightly.

"Remember what we've taught you, Grace," Priscilla continued. "You have the strength and knowledge to protect yourself. These encounters, they are a test of your will and your understanding of the balance between our world and the other. The entities you sensed are drawn to your power, but you can control that."

Priscilla stood and retrieved a small, ornate box from a nearby shelf. She opened it to reveal an array of crystals and herbs, their scents mingling in the air. She selected a few items and began to prepare a protective charm.

"Let's make sure you're well-guarded," Priscilla said, her hands deftly working with the materials. She handed Grace a small amulet, freshly imbued with protective energies. "Keep this with you at all times. It will help ward off any malevolent spirits."

Grace took the amulet, feeling its warmth against her skin. She nodded as she felt a sense of calm washing over her.

"Don't forget, Grace," Priscilla said, looking into her daughter's eyes with unwavering confidence. "You are not alone. Your father and I are here to guide you, and you have the strength within you to face these challenges. The spirits you encounter may be frightening, but they cannot harm you if you stand firm."

Grace nodded, feeling a newfound determination. The shadows of the day still lingered in her mind, but she knew she had the power to face them.

Priscilla wrapped an arm around Grace and pulled her close. They sat together for a long time, holding each other tight.

"Thank you, Mom," Grace whispered.

Priscilla kissed the top of her head. "Anytime, my love. Remember, you are stronger than you think."

As the night deepened, the oppressive shadows she had faced that day seemed a little less daunting. Grace knew that with her mother's wisdom and her father's teachings, she could face whatever darkness came her way. The world outside might be filled with unseen threats, but within the walls of her home, she found the strength to stand against them.

***

Despite her supernatural experiences, it was the relentless bullying that gnawed at her most. The group of girls, led by Amanda, a rich, white entitled piece of work, delighted in making Grace's life a living nightmare. One afternoon, as Grace was leaving her last class, Amanda, flanked by two other girls cornered her in the hallway.

"Hey, Ghost Girl," Amanda sneered, stepping closer, her voice dripping with hate. "This school would be a lot better if you'd just disappear like one of your stupid spirits!"

The other girls giggled, their eyes glinting with cruelty. "Go, Ghost Girl, disappear," one girl sneered.

Grace felt a surge of anger and helplessness, her hands trembling as she clutched her books. She could sense the energy around her shifting, a familiar hum that usually signaled the presence of something otherworldly.

"Leave me alone, Amanda," Grace said. "You don't know what you're messing with."

"Oh, is that a threat?" Amanda mocked, stepping even closer, her breath hot and sour. "What are you going to do, cast a spell and summon some kind of evil spirit to scare me?"

The laughter that followed was harsh and grating, echoing off the walls like the cackle from a witch's coven. Grace closed her eyes, trying to calm the storm building within her. But something dark and unexpected stirred, a fragment of the nightmare she had buried deep inside her mind.

Without warning, the air grew chilly, and the lights flickered violently. An instant later, a shadowy figure—a dark presence; an absence of light that seemed to suck the warmth from the air—appeared behind Amanda, its form shifting and undulating like smoke. The temperature in the hallway plummeted, and an unnatural silence fell over everything, as if the building itself was holding its breath. The girls' laughter died in their throats as they stared wide-eyed at the apparition, their bodies frozen in fear.

The menacing shadow towered over Amanda, its eyes glowing with an eerie light, a sinister delight flickering within them. It reached out a spectral hand towards Amanda, its fingers elongating into dark, smoky tendrils.

"Wh... what is that?" Amanda stammered, her voice shaking.

The figure's eyes gleamed with an intense brightness, and the icy tendrils coiled around Amanda's arm, sending shivers down her spine. A scream of pure terror escaped her lips as she stumbled back and crashed onto the floor. The other girls swiftly turned and fled, their footsteps reverberating through the hallway like the ghostly murmurs of the departed.

Grace opened her eyes, feeling the energy recede as quickly as it had come. The shadowy figure vanished, leaving only the chilling memory of its presence. Amanda lay on the floor, sobbing and shaking.

For a brief second, Grace took a certain amount of pleasure in seeing her greatest tormentor in such a sorry state. Then, her mother's voice popped into her head, admonishing her, *You're better than that, Grace.*

Whether it was actually her mother's voice, or her own guilt manifesting as such, the words were true. She looked at Amanda sadly and kneeled down. "I told you, Amanda," she said softly. "You don't know what you're messing with."

Amanda looked up at her, fear and confusion etched on her face. "What... what did you do?"

"I didn't really do anything. I just concentrated my energy and made it go away." Grace replied, helping her to her feet.

Amanda replied, "You helped me after all the shit I did to you. Why?"

Grace thought about it for a moment, "You may think I'm weird because of the things I believe, but you just got a little taste of what's out there in the shadows. Maybe now you'll think twice about hurting someone who's different."

When Grace turned to walk away, Amanda stood frozen in place, afraid to move for fear of another supernatural attack.

She had only made it a few steps when she felt the tug at her heart and stopped. Her shoulders dropped in resignation. *You're gonna make me do it, aren't you?*

Yep! her mother replied.

Grace walked back to Amanda and grabbed her hand. "Come on, let's get out of here."

***

The days that followed were cloaked in an oppressive, almost tangible tension. Whispers of the inexplicable event echoed through the hallways of Fairview High, blending with the dull hum of fluorescent lights and the metallic clang of locker doors. The rumors about Grace morphed into something darker, dripping with a mixture of awe and fear. Amanda and her clique kept their distance, their sneers replaced by furtive, wide-eyed glances. The school itself exuded an eerie energy, a mysterious tension hanging in the air and a palpable scent of unease filling the hallways.

Grace found herself propelled by a newfound sense of purpose, throwing herself into her studies with a fervor that bordered on manic. By day, she navigated the trivialities of high school, her eyes scanning the crowds for signs of any lingering darkness. By night, she immersed herself in the arcane, delving into dusty tomes and forgotten incantations. Her father's voice echoed in her mind, cautionary and guiding, while her mother's soothing whispers grounded her in moments of doubt.

The line between the ordinary and the supernatural had all but dissolved. The world of the unseen pressed in on her, demanding recognition. Grace's encounters with the otherworldly became more frequent, more intense. Shadows twisted and danced in her periphery, and the once familiar corridors of her school took on a sinister, labyrinthine quality. She could feel the weight of unseen eyes upon her, icy fingers brushing against her skin in the dead of night.

Every ghostly whisper and spectral touch added to her growing arsenal of knowledge, fortifying her against the encroaching darkness. She felt the power thrumming within her, a raw, untamed force that both frightened and exhilarated her. Her dreams were filled with cryptic visions and haunting specters, their meanings elusive but undeniably potent.

Grace's transformation was stark. The once timid girl, who had flinched at every cruel word and mocking laugh, now moved through the halls with a quiet, almost eerie confidence. Her eyes held a depth that spoke of battles fought in shadows, a steely determination etched into her every feature. The balance she sought was not merely between the mundane and the mystical, but between the light within her and the darkness that sought to consume her.

The ordinary world had not just blurred with the supernatural; it had become a part of her, and she of it. The shadows that once threatened to engulf her now seemed to acknowledge her strength, retreating but never disappearing. They lingered at the edges of her vision, a constant reminder of the battles yet to come.

Grace knew she had changed irrevocably. She was no longer the scared girl cornered by bullies. The darkness still loomed, ever-present and insidious, but she stood ready to face it. The halls of Fairview High were her domain now, and she navigated them with a sense of purpose and power. Whatever shadows dared to cross her path would do well to fear the light she carried within.

CHAPTER 48

Despite the adversity, Matthew's connection with the supernatural strengthened. Friendly spirits became his confidantes, providing solace in a world that failed to understand. Mary, torn between shielding her son from ridicule and encouraging his unique gifts, chose the path of denial. She convinced herself that Matthew's experiences would simply fade with time.

She couldn't have been more wrong.

Matthew continued to struggle in school as the other kids taunted and bullied him relentlessly. As a result, his grades weren't reflective of his natural intelligence. In parent-teacher conferences, the counselors dismissed Mary's concerns, ignoring her accusations against other students, instead attributing Matthew's struggles to a vivid imagination.

This pattern continued throughout his school years, and as he grew older, his dreams and nightmares, once benign, took a darker turn. Mary, haunted by memories of her past, recognized the signs all too well. As Matthew's abilities flourished, the whispers of malevolent entities mingled with the soft footsteps of friendly spirits. The delicate balance between the two teetered on the edge, and Mary, trapped between a mother's love and the fear of history repeating itself, maintained a deliberate silence.

The supernatural ballet continued for years, each pirouette echoing the fragile dance of a family caught between worlds, and Mary clung to the hope that ignorance could shield her son from the haunting legacy that lurked in the corners of their shared existence.

Then, as he approached adulthood, the nightmares intensified dramatically, eventually spilling over into every waking hour. He started seeing them everywhere, not just spirits trapped in this world because of some unfinished business, but evil entities looking to claw their way into the world, hell-bent on destruction.

Desperate to find an escape from the madness, he turned to things he knew he shouldn't; things that would tear his mom's heart apart if she found out. But the shadows only grew darker as he spiraled into a dangerous world where the supernatural and substance abuse collided.

In the heart of the city's twisted alleys, where shadows danced with the flicker of dying streetlights, Matthew, lost in the labyrinth of his own turmoil, wandered aimlessly. Each step was a stumble through the fog of whiskey, his senses dulled by the harsh liquor burning his throat. Hidden within the maze of buildings, a forgotten passage called out to him, tempting his curiosity.

Led by the formidable Raz, a large and rotund man, his gnarly band of scavengers skulked within the shadows, their eyes gleaming with mischief. Their worn leather outfits and ripped hoodies were a testament to their fierce dedication as they guarded their turf.

As Matthew stumbled into their domain, Raz's pack closed in. Matthew, barely coherent, attempted to apologize, but his words fell upon deaf ears.

"Look what we got here, boys," Raz's voice rumbled like distant thunder. "A lost little lamb in our den."

Matthew, his vision swimming, struggled to maintain his balance. "Sorry... didn't mean to intrude... just passing through."

Raz's laughter cut through the darkness like a blade. "Sorry don't cut it, kid. You're in our territory now."

Before Matthew could comprehend the danger, Raz's fist collided with his jaw, sending him reeling. Panic surged through him as he tried to defend himself, but his efforts were feeble against the onslaught of Raz and his gang.

The alley erupted into chaos, a symphony of violence that was quickly drowned out by the distant wail of sirens. When the police arrived a minute later, the assailants scattered like rats fleeing a sinking ship, leaving Matthew leaning against the brick wall bruised and bleeding.

A pair of police officers approached, the harsh beams of their flashlights casting long shadows along the narrow corridor. Matthew, disheveled and bewildered, was caught in their crossfire.

Officer Rodriguez, a stern-faced man with years of experience etched into the lines on his face, stepped forward. "What's going on here?" he demanded.

Matthew, struggling to focus, just stammered, "I... I don't know what happened? I was just walking through, minding my own business, and a bunch of guys jumped me."

Officer Simmons, a younger, more empathetic man, looked at Matthew with a furrowed brow. He shined his light on Matthew's face, revealing a swollen lip and red, dazed eyes. "Are you on something, kid?"

Matthew tried to ignore the officer and walked away, but Simmons stopped him. "Where do you think you're going?"

"Start talking, son," Rodriguez said.

"Like I said, I was just trying to pass through," Matthew insisted, his words slurred. "They... they started messing with me because I was on their turf... or something like that."

Rodriguez's gaze remained unyielding. "We got a call about a disturbance, and it looks like you're right in the middle of it."

"The other guy started it, I swear! I was just minding my own business!"

"Caught yourself in a pickle, ain't ya?" Rodriguez's voice was gravelly, thick with suspicion. Unconvinced, he instructed Simmons, "Check him for anything suspicious."

As Simmons began to pat Matthew down, the tension in the alley hung thick.

"You're making a big mistake," Matthew mumbled feebly.

Simmons, his flashlight illuminating the scene, scanned Matthew up and down. "What's this?" His hand clanked against the bottle concealed in Matthew's jacket.

Matthew flinched, a bead of sweat trickling down his temple. "It's... just a drink, officer. Needed to take the edge off."

Rodriguez's gaze bore into him. "Looks like you've been on more than just a stroll tonight, son."

A lump rose in Matthew's throat when he pulled the bottle out and looked at it. "How old are you, kid?"

Rodriguez sighed, his gaze unwavering. "Well, it looks like we're going for a ride. We'll figure this out at the station."

Matthew, his lip swelling, managed a weak nod. "I wasn't looking for trouble, officer. Just trying to find my way."

Caught between the merciless grip of the law and the consequences of his own reckless actions, Matthew found himself handcuffed and led away into the harsh glare of the streetlights.

The bitter taste of regret lingered on Matthew's tongue as

he faced the inevitable repercussions of his descent into the city's dark underbelly.

***

The flickering streetlights cast a dim glow through the air as Mary approached the imposing police station. Her heart pounded with a mixture of fear and sorrow, the harsh reality of her son's situation settling like a heavy fog. The night air seemed to carry whispers of regret, a mournful melody echoing through the desolate streets.

As Mary stepped into the stark interior of the police station, the cold, unforgiving atmosphere enveloped her. She made her way to the front desk, her footsteps echoing loudly through the corridor. The fluorescent lights buzzed overhead, creating an unsettling ambiance that heightened the gravity of the moment.

The duty officer looked up, his eyes weary from hours of monotonous paperwork. "You're here for Matthew, I presume?"

Mary replied quietly, "Yes, where is he? What happened?"

The officer hesitated for a second, "He's in holding. The charges are serious, ma'am. Assault, substance abuse, resisting arrest. It's not a good situation."

Mary's heart sank, the weight of each word settling heavily upon her. She followed the officer through a labyrinth of gray hallways until they reached a dimly lit area.

The sight that greeted her was heartbreaking. Matthew, once full of youthful energy and innocence, now sat on a cold, metallic bench with a haunted expression. His eyes were clouded with a mixture of confusion and remorse.

Mary's voice cracked as she spoke. "Matthew, what happened?"

Matthew held his head low, avoiding eye contact. "I messed up, Mom. I messed up real bad."

Mary's heart shattered as she watched her son, a mere shell of the boy she once knew, grappling with the consequences of his actions. The shadows that had haunted their lives seemed to converge in this cold, sterile cell.

As Mary approached the bars, an oppressive silence hung in the air. She could sense a presence, an otherworldly force that lingered in the corners of the room. The shadows seemed to writhe, mirroring the turmoil within both of their souls.

A whisper, soft yet laden with sorrow, echoed through the cell. "The choices made in the dark reverberate through the tapestry of life. The spirits bear witness to the pain etched in the threads of this fateful night."

Mary whispered nervously, "Who's there? What do you want?"

The voice lingered, an ethereal lamentation weaving through the atmosphere. "A mother's love, a son's descent. The balance trembles, and the threads fray. Will you break, or will you find strength in the shadows that dance around your heart?"

The spectral presence dissipated, leaving Mary with an unsettling sense of foreboding. She turned back to Matthew, his tear-streaked face reflecting the harsh reality of the situation.

Mary, choked back her tears as she reached through the cold bars. "We'll get through this, Matthew. I won't let you face this alone."

Once the bail was paid, the officer led Mary back to the holding area, and Matthew shuffled from the corner of the cell, harsh lines of sorrow and regret etched on his face.

CHAPTER 49

The moon hung high and full in the night sky, casting a pallid light through the ancient stained-glass windows of the chapel. The colored glass, once vibrant and filled with scenes of divine grace, now appeared sickly and distorted, casting grotesque shadows that danced upon the cold stone floor.

Gideon stood at the center of the hidden chamber, an unholy figure draped in dark robes. His eyes, now a piercing, unnatural shade, were closed in fervent concentration, his arms raised high above his head in a gesture of dark supplication. The air was thick with the acrid scent of incense mingling with the coppery tang of blood.

The chamber was illuminated by flickering candlelight. The figures around Gideon, cloaked in hooded robes, moved in a slow, deliberate circle. Their faces, hidden deep within their hoods, occasionally caught the candlelight, revealing fleeting glimpses of expressions contorted in ecstasy and madness. The floor beneath them was inscribed with intricate symbols drawn in fresh blood, forming a grotesque tapestry of arcane power.

Gideon opened his eyes, now burning with an otherworldly intensity. He took a deep breath, feeling the dark energy coursing through him, the intoxicating power that he had come to crave. Before him stood an altar, stark and ominous, adorned with black candles and relics that seemed to pulse with life. An ancient tome lay open upon it, its pages filled with blasphemous texts and forbidden knowledge.

He began to chant, his voice deep and resonant, carrying the words of a language long forgotten by the world of men. The robed figures echoed his incantation, their voices blending into a haunting symphony that reverberated through the chamber. The candles flickered and flared as if responding to the dark invocation, their flames casting eerie, dancing shadows on the walls.

As the ritual progressed, the air grew colder, and a palpable sense of dread filled the room. Gideon stepped forward, raising a ceremonial dagger high above the altar. Its blade was ancient, inscribed with runes that seemed to shimmer in the candlelight. His voice grew louder, more urgent, as he called upon the ancient forces that had promised him power beyond imagination.

The robed figures began to writhe and convulse, their voices rising in a frenzied chorus. The symbols on the floor glowed with an eerie light. Gideon's eyes gleamed with dark triumph as he felt the power building, a torrent of energy that surged through his veins.

With a final, triumphant cry, he plunged the dagger down, piercing the heart of a sacrificial offering laid upon the altar. The offering, a young lamb, bleated weakly as its life drained away, its blood pooling on the altar and flowing into the grooves of the carved symbols. The room shuddered as if the very foundation of the chapel was reacting to the dark deed. A blinding flash of light erupted from the altar, and for a moment, the chamber was filled with an overwhelming presence, an ancient, malevolent force that seemed to seep into the very stones of the building.

The robed figures fell to their knees, their voices rising in a cacophony of twisted joy and reverence. Gideon stood over the altar, his chest heaving, his eyes alight with the unholy power that now coursed through him. He had crossed the threshold, fully embracing the darkness that had beckoned him. The transformation was complete.

In the shadows, an artist lurked, his eyes wide with a mix of fear and inspiration. He had been compelled to witness the ritual, his hands guided by an unseen force as he sketched furiously on a large canvas. His brush moved with unnatural speed, capturing every detail with horrifying clarity. The likeness of Gideon emerged on the canvas, his eyes burning with otherworldly fire, the robed figures caught in their ecstatic worship, and the sinister altar standing as a testament to the dark ritual that had taken place.

The artist, once a man of faith, now found his soul tainted by the very act of creation. He knew that the painting was no mere depiction but a vessel, a conduit for the dark power that had been unleashed. As he added the final strokes, he felt a chill pass through him, a whisper of darkness that promised eternal torment.

The ritual ended with a sudden, deafening silence. The robed figures remained prostrate on the floor, their breaths ragged and shallow. Gideon lowered the dagger, his face a mask of grim satisfaction. He turned his gaze to the artist, who trembled under the weight of his stare.

"Bring it forward," Gideon commanded, his voice echoing with unholy authority.

The artist obeyed, dragging the heavy canvas toward the altar. As he approached, the symbols on the floor flared briefly, and the painting seemed to pulse with a life of its own. Gideon inspected the work, a cruel smile playing on his lips.

"It is done," he said, his voice filled with dark triumph. "This painting shall be hidden, a testament to our power and a beacon for those who seek the path of darkness."

The artist nodded mutely, his eyes hollow and haunted. He knew that his fate was sealed, his soul forever bound to the dark forces he had unwittingly served.

The painting was carried to a hidden alcove behind a tattered tapestry, its vibrant colors long since faded. There it would wait, a silent witness to the corruption and malevolence that now festered within the once-sacred walls of the chapel. And in the years to come, it would draw others, those with a hunger for power and a willingness to embrace the darkness, perpetuating the cycle of evil that Gideon had so willingly embraced.

CHAPTER 50

Time moved in elusive strides, and Grace transitioned from the innocence of childhood into the complexity of adolescence, leaving the nightmare of her possession buried deep inside her mind, locked away never to be opened again. Her teenage years unfolded in the dance of shadows, a delicate balance between the ordinary and the supernatural. Splitting her time between the care of her mother and the guidance of her father, Grace became a reluctant apprentice to the mysteries lurking beyond the veil.

With Priscilla's guidance, Grace discovered the subtleties of the supernatural. Underneath the moonlit sky, they would sit in the garden, surrounded by the fragrance of blooming roses. Priscilla, spoke of the unseen threads connecting the living and the spectral. Grace learned to sense the whispers of spirits, feeling the gentle caress of energies that traversed the boundary between realms.

Conversely, alongside Andrew, she explored the more practical aspects of the supernatural. The dusty tomes in his study held secrets of ancient incantations and protective charms. Together, they would embark on journeys into abandoned places, chasing the echoes of entities long departed. Andrew, with a mixture of caution and determination, imparted the skills needed to navigate the perilous waters of the supernatural.

As Grace matured, latent abilities began to stir within her. Andrew observed with a mix of pride and concern, as his daughter displayed an intuitive understanding of the occult. Objects responded to her presence, and the air seemed to hum with an energy uniquely hers.

Priscilla, with her own psychic gifts, recognized the blossoming potential within Grace. Together, they delved into the art of scrying and communicated with entities that lingered in the unsettled spaces. The psychic bond between mother and daughter strengthened, forming a bridge that connected the earthly and the metaphysical.

The dynamics between Priscilla and Andrew, once strained by the damage of their daughter's possession and exorcism, evolved into a delicate truce for her sake. Though marked by past wounds, they were united in their commitment to shield Grace from the encroaching darkness.

Grace, caught between the currents of her parents' divergent teachings, found a unique synthesis of the supernatural. The balance between Priscilla's ethereal insights and Andrew's grounded knowledge became the foundation upon which she built her understanding of the unseen forces that surrounded them.

The supernatural became more than a mere curiosity for Grace; it was a living tapestry that wove itself into the fabric of her existence. Late into the night, she would sit with Priscilla, deciphering the cryptic symbols that adorned ancient manuscripts. Then, with Andrew, she would venture into the heart of haunted places, unraveling the secrets buried in the whispers of the past.

Each encounter with the supernatural added layers to

Grace's growing knowledge. Her teenage years became a testament to the delicate dance between light and shadow, as she navigated the realms of the unknown with both caution and curiosity. While most girls her age were worried about boyfriends or the latest fashion trends, Grace was out hunting ghosts and communing with spirits.

***

The abandoned asylum loomed like a specter against the dying light of day, its decaying façade a testament to the tales of ghostly echoes that reverberated within its walls. Grace and Andrew, armed with flashlights that cut through the encroaching darkness, stood at the entrance, their breaths visible in the cold air. The distant howls of an unseen wind whispered through the corridors, amplifying the sense of desolation.

As they ventured further into the asylum, the oppressive atmosphere seemed to thicken. The air, heavy with the weight of forgotten anguish, carried with it the moans of tortured souls.

The flickering beams of their flashlights cast eerie shadows on peeling wallpaper and crumbling ceiling tiles. Andrew carefully guided Grace through the labyrinth of abandoned rooms, searching through the rubble and debris for the source of the building's anguish. It was in one of those forgotten chambers that they stumbled on a relic of the asylum's dark past.

In the corner, obscured by layers of dust and neglect, lay an old journal. Grace, drawn to it like a moth to flame, carefully retrieved the weathered tome. The leather cover crinkled as she opened it, revealing pages filled with faded ink and the remnants of long-forgotten secrets. The journal detailed rituals—sinister invocations and incantations—that sent a shiver down Grace's spine.

Grace whispered, "Dad, look at this. These rituals, they're eerily similar to something I've seen before."

Andrew's eyes narrowed as he scanned the arcane text, his flashlight casting an ominous glow on the pages.

Andrew replied, "This... this is dark magic, Grace. Something evil lingers in these halls. We need to be careful."

The air in the room suddenly seemed charged with an unspoken tension as they realized the asylum held more than just echoes of the past.

While poring over the journal, Grace's hand shook, her fingertips delicately tracing the faded words that seemed to emanate a sinister aura. Suddenly, a distant sound echoed through the corridors, like the scraping of metal against stone. Andrew glanced at Grace, his expression mirroring her growing fear.

"Did you hear that?" Grace whispered.

Andrew nodded grimly, his grip tightening on the flashlight. "We're not alone in here."

With cautious steps, they ventured deeper into the asylum, the shadows dancing around them as if alive with unseen horrors. Every creak of the floorboards sent shivers down their spines, every gust of wind through broken windows seemed to carry the whispers of restless spirits.

Then, in the dim light of their flashlights, they saw it—a figure, shrouded in darkness, lurking at the end of the corridor. Its silhouette was twisted and contorted, its presence exuding an aura of wickedness that seemed to suffocate the very air around them.

The figure began to move towards them, its movements jerky and unnatural. As the entity drew closer, its features became clearer in the wavering light of their flashlights. It was like nothing they had ever seen before—a twisted amalgamation of shadow and substance, its form shifting and contorting with each step.

Andrew stepped forward, his voice steady despite the fear gnawing at his insides. "Who are you?" he demanded, his flashlight trembling in his grip.

The entity remained silent, its presence looming over them like a specter of death. Then, with a voice that seemed to reverberate from the depths of the abyss, it spoke—a guttural whisper that sent shivers down their spines. "We are the forgotten ones," it hissed. "Trapped within these walls for eternity, feeding on the souls of the lost and the damned."

Grace's heart hammered in her chest as she realized that she was face to face with a creature born from the darkest depths of the asylum's history—an evil force that had festered within its decaying walls.

"We are not bound to this place!" Andrew declared. "You may have haunted these halls for centuries, but we will not be your prey!"

With that, he raised his flashlight high, casting a brilliant beam of light directly at the entity, while speaking a sharp incantation. The creature recoiled, its form writhing and contorting in agony as the light pierced through its shadowy facade.

Seizing the opportunity, Grace and Andrew turned and ran, their footsteps echoing through the empty corridors as they fled from the wraith that pursued them.

As they burst out into the cold night air gasping for breath, they knew that they had narrowly escaped the clutches of something far more sinister than they could have ever imagined.

But as they glanced back at the abandoned asylum, its looming silhouette against the night sky, they couldn't shake the feeling that they had only scratched the surface of the horrors that lurked within its walls. And somewhere, deep within the darkness, the forgotten ones awaited their next unsuspecting victims.

Once they had cleared the building, Grace turned toward her dad and handed him the journal. "Here, Pops. We may need to study this a bit so we know what we're dealing with in the future."

Andrew raised an eyebrow, "Pops?"

Grace just shrugged and smiled.

Andrew grabbed the journal and felt a soft prick of energy flow through him. A look of worry crossed his eyes before he quickly wrapped the tome in a black velvet cloth and deposited it inside a large leather bag.

CHAPTER 51

The road to Bleaker's Manor twisted through dense forests, the trees looming overhead like silent sentinels guarding the secrets of the past. Andrew gripped the steering wheel tight as the car bumped along the dirt road, his knuckles turning white against the leather. Grace sat beside him, her face etched with a mixture of excitement and trepidation.

The legends surrounding Bleaker's Manor were the stuff of nightmares, whispered tales passed down through generations. Curses, spectral apparitions, and dark rituals were said to plague the desolate estate, shrouding it in an aura of mystery.

As they approached the manor, its silhouette rose like a specter against the fading light of dusk. The once-grand facade was now marred by years of neglect, its windows boarded up like vacant eyes staring into the void. Ivy snaked its way up the crumbling walls, clinging to the stone like a parasite feeding off its host.

Stepping out of the car, Andrew and Grace were greeted by an eerie silence that hung heavy in the air. The sound of their footsteps echoed through the overgrown courtyard, each crunch beneath their feet sending shivers down their spines.

They made their way towards the entrance, the wooden door creaking open with a reluctance that seemed almost alive. Inside, the air was thick with dust and decay, the musty smell of neglect permeating every corner of the dilapidated structure.

As they explored the manor, Andrew and Grace felt the walls closing in around them, the oppressive energy pressing down heavy on their chests. Shadows danced in the dim light, twisting and contorting into grotesque shapes that seemed to taunt them.

"It feels like the very walls are watching us," Grace whispered, her voice barely audible.

Andrew nodded, his jaw clenched with determination. "We're getting closer. I can feel it."

It was in a hidden chamber, tucked away behind a tapestry that had long since lost its vibrant colors, that Andrew stumbled upon the painting. Gideon's likeness stared back at him from the canvas, his eyes filled with an otherworldly intensity that sent a chill down Andrew's spine. In the foreground, figures clad in robes gathered around a sinister altar, their features twisted into grotesque masks of ecstasy as they performed a ritual too dark to comprehend.

Grace gasped as she caught sight of the painting, her hand flying to her mouth to stifle a cry of horror. "Oh, my God! Is that... ?"

In that moment of frozen terror and disbelief, they were overwhelmed by the sensation of the chamber walls pulsing with a dark energy, as if it held the secrets of the horrors that had transpired within.

"We need to get out of here," Grace said, her voice trembling with fear.

Andrew shook his head, his eyes fixed on the painting.

"Not yet. We're close to uncovering the truth. I can feel it."

With a sense of urgency born of desperation, Andrew and Grace knew they had to uncover the truth behind the curse that bound Bleaker's Manor in its icy grip. For if they failed, they risked not only their own lives but the souls of all who dared to set foot within its haunted halls.

As Andrew and Grace stood in the chamber, the air grew heavy with an ominous presence. Suddenly, the painting began to emit a faint, pulsating glow, casting eerie shadows across the walls.

"We shouldn't stay here," Grace insisted, her voice tinged with urgency.

But Andrew's curiosity outweighed his fear. "We're on the brink of something big, Grace. We can't turn back now."

For a brief second, the irony of the situation resonated deep within Andrew as he recalled the very same situation in their own home long ago, the moment that had led to the nightmare that would end their marriage. It was then that he finally understood.

Before Grace could protest further, a low, guttural growl reverberated through the chamber, causing the floorboards to tremble beneath their feet. The sound seemed to emanate from the very walls themselves.

The glow from the painting intensified, bathing the room in a brilliant light. Shadows danced and writhed across the walls, taking on sinister shapes that twisted and contorted with a life of their own.

Suddenly, a voice echoed through the chamber, cold and filled with venom. "How dare you violate this sacred land?"

Andrew and Grace froze, their hearts pounding in their chests, as they exchanged a nervous glance.

"We mean no harm," Andrew called out. "We're only here to uncover the truth."

Laughter, dark and mocking, filled the chamber, sending chills down their spines. "The truth?" the voice sneered. "You know nothing of the truth. You are like insects crawling in the darkness, blind to the horrors that lurk within."

As the voice spoke, the shadows coalesced into a swirling vortex of darkness, enveloping the room in an impenetrable shroud. Andrew and Grace stumbled backwards, overwhelmed by the force that surrounded them.

But even in the face of such overwhelming evil, they refused to back down. With a defiant roar, Andrew raised his cross, the gleam of determination shining in his eyes.

"We will not cower before you!" he declared. "We will uncover the truth, no matter the cost."

With a sudden surge of movement, the shadows converged into a tangible form—a grotesque creature, its features twisted into a macabre semblance of humanity. Its eyes glowed with an unearthly light as it lunged towards Andrew and Grace.

Andrew swung his cross in a wide arc, the holy symbol cutting through the darkness like a beacon. The creature recoiled, hissing in agony as the cross burned against its flesh, but it quickly recovered, its primal fury fueling its relentless assault.

Grace pulled out a silver dagger forged with ancient runes. She lunged forward, her movements fluid yet desperate as she sought to fend off the creature's relentless attacks.

The chamber echoed with the clash of metal against flesh, the sound reverberating through the air like a battle cry. Andrew and Grace fought with a ferocity born of desperation, their minds focused solely on survival as they danced on the precipice between life and death.

But the creature was relentless, its strength seemingly endless as it pushed them to the brink of exhaustion. Andrew felt a searing pain shoot through his side as the creature's claw raked across his flesh, leaving a trail of blood in its wake. Almost simultaneously, Grace cried out as a sharp talon ripped a deep gash in her arm.

Despite their injuries, Andrew and Grace refused to yield, drawing upon reserves of strength they never knew they possessed. With one final, decisive blow, Andrew plunged his cross deep into the creature's neck, its unearthly shriek piercing the silence before dissipating into nothingness.

As the shadows receded, Andrew and Grace collapsed to the floor, both of them reeling from the attack, with each one wondering the same thing: what role did Gideon play in all of this?

CHAPTER 52

Priscilla found herself walking through a dense forest shrouded in an eerie stillness. The towering trees loomed overhead like ancient sentinels, their gnarled branches reaching out like skeletal fingers to ensnare any who dared to tread upon their sacred ground.

Mist clung to the forest floor like a ghostly veil, obscuring Priscilla's vision and adding to the sense of foreboding that hung heavy in the air. Every step she took echoed loudly through the silence.

The forest seemed to stretch on endlessly in all directions, its paths twisting and turning like the tendrils of an ancient creature. Shadows danced among the trees, their movements flickering and elusive, as if taunting her with their secrets.

Yet amid the darkness, there was a faint glimmer of light that drew Priscilla further into the depths of the forest. As she pressed on, the forest seemed to suddenly come alive around her, the sounds of unseen creatures breaking the silence through the trees. Leaves rustled in the breeze like whispers of the dead, and the earth beneath her feet seemed to pulse with a hidden energy, as if the very heart of the forest beat in time with her own.

In the distance, a figure materialized from the shadows—Emily, her form bathed in a ghostly light that flickered like a dying flame. But there was a darkness in her eyes, a haunted look that spoke of unspeakable horrors lurking just beyond the veil.

"Priscilla," Emily's voice echoed through the darkness, a ghostly whisper that sent shivers down Priscilla's spine. "You must listen to me. Grace and Andrew are in danger."

Priscilla's breath caught in her throat as she stared at her friend's spectral form, her heart gripped by a cold dread. "What do you mean?" she whispered in a trembling voice.

Emily's eyes bore into Priscilla's. "Gideon," she said, her voice laced with urgency. "He seeks to harness the darkness for his own twisted purposes. He will stop at nothing to achieve his goals."

Priscilla's blood ran cold as Emily's words echoed through the void. "What can I do?" she asked.

"Trust in yourself," Emily said, her voice fading into the darkness. "You have the power to stop him, but you must act swiftly. Time is running out."

As Priscilla reached out to embrace her friend, the forest seemed to shift and twist around them, its shadows closing in like a suffocating embrace. Then she was suddenly looking up at a dark and cursed mansion. "Bleaker's Manor," Emily's voice whispered before it went silent.

Priscilla suddenly jolted awake from her dream, her heart pounding in her chest as she bolted upright in bed. Immediately, she leaped to her feet and rushed from the room, the only thought running through her brain was that she needed to save Grace and Andrew at all costs.

***

* * *

As Grace and Andrew limped through the overgrown courtyard of the Manor, their bodies battered and bruised, the moon cast an eerie glow upon the dilapidated estate, its shadows twisting and contorting into grotesque shapes that seemed to mock their pain. "We need to get out of here," Grace whispered.

Andrew nodded grimly, his injuries throbbing with each labored step. "Just a little further," he muttered, his gaze fixed on the faint outline of their vehicle looming in the distance.

But before they could reach the safety of their car, a low, menacing growl echoed through the darkness, freezing them in their tracks. The sound seemed to emanate from the very shadows themselves, sending a chill down their spines.

With a sinking feeling in the pit of their stomachs, Andrew and Grace turned to see Gideon emerging from the darkness. His eyes glinted with a sinister light as he advanced towards them.

"You thought you could escape so easily?" Gideon's voice dripped with acid as he surveyed their battered forms with a twisted grin. "How amusing."

"Gideon, what are you doing here? And what's your involvement with these dark rituals?" Andrew's voice was tinged with fear and trepidation, for he suspected that his friend and mentor had betrayed him to the darkness.

Gideon, his mask of feigned innocence now shattered, responded with a twisted grin. "I see you've been quite diligent in your investigations. How charming. But do you truly comprehend the magnitude of the forces you've meddled with?"

Grace held out the journal from the asylum with a trembling hand. "Explain this, Gideon! You owe it to us. Why did we see an image inside there that looked just like you? What connection do you have to all of this?"

Gideon's laughter echoed through the night, chilling the very air. "You little insolent fuck! I owe you nothing! If anything, you should bow before me in gratitude for opening your eyes to the true power that hides in the shadows."

"We will bow before no man," Andrew replied. "You know deep down that Light will always conquer Darkness."

Gideon chuckled, "My friend, you've merely scratched the surface. The rituals are but a means to an end—a prelude to the grand convergence that awaits. Despite your blissful ignorance, you find yourself standing at the precipice of reality, where the darkness and supernatural merge into a terrifying abyss."

Andrew gritted his teeth. "We won't let you get away with this," he growled in defiance.

Gideon's laughter cut through the silence like a knife, sending shivers down their spines. "Oh, my dear children, you truly are entertaining. But you underestimate the power that resides within the shadows."

With a flick of his wrist, Gideon summoned a surge of dark energy, the air crackling around him with sinister force. Andrew and Grace staggered backward under the attack.

"We have to fight," Grace urged, her voice tinged with desperation.

Andrew nodded grimly, his mind racing as he sought a way to overcome the overwhelming odds stacked against them. With a silent prayer for strength, they braced themselves for the battle that lay ahead, knowing that their survival depended on their ability to face the darkness head-on.

As Gideon launched himself at them with unholy fervor, Andrew and Grace fought back with a ferocity born of desperation, their injured bodies pushed to the brink as they struggled to hold their ground against the relentless onslaught.

The shadows that clung to Gideon seemed to writhe with a life of their own as the battle spiraled into a descent that threatened to plunge Andrew and Grace into a realm of horror beyond their darkest nightmares. The vortex seemed to grow stronger, pulling them towards its swirling depths.

Desperation clawed at their hearts as they fought against the pull of the vortex, their strength waning with each passing moment. But just as all seemed lost, a voice rang out from the shadows, cutting through the chaos.

"Enough!"

The word reverberated all around them, causing the vortex to falter and dissipate into nothingness. As the dust settled, there, standing before them was Priscilla, with pure hatred radiating from her eyes. "Gideon!" she boomed. "Your reign of terror ends here!"

CHAPTER 53

Matthew's eyes snapped open, but instead of the familiar comfort of his room, he found himself engulfed in darkness. A chill seeped into his bones, gnawing at his very soul as he realized he was no longer in his bedroom. Panic clawed at his throat, threatening to suffocate him as he looked around at his surroundings.

He stood in the heart of a nightmare, a realm of unfathomable horror. The ground beneath his feet was slick with blood, and the air was thick with the acrid stench of sulfur. Jagged rocks jutted from the ground like the gnarled fingers of the damned.

And there, before him, loomed the courthouse of his darkest nightmares. Its walls were covered with grotesque carvings, twisted images contorted in eternal agony. The entrance beckoned like the gaping maw of a ravenous beast, promising horrors beyond comprehension.

As Matthew stepped forward, the ground seemed to tremble beneath his feet, as if recoiling from his presence. The whispers that had plagued him in his room now swirled around him like a sinister chorus, their words a cacophony of despair and madness.

He hesitated, but a voice, deep and guttural, echoed through the darkness, sending shivers down his spine. "Welcome, Matthew, to the halls of judgment," it rumbled, the words dripping with malice.

Matthew turned, his eyes widening in terror as he saw the source of the voice. Before him stood a creature of nightmares, a towering behemoth with horns that curled like blackened tendrils and eyes that burned with the fires of Hell itself.

The demon judge looked at him with contempt, its gaze piercing through Matthew's very soul. "You stand accused of crimes against the natural order," it intoned, its voice a symphony of suffering. "In this court, there is no mercy, only punishment."

Matthew's heart hammered in his chest as the demon judge gestured toward the courtroom doors, which swung open with a deafening creak. Reluctantly, he stepped forward, the weight of his sins pressing down upon him like a suffocating blanket.

Inside, the courtroom was a vision of hellish torment. The walls pulsed with a sickly glow, and the air was thick with the wails of the damned, their cries echoing through the chamber like a chorus of the forsaken.

The demon judge took its place upon the throne of bones, its eyes burning with unholy fervor as it surveyed its domain. "You will be judged," it proclaimed, its voice reverberating through the chamber like the tolling of a funeral bell. "And your punishment shall be swift and severe."

As the trial began, Matthew felt the weight of his sins bearing down on him like a crushing weight. The accusations flew like arrows, each one striking a blow to his very essence. And with each damning verdict, the demon judge's laughter echoed through the courtroom, a chilling reminder of the horrors that awaited him in the afterlife.

Just as Matthew felt himself being consumed by the darkness, a voice pierced through the cacophony of horror. It was a voice he knew, a voice filled with love and desperation.

"Matthew, wake up! Please, you're having a nightmare!" Mary's voice broke through the veil of terror, pulling him back from the brink of the abyss.

With a gasp, Matthew's eyes flew open, the nightmare melting away like mist in the morning sun. He found himself back in his room, the comforting glow of dawn seeping through the curtains.

Shaken and drenched in sweat, he clung to his mother tightly, wondering if he'd ever be free of the torment? Deep down, he already knew the answer.

***

The following day, the journey to the courtroom was a silent one, both of them lost in their thoughts. As they entered the building, the atmosphere shifted, becoming heavy with an eerie tension, as unseen eyes seemed to follow their every move.

The court proceedings unfolded with an almost surreal detachment. The judge's voice echoed through the room, laying out the charges against Matthew. Mary, sitting closely behind him, held onto the fragile hope that justice would be kind to her son.

As the lawyers presented their arguments, Matthew's vision wavered. The edges of the courtroom blurred, and ghostly images flickered in and out of existence. Faces from the past, shadows of regrets, and the lingering spirits of those who had faced the harsh judgment of the court crowded around him.

Matthew turned around in his chair and looked at his mom, his eyes wide and his voice shaky as he said softly, "Mom, do you hear that? The whispers?"

Mary strained to hear, her senses on edge. A chilling breeze seemed to sweep through the courtroom, carrying with it disembodied murmurs and anguished sighs. The atmosphere thickened, and the temperature dropped.

Suddenly, the spectral figures materialized with unsettling clarity. Pale faces contorted in pain, ethereal hands reaching out as if begging for mercy. Hollow eyes locked onto Matthew, pleading for acknowledgment, for recognition of the injustices they had suffered.

Mary's voice trembled, "Matthew, what's happening?"

Matthew, his eyes wide with astonishment, replied, "They're here, Mom. The ones who suffered in this place. They want me to see."

The judge's stern voice became distorted, melding with the ghostly wails that echoed through the courtroom. Then the gavel fell with a resounding thud, sealing Matthew's fate in the eyes of the law. He had been found guilty on all charges. The spectral figures seemed to convulse in response, their torment intensified by the judgment. His only saving grace was the leniency of the sentence: six months house arrest and two years of probation.

As the court session ended and preparations made for Matthew's sentence, Mary guided him out of the courtroom, the ghostly apparitions trailing behind them like lingering shadows. The air felt heavy with the weight of unseen suffering, the cries of the unjustly condemned reverberating in Matthew's ears.

In the corridor outside the courtroom, the apparitions grew more confident. Wisps of icy fingers brushed against Matthew's skin, and agonized faces pressed closer. The temperature plummeted even further, and the flickering overhead lights cast eerie shadows that seemed to dance with the tormented spirits.

Mary's voice became desperate, "Matthew, we need to get out of here."

They hurried through the chilling corridor, the ghostly apparitions clinging to the edges of their reality. Matthew could feel their tendrils tightening around them, a palpable manifestation of the courtroom's dark history.

As they stepped out into the frigid night, the echoes of the specters faded, leaving behind an unsettling silence. They walked slowly toward their car, each of them with their arms wrapped tightly around the other, both as a shield against the darkness and as a promise of love to weather the storms ahead together.

CHAPTER 54

The air outside reeked of the evil forces Gideon sought to command as he chanted words in a deep and guttural language that descended into the depths of Hell itself.

Gideon's voice then cut through the air like a serrated blade. His mouth twisted with a malicious grin. "Oh, Grace, you thought we were allies in this pursuit of the unknown. How naïve. Not only am I not your ally, but in actuality, I'm the architect of your destruction."

Andrew struggled to comprehend the magnitude of Gideon's words. "Grace, what does he mean?"

Grace, her eyes wide with fear, felt a chill seep into her very soul. "What have you done, Gideon?"

Gideon replied, "Your father, dear Grace, has been my unwitting pawn. I guided him, like a lamb to the slaughter, down this treacherous path. And you, Andrew, you believed in the righteousness of our cause."

The revelation hung in the air like a poison, seeping into the very core of their beings.

As the truth of Gideon's betrayal settled over them, the shadows deepened, foreshadowing a revelation more sinister than they could fathom.

"But that's not the end of your tale," Gideon continued. "Oh, no. You see, dear Grace, your innate abilities make you the linchpin in our plan to usher in a new age of darkness."

Andrew's eyes widened in disbelief. "What... what do you want with Grace?"

"Grace is the key, the vessel through which the darkness shall manifest. The shadows have already tasted her sweetness, and now yearn to consume her completely."

Grace looked at her mother and father in complete shock, her lips trembling as she spoke, "What does he mean?"

Priscilla looked at Gideon with pure hatred radiating from her eyes, before she turned to Grace. "I put a wall up around your memories to shield you from having to relive the horrors you went through. But maybe now it's time to remove that barrier so that you may use the experience as a force to conquer that same darkness."

She put her hands on Grace's temples and closed her eyes as she softly spoke a series of cryptic syllables. Instantly, every moment of her horrifying possession came flooding back in full force. Grace felt the icy tendrils of the shadow demon wrapping itself around her soul, squeezing tightly as it sought to extinguish her flame and replace it with darkness. Then she remembered the hateful words she had spoken to her parents, and she realized at that moment, regardless of the fact that it was the demon speaking through her, that she was the cause of their divorce.

Grace turned toward Gideon, her voice trembling, "Why? What do you gain from such darkness?"

Gideon replied simply, "Power, my dear. Power beyond mortal comprehension. I shall ascend to a plane of existence where the boundaries between light and shadow cease to exist."

The revelation hung heavy in the air, a suffocating power

that threatened to consume them. Gideon, reveling in his triumph, exclaimed, "Now, witness the true power of the convergence!"

The shadows lunged, morphing into grotesque shapes that seemed to pulsate with evil. Ethereal tendrils reached out, grasping for flesh with a hunger that chilled the bone. Priscilla quickly summoned a protective barrier around them, its shimmering form flickering like a fragile flame in the midst of a storm.

Beside her, Andrew stood firm, his ancient cross clasped tightly in his hand, the weight of the bible pressing against his palm. With a fervor born of desperation, he recited numerous protective scriptures, each word a defiant challenge to the encroaching darkness.

Amidst the chaos, Gideon's laughter echoed through the night like a sinister anthem, his voice dripping with venom. "You cannot defy the inevitable!" he taunted.

In a desperate move, Andrew, Priscilla, and Grace united their powers, their souls entwining in a surge of defiance against Gideon's grasp. The air crackled with energy as the battle intensified, the very fabric of reality quivering under their fierce struggle.

Gideon, sensing an opportunity, turned his attention to Grace. With a violent twist of his wrist, his dark ethereal tendrils ensnared her. Grace's screams of pain cut through the night, as her body twisted and shook under the onslaught.

Andrew, with a fierce cry, leaped forward and unleashed a torrent of attacks as he pulled a long, silver dagger from his waist, thrusting it violently through the air at Gideon repeatedly.

Priscilla quickly summoned a wave of elemental energy, the air crackling with electricity as it surged forward. But

Gideon deflected the attack easily, the tendrils of darkness forming a shield against the storm.

Then, in the midst of the chaos, Emily's spectral form suddenly materialized, a beacon of hope amidst the encroaching darkness. With a silent nod toward Priscilla, she unleashed a surge of spectral energy that struck Gideon with all the force of a vengeful spirit.

The darkness recoiled in terror as the blast found its mark, sending Gideon stumbling backward with a cry of pain. Wounded and weakened, he struggled to regain his footing, his twisted form contorted in agony.

With a final, decisive blow, Emily unleashed a force of energy that enveloped Gideon in a blinding light. The shadows that had once cloaked him dissipated, revealing his true, twisted figure beneath. With a guttural roar of frustration, as his strength waned with each second, Gideon quickly retreated into the darkness.

As the echoes of the battle faded into the night, the air grew still once more, the scent of victory mingling with the metallic tang of blood. Grace lay crumpled on the ground, her body battered and bruised.

Andrew and Priscilla rushed to her side, their eyes frantic with worry. They both breathed a sigh of relief when she slowly opened her eyes and let out a stifled cough.

Priscilla felt a soft touch on her hand and looked up to see Emily's flickering image next to her. A gentle smile played across her lips before her form slowly faded away. Priscilla felt a slight tug on her heart as the realization hit her that Emily was gone.

CHAPTER 55

The cozy coffee shop hummed with the sounds of casual chatter and the gentle clinking of cups. Solomon sat at a corner table wearing his customer tie-dye shirt, scanning the room anxiously. His normally calm demeanor replaced with an air of concern. When Andrew and Grace entered the building and stood at the front looking around, he waved them over.

"Solomon?" Andrew asked as they walked over to meet him.

Solomon nodded and took his hand, "I prefer Sam. It's much more... current. It's a pleasure to finally meet you, Andrew. After our extensive amount of long-distance correspondence, it's finally good to put a face with a name."

Andrew replied, "Likewise. And this is my daughter, Grace."

Solomon took her hand and smiled, "You, my dear, are one of the strongest people I've ever met. To experience the horror that engulfed you and come out of it unscathed is truly remarkable."

Grace pulled her hand away, her eyes fixated on the floor as she tried to gather her thoughts. "I'd hardly say I came away unscathed. In fact, I'm pretty fucked in the head right now. And, how do you know about that anyway, unless Pops here told you?"

Andrew snapped at her, "I told you I don't like that name."

Solomon chuckled as he sat back down and invited them to sit across from him. "I can tell the three of us are going to have an excellent working relationship. And to answer your question, Grace, your father didn't have to tell me what happened. I already knew. My job as protector of this world is to be aware of everything that happens so I can try to stop the evil before it grows."

"That's a little dramatic, don't you think?" Grace replied. "There's no way anyone can know everything."

Solomon was thoughtful for a second before answering, "I guess if you look at it that way, you're right. One person can't possibly know everything, or they, in essence, would be God. And we know there's only one. But there are other methods to acquire intel, and that's where you, and others like you, come into play."

Grace's mind was spinning. "I don't follow?"

Andrew spoke up, "What he's getting at, is that we're basically being recruited."

Solomon nodded with a smile.

"Recruited for what?" Grace asked.

Solomon replied simply, "To help save the world from total destruction."

Grace's jaw dropped as she tried to comprehend Solomon's words. "Say what?"

Instead of answering, Solomon rose from the booth. "I think a cappuccino sounds good right now. You guys want anything? It's on me."

Andrew answered, "Two coffees, black. Thank you."

As soon as Solomon left the table, Grace turned to her father, "Who the hell is this guy? He's like some weird, hippie, peace and love freak."

"He is who he says he is... or at least I believe he is."

"Are you telling me that this guy is the Solomon from the bible?"

"Judging from the conversations I've had with him and talking with him right now, I'm starting to think he actually is."

"But that would make him over three thousand years old!"

"Approximately," Solomon said as he returned with their drinks. "I don't really like to divulge my true age too often. Plus, you're only as old as you feel, right?"

Grace's eyes glazed over as her head swam with the possibilities. "But, how?"

"Without going into too much detail, it involved a lot of personal spiritual growth, along with a measure of divine mercy. But, that's a story for another time. Andrew, do you have the information I requested?"

Andrew nodded, his brow furrowed as he brought out a beat-up journal and laid it on the table. "I've been digging into some old texts, asking around. There's talk of a disturbance, something brewing on a scale we haven't seen before."

Solomon sighed, his gaze intense. "There's a storm building on the horizon, and I have a good idea what's causing it."

Andrew sipped his coffee thoughtfully, before opening the journal. "Grace and I have been tracking anomalies, checking out places where the energy is spiking. Whatever it is, it's not natural, and it's definitely not good."

"I know what it is, and you're right, it's not good at all. Two of my scouts reported incidents involving a demon named Vizibir. I just couldn't verify their accounts before something unfortunate happened."

Grace's lips trembled. "Something happened to them?"

Solomon was silent for a moment, before he replied quietly, "They were both involved in terrible accidents."

Then he quickly changed his tone, "We need to be vigilant and approach the situation with urgency."

Andrew nodded, a determined look on his face. "I've got contacts who might have seen or heard something. We'll pool our resources and piece this puzzle together."

"And if the name Vizibir surfaces, even in the slightest implication, I need to know immediately."

"How do we stop this demon once we find it?" Grace asked.

Solomon replied, "I have a plan in place, and it involves a young man named Matthew."

Grace raised an eyebrow toward Solomon. "I've heard this story before. Let me guess, he's the Chosen One, right?"

Solomon chuckled at her response. "Something like that."

As they continued their conversation at the corner table, the patrons surrounding them had no idea that they were living in a world on the brink of a potential catastrophe, a storm of dark energy looming on the horizon that threatened to destroy everything they held dear.

The End

Book Four Preview

Hellish
Book Four:
Vizibir

By Scott Dokey

CHAPTER 1

Sometimes the forces of evil work in ways that are open for the entire world to see, their atrocities laid bare before God and man; individuals like Hitler and Stalin, who personified evil in its purist form. Usually, though, the evil works just under the surface of our reality, spreading its icy tentacles into all that is good. At first, it feels like nothing more than a slight tickle, only mildly irritating, but before long, it becomes a maddening itch that can never be scratched. That's how it started with Jeremy.

On a warm Saturday morning in June, little Jeremy Daniels bounded out of bed and rushed to his bedroom window, smiling wide when he saw a cloudless, blue sky overhead. As fast as a six-year-old kid can dress himself, he pulled on a pair of jeans, two mis-matched socks, and a t-shirt—that may, or may not have been dirty—then raced downstairs.

He held the carton of milk tightly with both hands and gingerly poured it into his bowl of Cheerio's, proud of the fact that he'd only spilled a few drops onto the table, all while glancing back and forth at the picture of the hungry lion splayed out next to him. A dribble of milk ran down his chin after shoveling a couple of huge bites into his mouth, almost more than his mouth could hold, then he flipped the page to a giraffe with its long tongue snaking out and eating hungrily from the hand of a small boy about his age. He smiled.

Jeremy had just plunked another huge spoonful of cereal into his mouth, turning the page to show a troop of monkeys whispering classified secrets to each other, when his dad entered the room.

A tall and thin man, who wore a serious face most of the time, Nathan Daniels was unusually happy and upbeat as he passed behind his son on the way to the counter, where the coffee maker sat with a freshly brewed pot in its belly. After pouring himself a cup, he sat down across from Jeremy, taking a long sip before putting the cup down. "Are you excited for today?" he asked.

Jeremy nodded. "First, I wanna see the lions, then the elephants, then the snakes, then the—"

Nathan chuckled, "Wow, slow down, kiddo. We'll have plenty of time to see everything."

Jeremy pouted for a second. "I know. It's just that, we don't get to do stuff like this very much. And I want today to be special."

Nathan looked at his son. "I know, but you have to understand how important my work is."

"More important than me?"

Nathan was silent for a moment. Then his phone rang.

Jeremy listened with the familiar uneasiness coiling up in his stomach as his dad answered the call while rising from the table, and walked to the corner of the kitchen, talking in his distinct business tone to the person on the other end.

Nathan looked at Jeremy for a second before he turned and walked out of the room, where he continued the conversation.

"Sorry, kiddo," Nathan said when he returned a few

minutes later after the call was done. "I'm afraid I have to go in to the office for a while today. Something's come up in this case I'm working on. I'll have to take a rain check on the zoo."

For a few minutes, Jeremy tried to be brave; tried to hold back the tears. If he had been older, he might've understood what the name Nathan Daniels meant among prosecuting attorney notoriety. But he was just a child, with childish hopes and childish dreams. He didn't know the world of grownups; didn't want to know; didn't deserve to know. Not at his age.

Finally, the dam burst and he ran to his room, crying like he had done so many times before.

That's when it all began.

***

A soft sound, like the flutter of tiny wings, drifted to Jeremy's ears, breaking through the sadness and jolting his curiosity. He looked up from his tear-soaked pillow and was surprised to see a soft, green point of light hovering a few inches from his face.

His first thought was that a firefly had somehow found its way into his room. Then he realized two things: first, it was morning; and second, the thing floating in front of him had no visible body. It was just a glowing orb that hung there in the air for a minute before it suddenly disappeared. But right before it did, it whispered his name.

Instantly, Jeremy forgot about his dad's broken promise and ran to his mom to tell her about the glowing light. Unfortunately, the condition he found her in was one of a drunken stupor, with an empty bottle of whisky on the end table next to the couch where she laid, the television blaring away and her cloudy eyes trying to focus on whatever show was playing. A cigarette dangled in her fingers, threatening to drop a pile of ashes onto the floor. Barely able to lift her head from the arm of the couch, she looked at him in a confused way while he recreated his close encounter for her.

Her words were slurred as she spoke. "What in the hell are you talking about, boy? Are you going crazy? If it's attention you're after, I'll give you attention! How 'bout I beat your ass and really give you something to think about?"

In the span of a minute, Jeremy's heart was ripped out and thrown back into the void where his father had tossed it only a short time before. Jeremy ran back to his room, which had become his harbor of refuge from this hurtful world he had been forced to live in.

As soon as he buried his head back into his pillow again, the soft buzzing drifted to his ears once more, lifting him from his saddened state and bringing a smile back to his lips. This time, the creature seemed to shine a little brighter, buzz a little louder, feel a little warmer. It darted back and forth in front of Jeremy a few times, like a crazed, happy-go-lucky insect. It flitted around, tickling the end of his nose, brushing against his cheek, and nuzzling up to his ear.

A soft voice then whispered into his ear a single word, "Vizibir."

CHAPTER 2

A soft knock sounded on Jeremy's bedroom door and immediately his little alien friend vanished.

His door creaked open slowly, and his dad peaked his head in, trying his hardest to look apologetic. "I've got to go, kiddo. Hopefully, this will only take a few hours and I'll be home before you know it. Maybe we'd still have time to go out for ice cream, or something?"

These were hollow words that Jeremy had heard numerous times before.

"Since Janice has decided to drink her breakfast today, I've asked your Aunt Sophie to come over and watch you until I get back," Nathan continued.

Sophie stepped from the hallway. She was a young lady with short, blond hair, and bright blue eyes. She resembled a younger version of his mother, only she had a clear head and a sense of self-pride—and she was sober. A pixie-like demeanor radiated from her.

"Hey, Jeremy," she said. "How's it going?"

"Okay, I guess," he lied.

Nathan turned to Sophie, "You have my number in case you need to reach me?"

"Yep, sure do."

She looked over at Jeremy. "Don't worry, Sweetie, we're going to have lots of fun today. I promise. I figured we'd watch a couple of movies, maybe make some popcorn, order a pizza? How's that sound?"

Even in his state of hopelessness, Jeremy's eyes lit up, just a little, at the mention of popcorn. The buttery smell, the salty flavor, even the popping sound echoing through the kitchen was a weakness of his. The very thought of that melted butter flowing down his throat as he crunched on a handful of the magic corn had him thinking that maybe this day wouldn't be so bad after all.

He couldn't have been more mistaken.

After a few minutes, he heard the front door close and his dad's car backing out of the garage. As he walked out of his bedroom toward the family room, he noticed that his mom no longer occupied the couch in the living room. For a long moment he was lost in sadness, not because his mother had moved, but because in his eyes, she was never really there to begin with.

Jeremy was a little more enthusiastic, even anxious, as he sat down in front of the TV, waiting for the pizza party to start. Sophie had that way about her, making everything just a little brighter during the darkness. His stomach started to rumble a little, trying to coax the pizza delivery guy through some arcane hunger communication to get there as fast as possible.

Sophie walked over to him, carrying a couple of movies in her hands.

"Okay, kiddo, which would you prefer, 'Toy Story' or 'The Lion King'?

"Those movies are for babies!" Jeremy said. "I'm six-and-a-half now. I want something with action, like the 'Power

Rangers'."

She giggled, "Six-and-a-half now, is it? When did you get so big?"

After rifling through the large collection of movies, which filled one large bookshelf in the corner of the family room, she finally pulled one out.

"If it's 'Power Rangers' you want, then it's 'Power Rangers' you'll get."

A minute later, Jeremy was watching his favorite show and thinking that this day might turn out pretty great after all. Then he realized that it was his aunt, and not his mother, that he was enjoying this moment with. Suddenly, it wasn't so fantastic anymore.

He looked at his aunt for a second, taking in her carefree, fun-loving essence, and thought that his mom was probably like that at one time. Then, somewhere along the road, the pressures of life, marriage, motherhood, took their toll and zapped all the joy from her spirit.

The ring of the doorbell snapped him from his moment of wistful thinking, and immediately he smelled the scent of pepperoni pizza wafting through the house. Apparently his stomach communication trick had worked pretty quickly.

A minute later, he heard Sophie's voice shouting from the living room; "I said, take your hands off me, now!"

Jeremy jumped from the couch and ran toward her cry. As he rounded the hallway, he saw her struggling in the doorway, trying to escape the delivery guy's grasp. Even though he wore the uniform of one of the most important people in this world, the look in his eyes and the tone in his voice was more fitting to that of a hardened criminal.

"Listen, bitch," he said. "I want my stuff back, and I want it now!"

Sophie yelled back, "You'll get your stuff back, asshole,

when I'm fucking ready to give it back, and not before!"

The not-so-nice delivery guy responded by slapping her hard across the face, sending Sophie slamming backward against the wall with a mixture of shock and rage on her face. Jeremy ran forward and kicked him as hard as a six-and-a-half-year-old could kick.

Once again, the guy's hand swung around, this time catching Jeremy on the side of the head and sending him sprawling to the floor.

As Jeremy lay there on the floor crying, with blood seeping from a cut on the back of his ear where the man's nails had caught his flesh, he heard the familiar buzzing echoing in his ear, and saw the mysterious green light fluttering before him, bigger than before. Then it shot forward and struck the delivery guy in the middle of the chest, sending him flying backward into the stone pillar that supported the roof covering the front porch. His body slumped to the ground, leaving a streak of blood behind to mark where his head had hit.

Somehow, at this time, Janice had managed to arouse herself from her drunken stupor in response to Sophie's outcry, and peeked her head into the living room.

"Oh my god," she cried. "What in the hell happened here?"

By this time Sophie was sitting up, propped against the wall. "I'm not sure. It all happened so fast."

She turned to me. "I saw it. I saw the light, right after he hit you. It flew forward and hit him right in the chest."

His mother, in all her alcohol-induced splendor, looked at Jeremy with disgust written all over her face. "What have you done, Jeremy?"

Author's Bio

Growing up in the shadow of Notre Dame's Golden Dome, Scott Dokey developed a strong affinity for the arts, learning at a young age the joy of transforming an empty page into something magical. Eventually, as an adult, his creative endeavors expanded to include writing and filmmaking. Focusing primarily on subjects with horror and supernatural aspects, he became an award-winning screenwriter, and has produced and directed three short films and a no-budget feature film.

Scott currently lives in Southern California with his wife, Jennifer, and their daughter, Kaylee, enjoying the sweltering 120° summer heat. Of course, 85° in January more than makes up for it.

To find out more about his work visit his website at www.scottdokey.com

Be sure to check out:
   Hellish Book One: Tortured Souls
   Hellish Book Two: The Chosen